Big Lake Ninja

By Nick Russell

Also By Nick Russell

Fiction

Big Lake Mystery Series
Big Lake
Big Lake Lynching
Crazy Days In Big Lake
Big Lake Blizzard
Big Lake Scandal
Big Lake Burning
Big Lake Honeymoon
Big Lake Reckoning
Big Lake Brewpub
Big Lake Abduction
Big Lake Celebration
Big Lake Tragedy
Big Lake Snowdaze
Big Lake Fugitive
Big Lake Wedding
Big Lake Ninja

Dog's Run Series
Dog's Run
Return To Dog's Run

John Lee Quarrels Series
Stillborn Armadillos
The Gecko In The Corner
Badge Bunny
Mullets And Man Buns
Strawberry Slugbug

Standalone Mystery Novels
Black Friday

Nonfiction
Highway History and Back Road Mystery
Highway History and Back Road Mystery II
Meandering Down The Highway; A Year On The Road With Fulltime RVers
The Frugal RVer

Work Your Way Across The USA; You Can Travel And Earn A Living
Too!
Overlooked Florida
Overlooked Arizona
The Gun Shop Manual

Keep up with Nick Russell's latest books at
www.NickRussellBooks.com

Author's Note

While there is a body of water named Big Lake in the White Mountains of Arizona, the community of Big Lake and all persons in this book live only in the author's imagination. Any resemblance in this story to actual persons, living or dead, is purely coincidental.

Chapter 1

"Well, what do you think?"

"It's beautiful," said Big Lake Sheriff's Department administrative assistant Mary Caitlin as she admired the new Mustang. "It's the same color as your old one, isn't it?"

"Pretty close. They call it ingot silver. This one has the EcoBoost four-cylinder turbo instead of the V-8 my old one had. But it's pretty darn fast," Deputy Robyn Fuchette said.

"Fast enough that I thought we were going to get a ticket coming home from the Valley in it," her husband, Sheriff Jim Weber, added.

"Well, congratulations," Mary said. "A new husband and a new car. Life just doesn't get much better than that, does it?"

"I think that the car's got a lot less miles on it than the husband has," Weber said with a smile.

"That's okay, as long as she keeps both of you well lubed and exercises you on a regular basis, you'll be fine," FBI agent Larry Parks joked.

"It's sure a nice looking car," Deputy Dolan Reed said.

"She needed a replacement, since I kind of killed hers on our wedding day," Weber said.

"Pretty wife and a pretty car. You're a lucky man, Jimmy."

Their conversation was interrupted when a maroon F-150 pickup truck pulled into the parking lot of the Sheriff's Department and a man got out, quickly approaching them. From the look on his face, Weber knew it wasn't a social visit. When he got closer the sheriff noted he was breathing hard and seemed visibly shaken.

"Hi, Sheriff. Got a minute?"

"Sure. What can I do for you, Doug?"

"This is going to sound crazy, but I think a ninja just tried to kill me."

Weber looked at him quizzically. "What do you mean, a ninja tried to kill you?"

"Just that. Like I said, I know it sounds crazy. But it was pretty scary there for a while."

"What the hell happened, Doug?"

"I was headed out to the Neufield place to give them an estimate for replacing some fencing, and there was a big cardboard box sitting in the middle of the road. I didn't want to hit it, not knowing what was in it, so I got out to move it. I was just bending down when I heard a sound, and when I turned around there was this ninja with a sword. He had it in both hands and took a swing at me with it, like he was trying to cut my head off."

"You're kidding."

"I swear to God, Sheriff."

"What happened then?"

"I jumped backwards and tripped over the box and fell on my ass. I could feel the wind as the blade went over my head. It was that close!"

"Then what happened?"

"He came at me again and tried to cut me in half with that damn sword."

"Really?"

"I swear it's true, Sheriff. I managed to get up on my feet and I ran away. When I turned around he wasn't there anymore."

"Did you see where he went?"

"No, sir. I waited a few minutes to catch my breath and to see if he was coming back, and when he didn't, I got back in my truck and hauled ass out of there and came here to tell you about it! I'll tell you what, I about crapped my pants when he came at me with that big old sword!"

"Where exactly did this happen, Doug?"

"On Providence Road, just past where the Turner place used to be. I came around the curve, and like I said, there was this cardboard box sitting there in the middle of the road. It was like he set me up. Wanted me to get out of the truck so he could try to kill me."

"Let's take a ride out there," Weber said. "We'll follow you. I want to see exactly where this happened, Doug."

~~~***~~~

"See, there's the cardboard box," the man said when they arrived at the scene of the attack, pointing at a box on the side of the lightly traveled road. He was still breathing heavily from fear or maybe the adrenalin rush of fleeing his attacker.

Weber walked over and picked up the box. It was about 36 inches square and folded closed. It felt empty, and when he opened it there was nothing inside.

"The box was just sitting in the road when you pulled up to it?"

"Yep. It was like someone put it there to stop me when I came along."

"And then the ninja came from out of the woods. What direction did he come from?"

"I really don't know," Doug said. "I was just bending down to the box and he came at me."

"Where were you standing exactly? Which direction did he come from?"

The man thought for a minute and then said, "Right here. I got out of my truck and walked up to the box. I was bending down, and all of a sudden I heard a noise. I looked up and this crazy person dressed all in black was running toward me with a sword."

"Then he approached you from your left side?"

"Yeah, I guess. Like I said, I think he was there to ambush me. I don't know."

"Then what happened?"

"I fell down and scooted to the side of the road. I guess I still had the box with me, I don't know. It all happened so fast."

"And that's when he tried to cut you again? There by the shoulder of the road?"

"Yeah, right there," the man said, pointing. "He raised the sword over his head and swung it down at me. I don't remember exactly what happened. Maybe I rolled to the side or something to get out of the way. Then I got up and ran like hell."

"Did he chase you at all?"

"If he did, I didn't know it. I wasn't looking backward. I ran all the way to the curve before I finally stopped. I swear to God, Sheriff, it was the craziest thing that's ever happened to me."

"Doug, do you have any enemies that you know of? Anyone who would want to harm you?"

"Gosh, no, Sheriff. I pretty much get along with everybody."

"And you have no idea why you were singled out like this?"

"No, sir, I don't. I keep asking myself why somebody would do something like this to me, and I keep drawing a blank."

"Can you give me any idea of what this person looked like?"

"He looked like a ninja. All dressed in black with a hood over his face with two eye holes in it."

"Was he tall or short? Any idea what he might have weighed?"

Doug thought for a minute and said, "To be honest, I couldn't guess. It all happened so fast. I don't think he was very big."

"Did he say anything at all?"

"Nope, not a word."

Looking around again, Weber walked to the side of the road where Doug said the attacker must have come from. There were no footprints or anything else to indicate who had been there or when. Thick Ponderosa pines grew almost to the edge of the road. It would have been easy for someone to hide behind one of them, waiting to attack, if that's what happened. Weber had no reason to doubt the man. Doug Mullins was a good citizen, a respected businessman, and not one prone to making things up or exaggeration.

Weber looked at Parks and said, "This has gone way beyond kid stuff, hasn't it?"

"I guess it could be a prank," Parks said. "But if it is, it's the kind of prank that can get somebody hurt. Or killed."

4

"He keeps saying someone was trying to kill him," Robyn said. "Do you think he was singled out, or was he just the person who happened to come along?"

"That's a good question. Whether he was the person this ninja was trying to get to, or just a random target of opportunity, I imagine it seems pretty personal either way when someone's trying to chop you up with a sword."

They walked back out onto the road and Weber said, "Why don't you go ahead and take off, Doug? If you would, stop by the office and fill out an incident report and give it to Mary. We're going to poke around here for a little bit longer. If you think of anything else, give me a call."

The man walked to the door of his truck and opened it, then turned around and asked, "Why me, Sheriff? I don't bother anybody. I just do my job and go home at the end of the day. Why would somebody want to kill me?"

"If it's any comfort to you, I don't think that you were the intended target," Weber said. "We've had several reports of somebody dressed like a ninja running around causing mischief. I think whoever is doing it is some stupid kid who has escalated things way too far."

"I don't know if it was a kid or a grown-up," Doug said. "But whoever it is, I think I'm going to be seeing him over and over again in my dreams for a while."

He nodded at the sheriff, got in his truck and started it, then made a U-turn and drove away. Watching the pickup disappear back around the curve, Weber hoped that whoever was pulling these dumb stunts wouldn't make the mistake of doing it again. Doug was a pretty mellow guy, but there were plenty of people around Big Lake who carried guns on their person or in their vehicles, and the next time something like this happened, it could turn out tragically for everybody involved.

At the time, the sheriff had no idea of the tragedy to come, and he would wonder afterward if there had been a way to prevent it.

Chapter 2

The first report of the ninja had come from Hazel Fuller, and as was normal, no one really paid any attention to it. The elderly busybody was well known to the Big Lake Sheriff's Department. She was always calling to complain about suspicious activity, with the focus on prostitution. For some reason nobody could ever figure out, Hazel was obsessed with prostitutes and believed they were taking over the small mountain town. According to her many calls to the Sheriff's Department over the years, ladies of the evening frequently solicited business at the boat launch in town, worked out of the library's bookmobile, and took jobs as convenience store clerks on the night shift so they could ply their trade with customers who came in to purchase beer, cigarettes, or gasoline and found something more available that they never expected in a place like Big Lake.

So when Hazel called to say that someone dressed all in black, with a black hood over their head, was prowling around her back yard late one night, Deputy Chad Summers had finished the cup of coffee he was drinking in the parking lot of the Fast Stop convenience store, where he had seen no indication of prostitution or any other suspicious activity going on, gone inside to relieve himself in the store's bathroom, and then had driven to her house to see what her latest problem was.

"He was right back there beside the garage. I don't know what he was up to, but it was no good," Hazel told Chad upon his arrival. "No good at all."

Chad had walked around the property, not expecting to find anything or anybody, and he wasn't disappointed when he didn't. Hazel was always seeing things that weren't there. He couldn't help but wonder if maybe the apparition she had reported was a ninja prostitute. Did ninja prostitutes even exist? He wasn't sure, but he thought that this was simply another case of Hazel imagining things that went bump in the night.

Two days later, Imogene Buckley called to say that she had just gotten out of the shower when she saw movement at her bedroom window. The tall, pretty strawberry blonde schoolteacher reported that she had quickly pulled a robe on and gone to the window just in time to see someone dressed in black with a hood or mask over their face running through the backyard and into the forest behind her property. Imogene lived on a country road with no close neighbors, and when deputies Dan Wright and Jordan Northcutt responded to the call, they were not able to find anybody in the area.

"I swear I saw somebody," Imogene had told them. "I usually close my curtains when I'm getting ready to undress, but I had just gotten home from visiting my sister in Show Low and forgot. She's got three cats that crawl over you and I just wanted to get out of my clothes and wash the cat hair off. I won't make that mistake again!"

"Could you tell if it was a man or a woman? Short, tall, fat, skinny? Anything about them at all?" Dan had asked. A single man, he couldn't help but notice the fact that the white terrycloth robe did little to hide the schoolteacher's shape and accentuated her long legs.

"To be honest, I can't give you much of a description. I would say average height and weight at most. And I'm pretty sure whoever was out there was male."

"What gave you that impression?"

She shrugged her shoulders and said, "I don't know. But why would a woman be peeking in the window at me?"

The thought had crossed Dan's mind that a good looking woman like her might attract all kinds of admirers, but he didn't say that. Instead, he asked, "I know it's hard to say when someone is dressed up like that, but do you think it was an adult or a kid? You said the person was average height. Do you mean average height for an adult or for a teenager, maybe?"

Imogene had thought about it for a moment and replied, "I really can't say. I mean it sounds like something a kid would do, but I just don't know."

"No problem. Look, I'll make it a point of driving by every so often, just to make my presence known in case whoever it was decides to come back, okay?"

"I'd really appreciate that, Deputy," Imogene had told him. "Thank you so much."

Dan wrote something on the back of one of his business cards and handed it to her, saying, "That's the office number on front, and I wrote my cell phone number on the back. Anytime you need something, you call me. I promise, I'll be right here as soon as I can."

Imogene had rewarded him with a nice smile and said, "Thank you Deputy. That makes me feel a lot better."

When they walked back out to their vehicles parked in her driveway, Jordan had grinned and asked, "Was that strictly professional, all that promising to keep driving by and checking in on her and telling her to call if she needed anything?"

"What? That? Just doing my job, son," Dan had told the younger officer. "To serve and protect, that's why we're here, isn't it? Says so right there on the side of our cars and on our badges."

Jordan glanced back at the house, where Imogene was still standing in the doorway, the robe pulled tightly around her, as the big deputy got into his vehicle. "Yeah, Dan, that's what it was all about. I'm sure."

"Well, all right then," his friend said. "I'm glad we got that cleared up."

He had looked back at the house, where Imogene smiled again and waved at him, and he had waved back. Yes indeed, Deputy

Wright would make sure to make his presence known around Imogene Buckley's place.

There had been three other incidents. A couple from Tucson who had a weekend cabin in town had reported arriving late on a Friday night and surprising someone dressed like a ninja in their driveway. They said the person had run off as soon as the headlights hit him. Then, Burl Pierce and his wife Sharon called to report seeing not one, but two ninjas, fighting with swords or sticks or something like that at the playground of the middle school when they drove past at twilight a few days later. The last reported sighting had been just two days before the ambush on Doug Mullins. In that case a rural mail carrier named Clyde Gardner had called to say he had seen a ninja character lurking at a summer home on Appaloosa Trail. In every case, responding deputies had not found anyone or seen any evidence of suspicious activity.

"What do you think is going on with all this nonsense?"

They were back at the sheriff's office and Deputy Dolan Reed said, "It's got to be kids, Jimmy."

"Maybe so," the sheriff agreed. "But swinging a sword at somebody isn't kid stuff. Not by a long shot."

"No, that kind of crap will get you killed if you try it on the wrong person," Deputy Ted "Coop" Cooper said.

"Well, whoever's doing this, we need to find them and put a stop to it before somebody does get hurt," Weber said. "I need you guys to ask around and see what you can come up with. See if anybody has heard anything that might lead us to whoever's doing this. Because the next guy who crosses paths with this clown may be packing and blow him away. Especially when news gets out about the sword. It's one thing to be wandering through people's yards and peeking in windows, but when you start threatening people with weapons, that's a whole different story."

Chapter 3

The next afternoon Weber was cruising through town, just letting the citizens know that the Sheriff's Department was on the job, when a white convertible with the top down passed him going the opposite direction at a high rate of speed. He made a U-turn, flipped on his Explorer's roof lights, and took off in pursuit. The driver didn't see or chose to disregard his flashing red and blue lights, so he blipped the siren to get his or her attention. When that didn't work, he turned the siren on. The turn signal on the car, a Camaro with an Arizona license plate, came on and it pulled to the shoulder of the road.

Weber got out and approached it, following standard protocol of putting his hand on the trunk lid to leave his fingerprints in case things were to go bad during the traffic stop. But seeing the four young women in it, he really didn't expect any problems. He was wrong.

"Good afternoon, ladies. I'm Sheriff Weber for the Big Lake Sheriff's Department. How are you today?"

"Why are you stopping us?" The person asking was the front seat passenger, who was pointing her cell phone toward the sheriff. "And just so you know, I'm recording this whole thing."

"That's certainly your right," Weber told her, then addressed the driver, "I need to see your license, registration, and proof of insurance, please."

"I asked why you stopped us," the passenger said. "We've got a right to know."

"I'll get to that in a minute. Now, may I see that paperwork?"

"It's a free country, she doesn't have to show you anything," said one of the backseat passengers.

Weber ignored her and waited patiently while the driver decided whether or not she was going to comply. When she simply looked at him with a condescending glare, he repeated the request a third time.

"I said she doesn't have to show you anything," repeated the backseat passenger.

"Actually, yes she does. I'm not going to ask you again, ma'am. Drivers license, registration, and proof of insurance."

"Ma'am? Do I look like an old lady to you?"

"I don't know how old you are, but once you give me your drivers license, I will," Weber said, trying to keep things light.

"What if I don't?"

"What if you don't show me your paperwork?"

"Yeah. My friend says I don't have to."

"Well, I'm not sure where your friend got her law degree, but she might want to go back for some remedial education," Weber replied. "The law says you have to provide me with your identification, registration, and proof of insurance."

"And what if I don't?"

"Don't go there," Weber told her. "Look, this is just a traffic stop. There's no reason to turn it into anything else."

"You didn't answer my question. What if I don't?"

"Then I arrest you and I take you to jail and I have someone come and tow your pretty car away. And your friends here can figure out how they are going to get to wherever they're going."

"You would arrest me?"

"Yes, ma'am, I would. I'd prefer not to, but it kind of looks like you're not going to leave me any choice."

"Ma'am again?"

"Well, if I said missy it would be sexist, and so far you haven't given me any reason to think you're a lady, so I guess we're stuck with ma'am for right now. So, which is it going to be, *ma'am*? You show me the paperwork or you go to jail. End of discussion."

She sighed and reached toward the glove compartment. Weber instinctively moved his hand to the butt of his holstered Kimber .45 semiautomatic pistol.

"What? You're going to shoot her now? Remember I'm recording this whole thing," the front seat passenger reminded him.

"Shut up, Julie, or else he might shoot all four of us," said the other backseat passenger, who had remained silent until then.

Weber ignored them and took the paperwork from the driver, going back to his car. He called the dispatcher and ran the car's plate and the driver's license number. Both came back clean. Just out of orneriness he sat in the Explorer for several minutes more, watching the young women fidgeting impatiently in the Camaro. He called Dispatch again and asked where Robyn was, and requested she come to his location.

When he walked back to the car, he said, "So, Miss Tabatha Charleston, do you know why I stopped you?"

"Because you're an asshole?"

"No, ma'am, because you were doing 61 miles an hour in a 40 mile per hour zone."

"I don't think so."

"That's what I clocked you at."

"Do you stop everybody who drives through this town, or just the pretty ones?" the front seat passenger asked.

"It's probably the only way he ever gets to talk to pretty girls," the self-styled lawyer in the backseat said. "That's why you became a cop, isn't it? So you can hassle people who are minding their own business?"

"Actually, I'm a cop because I like the job," Weber replied. "I get to meet some really nice people. And then, I also get to meet people like you."

"What's that supposed to mean?"

Weber ignored her and began writing the driver a citation for speeding.

"Really? You're going to give me a ticket?"

"Yes, ma'am, I am. Being pretty doesn't get you a pass for breaking the law or being snotty in my town."

"My dad's attorney makes more in a day than you do in a month," the young woman sneered.

"Well goody for him. Sign right here on the line next to the X," Weber told her. "This isn't an admission of guilt, just a promise to appear in court on the designated day."

"What if I don't sign it?"

"Then your daddy's attorney gets to earn his salary."

Robyn pulled up behind his Explorer and got out, walking up to the passenger side of the Camaro.

"What, you need backup? Do you think we're going to resist arrest or something?"

"None of you are under arrest at this point," Weber told the passenger. "But I would like to see all of your identifications, please?"

"What for? We're not driving."

"It's just routine."

"I'm not showing you anything," the wannabe attorney said. "I know my rights."

"By law, in the State of Arizona, you have to provide proof of identity to a police officer when he asks for it," Weber told her.

"That's bullshit."

"Okay, last chance. ID or jail, you three decide what it's going to be."

"I want to talk to my attorney."

"You can do that once I arrest you. Step out of the car, please."

"Nope, not going to happen," the young woman said, shaking her head defiantly.

Robyn leaned in to push the button to release the lock, then opened the passenger door. "Out of the car," she ordered the front seat passenger. When the woman hesitated, Robyn took her arm and pulled her out. "You go up there by the front bumper and you stand right there and don't move," she ordered.

"I'm filming this whole thing."

"Great, be sure you get my good side. Now do what I told you."

14

"Oh, this is going to be one hell of a lawsuit," the woman said, but at least she complied and moved to the front of the car.

"Okay, your turn," Robyn told the backseat passenger who had refused to get out. "I'm only going to tell you once."

"Go to hell, bitch."

Robyn pushed the back of the front passenger seat forward and reached for her arm. The woman slapped her hand away and shouted, "Don't touch me!"

"That was a big mistake," Robyn told her. She grabbed the woman's arm and started to pull her out of the seat. When the woman slapped at her again, Robyn pulled her can of pepper spray from the pouch on her belt and said, "Stop resisting or I'm going to spray you."

"I'm not resisting. I'm just not going to do what you tell me to do."

"Out of the car," Robyn ordered one last time. The young woman defiantly crossed her arms over her chest and shook her head. Robyn reached for her again and she pulled her foot back, ready to kick the deputy. Robyn looked at Weber, who nodded, then she sprayed a burst of pepper spray in the woman's face.

"What the hell are you doing? You're going to kill her!"

Robyn ignored the driver as she pulled the passenger out of the car and forced her to the ground, face down.

Meanwhile, Weber opened the driver's door and said, "You two. Out now. We're done playing games here."

They protested stridently, but neither one wanted to join their friend on the ground where she was gagging and screaming that her face and eyes were on fire. Weber ordered them and the front seat passenger to the rear of the Camaro and faced them towards it, hands-down on the trunk lid. While Robyn handcuffed them and patted them down, he used his portable radio to notify Dispatch that they needed an ambulance at his location.

Robyn had set the woman who had been pepper sprayed upright, then got a bottle of water from her patrol car and splashed some onto the woman's face. "This will hold you until the paramedics get here," she said.

"Why did you spray me? I wasn't doing anything!"

15

"You refused to obey a lawful order from a police officer and then you tried to assault me," Robyn said.

"I wasn't under arrest, I didn't have to obey you!"

"Well, you're under arrest now," Robyn told her, then recited her Miranda rights.

"This is crazy," sobbed the driver. "What kind of people are you, anyway? We were just minding our own business."

"None of this had to happen," Weber said. "You chose to speed. You chose to ignore my flashing lights. And you chose to give me a bunch of attitude. And your friend there chose to resist a lawful order from Deputy Fuchette. All any of you had to do was comply, but you all had to make an issue out of it instead."

"Are we all under arrest?"

"Not at this point. And my advice to you would be to shut your mouth and keep it shut," he told the front seat passenger. "And yeah, I know you recorded the whole thing. That's okay, so did we. That's why we have dash cameras and body cameras."

The ambulance arrived and Robyn walked the handcuffed prisoner to the back of it where paramedic Rusty Heinz flushed the woman's eyes and face. She was no longer defiant, instead crying and saying she didn't want to go to jail. Rusty, a stocky bald man with a goatee and a silver hoop in his left ear, just rolled his eyes and looked at Robyn, shaking his head. Nobody ever wanted to go to jail and nobody ever thought they should have to, no matter what their actions were.

Robyn joined Weber, who was searching the Camaro. "Are we taking them all or just the one?"

"I don't find anything illegal, so just the one," he told her. "Hopefully the others will have learned a lesson seeing what happened to their friend."

"Don't hold your breath," Robyn said. "Girls like that never learn. They think being pretty and being from families with a lot of money is a license to do anything they want and it's okay."

"I don't know about that," Weber said. "You're pretty, and you don't have a piss poor attitude."

16

"Well, I guess we can both thank God I wasn't from a rich family," she told him, then added "And you've told me more than once that I have an attitude."

He returned her impish smile and said, "It's an attitude I've gotten used to. How about you uncuff those three and we'll send them on their way? Once Rusty is done with the prisoner, you can take her to jail."

"Oh sure, I get to stink up my unit with pepper spray instead of yours."

"It's one of the perks of being sheriff," Weber told her with a grin. "I give the orders and you follow them."

"That's just until we get home and take off the uniforms, mister. Don't you forget that."

"I've seen you take your uniform off a lot of times," Weber replied with the same grin. "And believe me, it's something I'll never forget."

Chapter 4

By the time Robyn got the prisoner lodged in a cell and gave her an orange jumpsuit to wear, her family's attorney had already called, demanding that his client be released. Mary explained to him that she would be taken before the judge the next morning and gave him the court date and time so he could be in attendance. He was still telling her how important the young woman's family was and how many connections they had in high places, and about all the different lawsuits he would be bringing forth against the Town of Big Lake, the Sheriff's Department, and the officers involved when Mary hung up on him.

"I guess her friends didn't waste any time calling their daddies, did they?"

"That's fine. As long as they are whining to them, they're not sassing us," Robyn said.

"That's true," Mary said, rising from her seat at the dispatch desk. "I need to make a pitstop. Would you cover the phones for me?"

"You're just afraid that lawyer's going to call back, aren't you?"

"I've lived with Pete Caitlin longer than you've been alive," Mary said. "I'm not afraid of anybody."

The bathroom door down the hall had barely closed when the phone rang. Robyn answered and the caller was someone who identified himself as John Pelszynski. He told her they had rented a cabin for the summer, and that his wife and two children stayed there to escape the desert heat while he returned to Phoenix during the workweek and came back up to the mountains on the weekends.

"I know this is going to sound crazy," he said. "But I'm down in the Valley and my wife said she took the kids to the lake, and when she came back there was somebody dressed in black pajamas with a hood over their face looking in one of the windows."

"When did this happen?"

"She just called me. Said her and the kids are still in the car and they left and are parked down the block because she's afraid of whoever it is."

Robyn got the address from him and assured him that deputies were on the way. Then she got on the microphone and said that every unit available was needed at that location. Dan Wright, Coop, and Weber responded that they were all on their way.

Coop was the first officer on the scene, stopping long enough beside the woman's minivan to ask if she had seen the trespasser again since they left the house. She told him no and he instructed her to stay where she was with her children while they checked things out. By the time he pulled into the driveway, Dan was right behind him. They got out and approached the cabin from both sides. Weber arrived a moment later and drove past, made a right turn and then went to the street behind the location, looking for anybody matching the description. He drove down the next two streets, carefully peering into yards and seeing nobody. Returning to the cabin, he found Coop and Dan were standing in the driveway.

"Anything?"

Both deputies shook their heads.

"Not a thing," Coop said. "Whoever was here is long gone now."

Weber went out into the street and called to get the woman's attention, then waved her forward. She was a typical soccer mom, dressed casually in a purple T-shirt and white shorts, with a worried expression on her face. The children, a boy and a girl who looked like they were probably middle school age, were wide-eyed with fear and excitement.

"Ma'am, I'm Sheriff Weber. I'm sorry you were bothered like this. Can you tell me what happened?"

The woman, who identified herself as Janie Pelszynski, said that she had made the children breakfast, and then they had gone to the park on the shore of the lake and spent several hours there. The little girl, whose name was Charlotte, added that she had caught a fish but that her brother Bobby had not.

"Well, that's fishing for you," Weber said. "How big was the fish you caught?"

"It was this big," the girl said, holding her hands apart to indicate the size.

"No, it wasn't," Bobby disagreed. "It was a lot littler than that."

"Was, too," Charlotte insisted.

"There's some big ones in there," Weber said, then turned back to their mother. "So, you came back here and then what?"

"I was pulling in the driveway when I saw him," she replied. "He was at that window there. The one all the way in back on this side."

"Was he trying to get in?"

"I don't think so. It was more like he was looking inside to see if anybody was there."

"And he was dressed all in black?"

"Yes, sir. Black pants, black shirt, and some kind of black thing over his head."

"You said over his head. Like a mask or more like a hood?"

She thought for a moment and then said, "Both, I guess. He turned his head and looked when he heard the car and his whole face was covered. Then he turned around and ran away, but I couldn't see his hair."

"You said he. Do you know for a fact that it was a male?"

She shrugged her shoulders and said, "No, I guess not. I mean, I didn't see any boobs or a shape that told me it was a woman, so I just assumed it was a man."

"That's fine. Let me ask you this, Mrs. Pelszynski. Could you tell anything about his age? Like, was it a kid or an adult? Or a teenager, maybe?"

"I'm sorry," she said, shaking her head. "I really don't know. He moved quick, more like a teenager than an adult maybe, but I can't say for certain. Like I said, he was all in black and I couldn't see his face. I'm sorry, I guess I'm not a very good witness, am I?"

"You're doing fine," Weber assured her. "Nobody expects to come home and see something like that. And from the way you describe him, there wasn't much to see."

"Well, I saw enough to scare the bejesus out of me, I can tell you that!"

"That's perfectly understandable. Would you mind if we have a look through the house before you and your kids go in?"

"You don't have to worry about that," she assured him. "I have no intention of going back in there ever again. Or taking my children in there!"

"Just sit tight for a bit longer. I'm sure there's nobody in the house, but we just want to be certain, okay? May I have the keys?"

Robyn had arrived on the scene and she stayed with the mother and her children while Weber and the two deputies approached the cabin. Dan went to the rear to block any exit attempt someone might make if they were inside while Weber and Coop made entry.

It was typical of the many summer cabins that had transformed the once sleepy little mountain town into a resort community. A living room in the front with two small bedrooms on the left side, a larger bedroom and bathroom on the other side, and a kitchen in the rear. A card table in the living room held a kids boardgame and there were a scattering of toys around, but otherwise the place looked neat and tidy. They cleared every room and then went back outside.

"There's no sign of forced entry and nothing looks out of place," Weber told the woman. "I'm sure whoever it was didn't get

22

in. And after you scared him away, I doubt he's going to be back. But I will make sure that we have a deputy driving by on a regular basis."

"There's no way I'm going to be staying here with just my kids," Mrs. Pelszynski said. "Not without my husband here. We're going back home."

"Home? I thought we were going to be here all summer. I don't want to go home," the little boy said.

"Neither do I," his sister added. "I want to catch another fish."

"Look, ma'am, it's after 3 o'clock now," Weber said. "There's no way you're going to get all the way back to Phoenix before dark. I promise you, we'll keep an eye on things and you're going to be okay."

"Maybe we should stay in a hotel, at least for the night. Then tomorrow…"

"That's an option," the sheriff agreed. "But this time of year there are not that many places with rooms available, and they're not cheap. Like I said, we'll have somebody driving by on a regular basis. And if you see or hear anything at all, you call us and we'll have somebody here right away."

"I don't know," she said, still not convinced. "Are you sure it's going to be okay?"

"If I wasn't sure I wouldn't tell you it was okay. We've got at least one, maybe two kids running around playing ninja. This isn't the first incident that's happened like this. I know it was scary for you and your little ones, but I'm sure it was just a harmless teenage prank."

He didn't tell her about the attack on Doug Mullins. He was sure that was an isolated incident, and he was just as sure that if she knew about it, she would be heading back to Phoenix so fast that she would put herself and her children's lives in danger on the mountain roads between Big Lake and home.

She nodded her head somewhat reluctantly and said, "Okay. But promise me you guys will be around."

"You have my word on it," Weber told her. He took a business card from his pocket and wrote his cell phone number on the back. "If you hear anything at all, even if you're not sure, you call 911 right away. And that's my cell phone. Don't hesitate to call me night or day. We'll be here, I promise."

"Okay, we'll give it a try."

Weber watched as she herded her kids into the house, both of them excited by the police cars and all of the activity happening around them.

"Whoever's pulling this shit, we need to put a stop to it," Coop said once the woman and her children were safely inside. "Sooner or later this clown is going to come across the wrong person and somebody is going to get hurt."

"I don't doubt that for a minute," Weber said. "Not for one minute."

Chapter 5

"This is crazy crap, man," Larry Parks said that evening as they waited for their dinner at Mario's Pizzeria. "What's next, Bigfoot hitchhiking through downtown?"

"I don't know," Weber replied. "I keep thinking it's just kid stuff, but when they start going after somebody with a sword it's a lot more than kid stuff."

"I was talking to Tracy Mullins at the beauty shop today," Marsha Perry said. "She told me that Doug was so shaken up by what happened that he couldn't sleep. He was up and down all night long, checking the doors and windows to make sure they were locked. She said they never locked their doors before this happened."

"I remember a time when nobody ever locked their doors in this town," Christine Ridgeway said. "Shoot, I don't know if we even had a lock on our front door when I was a kid."

"Me, either," Weber said. "And even with all the newcomers, a lot of the old timers still don't."

"Why would anybody go after Doug, of all people? He's one of the nicest guys I've ever known," Christine said. "Do you know that he came up and fenced off an area next to the house to make a dog run for our residents and didn't charge a penny for it? He said it was leftover material from another job, but even so, he worked on it for almost two days."

"A dog run? Why does a women's shelter need a dog run?"

"Surprisingly, there are women that won't leave their abusive home for fear of leaving their pets behind. And having them there, especially if they have kids, too, helps to make them feel more comfortable. At least something in their life hasn't changed."

"I guess I don't get that," Marsha said.

"That's because you've never been a pet owner," Christine told her. "For a lot of people, they are as much a part of their family as their kids are. Haven't you ever heard the term fur babies?"

"Yeah, but I thought they were talking about big hairy kids."

"You really need to get a dog, Marsha," Robyn said.

"No way! I work in the shop all day long and then I come home and have to take care of this fool," her friend replied, nudging Parks in the ribs. "What's it been, two or three years now? And I still haven't gotten him housebroken."

The batwing doors to the kitchen opened and Salvatore Gattuccio came through with a large pizza in each hand, setting them on metal holders on the table.

"Here you go, my dear friends. Dinner is served," the big man said with a bow. "Please, eat and enjoy."

"You park your butt right here in this chair next to me and you eat with us, Sal," Christine said. "That's our deal, right? You get to be the fancy restaurateur the rest of the time, but when we're here you eat with us."

"Restaurateur. That's a fancy word for a fancy man," Sal replied. "Me, I'm just a fat man who makes pizzas in a little town."

"You hush up," Christine told her boyfriend. "You are not fat, and neither am I. We're just fluffy."

The big man laughed and shook his head, sitting down beside her. "No, my love, you are fluffy. Sal? He is fat."

Christine put her arms around him and squeezed, saying "That just means there's more of you to love."

"Would you two get a room? People are trying to eat here," Marsha said with a smile as she used a spatula to put two slices of pepperoni pizza on Parks' plate.

"You hypocrite," the FBI agent said. "You just about raped me on the kitchen table last night before dinner."

26

"You can't rape the willing," Marsha told him as she put two slices on her own plate.

"Ewww. On the kitchen table? We eat off that table when we have dinner at your place," Robyn said.

"Yeah, and you sit on the couch and recliner, too," Marsha replied. "What's your point?"

"Well, my point was that I should probably buy you some of those folding TV trays, but now I think you need all new furniture."

"Oh, those TV trays don't work, Robyn," Parks told her. "They fall apart as soon as you put any weight on them. Talk about a mood killer."

Robyn looked at Sal and said, "Please tell me you guys don't do the nasty on these tables."

Sal blushed, but Christine said, "Of course not. We're not animals doing it right out here where anybody could walk by and look in the window! Not when Sal's got that big prep table in the kitchen. It's sturdy and out of sight."

"I think I'm just going to become a vegetarian," Robyn replied.

Marsha grinned at Parks and said, "Guess I shouldn't tell her about what happens in the garden, should I?"

Their laughter was interrupted when the door opened and a balding gangly man dressed in overalls with a long-sleeved green T-shirt under them came through the door and to their table.

"Hey, Jimmy. I hate to interrupt your dinner, but I have something I want to show you. I stopped by the office and the dispatcher said you were here. She said it was something she was pretty sure you would want to see."

"What have you got, Wes?"

"A while back I put a couple of trail cameras up behind the house because my wife likes to feed the squirrels and birds that come around and I thought she would like to have some videos of them. But one of the cameras picked up something else. I just happened to see it a little while ago when we were looking at the videos. Here, I'll show you."

He pulled a smart phone from his pocket and said, "I put it on my phone so you could see."

He pushed the button to start the video and handed the phone to Weber. The scene opened with a view of a well tended backyard with three posts sunk into the ground that held feeders stocked with seeds and nuts. Then, about 45 seconds into the video, Weber saw something that took him by surprise. Apparently wildlife wasn't the only thing out and about. The screen showed a person dressed all in black with a hood over their head that left just a slit for the eyes walking out of the tree line behind the house, pausing to look in both directions, and then going out of view as they passed under the camera. Less than a minute later the same mysterious stranger made a hurried exit from the yard and the video showed why. Wes Manchester's medium-sized mixed breed dog was chasing the intruder, nipping at his or her heels.

"I'll be damned," Weber said, passing the camera to Robyn. "Check this out."

Parks leaned over to see the video, too, while Weber asked, "Any idea when this was taken, Wes?"

"Yeah, there's a timestamp down there on the bottom. This happened this afternoon, 2:21 according to the timestamp."

"That's interesting. You live on Whippoorwill Way, right?"

"Yeah. 411 Whippoorwill. What's that got to do with anything?"

"That means you're one street over from Redbird Road. We had a call this afternoon about someone dressed just like the person in this video peeking in the window of a summer cabin on Redbird. 419 Redbird, to be exact."

"That's almost directly behind my place," Wes said. "One of those summer cabins they put up a couple of years ago."

"Is this the only video you have of whoever this character is, Wes?"

"Gosh, I don't know, Jimmy. I saw that and thought it was some kid probably trying to break into my place. That's why I took it to the office. I wanted you to see it. Do you think it's a burglar?"

"Have you heard anything about someone pretending to be a ninja running around town getting into mischief, Wes?"

He shrugged his shoulders and said, "No, but neither one of us has been out of the house much the last few days. Charlene's got IBS and it has been kicking up lately. In fact, the only time we were gone was today when we drove over to Show Low to the doctor's office. He wants to change her medication and we're hoping that will help her. Sorry folks, that's not really something you want to hear about when you're having dinner."

"It's okay," Robyn assured him. "No problem."

"When did you leave and when did you get home, Wes?"

"Let me think for a minute, Jimmy. We left sometime before noon. We needed to stop at the Lowes in Show Low because Charlene wants to put that laminate floor stuff in the kitchen and hallway and we wanted to see what they had. We did that, then went to her doctor, and then on the way home we stopped at Jack-in-the-Box to grab something to eat. I would say it was probably close to five when we got home. Charlene really likes seeing all the animals, so once we were back home, I went outside and got the SD cards out of the cameras and popped them into the computer. That's when I saw this. It's a good thing that fool didn't come around when we were home. He might have gotten an ass full of birdshot."

"Yeah, that wouldn't be a good idea," the sheriff said. "I think this is probably some goofy kid playing games. I don't think it's a real threat."

"Maybe not, Jimmy. You know me, I wouldn't just shoot somebody for the sake of shooting them. I'm just blowing off steam. But it does aggravate me that someone is trespassing on my property like that."

Weber did know Wes Manchester and his wife. Their families had lived in Big Lake forever and they were solid citizens. Wes worked at the water department, and before Charlene's IBS got so bad that it was almost incapacitating at times, she had worked at the grocery store.

"I'd be aggravated, too, if somebody was snooping around my place. Is there a way I can get a copy of this video, Wes?"

"Yeah, I can email it to you. Here, hang on a second." He took the phone back from Robyn and asked, "What's your email address, Jimmy?"

Weber told him, and a moment later his phone alerted to tell him he had a new email. He opened it and pushed the attachment icon that showed the video was there.

"Would you do me a favor, Wes? When you get home, would you check the card from the other camera and see if you can come up with anything else? And if you do, can you let me know right away?"

"Sure, Jimmy. I'll go check right now."

Weber wrote his cell phone number on the back of the business card and handed it to him. "If you find something, let me know."

"Will do. Again, sorry to interrupt your dinner. I just thought you might want to know."

"Not a problem. Anytime you have something suspicious like this going on, let me know, Wes."

The man started for the door and then stopped and said, "Jimmy, I don't want you to think I would just blow somebody away if they walked into my backyard. I know better than that."

The sheriff smiled at him and said, "I'm not worried about you doing something like that, Wes. We're good."

When he was gone, Robyn and Weber looked at the video again, then passed the phone around to the other people at their table. Nobody recognized whoever was inside the black costume.

"I have no idea who that could be," Marsha said.

"Me, neither. It's hard to even tell if it's a man or a woman," Christine said.

"I don't know who it is either," Weber said, taking the phone back, "But I damn sure intend to find out."

Chapter 6

After dinner, Weber and Robyn drove back to the cabin on Redbird Road. It was almost 8 PM and he wasn't sure how late Janie Pelszynski and her kids might be up, but there were lights on inside the cabin as well as yard lights on in the front and back. He could hear a television playing inside, and when he knocked, he heard someone moving toward the door.

"Who is it?"

"Mrs. Pelszynski, it's Sheriff Weber and Deputy Fuchette. We were here earlier. We just need a couple minutes of your time."

A curtain at one of the windows moved aside and he saw the woman looking at them tentatively. When she recognized who they were, a look of relief came over her face. She opened the door and said, "Please, come in. Sorry to keep you waiting. I guess I'm paranoid with everything that happened."

"No problem," Weber assured her. "I'd feel the same way if I was in your shoes."

While their mother might have been skittish, her children were not. The boy and girl both greeted them with smiles and all kinds of questions.

"Did you find the bad guy?"

"Did you put him in jail?"

"Is that a real gun? Can I see it?"

"You two hush," their mother said, then turned back to Weber and Robyn, "I'm sorry. This is all new to them."

"No problem," Weber said, then addressed the children. "No, we haven't caught the bad guy yet, but we're working on it. And yes, it's a real gun, but you can't see it. Sorry."

"Did you ever shoot anybody?"

"Bobby! That's a terrible think to ask somebody."

The boy's mother looked at Weber and said, "I'm sorry."

"That's okay," he told her. "Kids are curious about everything."

Charlotte had been studying Robyn carefully. Finally, she spoke up. "You're a girl, right?"

"I was the last time I looked."

"I didn't know girls could be cops."

"Girls can be anything they want to be," Robyn told her. "What do you want to be when you grow up?"

"I was going to be a doctor, but now I think I want to be a cop just like you."

"You might want to rethink that," Robyn told her. "Doctors make a lot more money than cops do."

"Yeah, but they don't get to have guns and cars with lights and sirens and stuff on them."

"I guess that's true. Everything in life is a trade-off."

"If I can't see your gun, can I see your handcuffs?"

"Bobby…"

"I think that's fair enough, as long as it's okay with your mom," Weber said. Though they were dressed in civilian clothes, both he and Robyn carried handguns in inside the waist holsters and handcuffs tucked behind their belts.

"Can I, Mom? Can I really see them?"

"Okay," she said. "But then I need both of you to be quiet so we can talk."

Weber pulled his handcuffs loose and handed them to the boy, who looked at them in fascination.

"They're heavy."

"I want to see them, too. Show me, Bobby," his sister said.

While the kids were occupied with the handcuffs, Weber showed their mother the video from Wes Manchester's trail camera. "Does this look like the person you saw here earlier today?"

"Yes, that's him. I'm sure of it. Where was this taken?"

"One of your neighbors on the street behind you has a couple of trail cameras set up in his backyard. According to the timestamp, this was at 2:21 this afternoon."

"That sounds about right. I think that's just about the time we got home from the lake. Hang on a second."

She went to an end table and picked up her own phone and came back, scrolling through the screen. "Yeah, right here. See? I called my husband at 2:17, as soon as we backed out of the driveway and drove down the street."

Weber looked at the call log on her telephone and nodded his head. "That means whoever it was left your place and went through the woods behind here and into the Manchester's yard. Then their dog scared him away."

"Do you have any idea where he went from there?"

"No, ma'am. Not yet. But we're working on it."

The woman wrapped her arms across her chest and shivered. "I'm still not sure I made the right decision, staying up here."

"Mrs. Pelszynski, we understand completely," Robyn told her. "And if either the sheriff or I believed you and your children were in any danger at all, we would tell you. But we both think this is some kid playing pranks."

"It may be a kid playing pranks, but it still scared me to death."

"I'm sure it did. It would me, too, if I was in your place."

There was a sound of a car pulling in the driveway, and a moment later Deputy Buz Carelton knocked on the door. Weber opened the door and let him in.

"I was driving by and saw your unit here, Jimmy. Everything okay?"

"Yeah," the sheriff told his longtime deputy. "Take a look at this."

He handed Buz his cell phone so he could see the video. Buz, who was in his 40s, had earned his nickname as a schoolboy because of his long, skinny neck and hawk-like nose, which made the other kids say he was part buzzard. He looked at the video and shook his head.

"No way to tell who it is under that getup."

"Well, keep an eye out and keep driving by here, will you, Buz?"

"I sure will."

Bobby, who had by now lost interest in the handcuffs, was staring at the newcomer.

"How come you've got such a big nose?"

"Bobby!"

"It's okay," the deputy assured the boy's mother, then squatted down to be on eye level with the curious child. "Well, here's what happened. Did you know that when babies are born, the doctor slaps them on their butt? The reason the doctor does that is to make them cry, which cleans out their lungs so they can breathe easier."

"Okay."

"Well, when I was born, the doctor was having a real bad day. I mean, real bad. He had a flat tire on the way to the hospital, and after he changed the tire, he was driving real fast to get to the hospital and Sheriff Weber here pulled him over and gave him a ticket for speeding."

"My daddy got one of those," Bobby said. "Mommy was real mad at him."

"That happens sometimes," Buz told him, then continued his story. "The same thing happened when the doctor got to the hospital. This mean old nurse named Thelma was yelling at him for being late and getting a ticket and that made the doctor kind of mad. So when I was born, he picked me up and slapped my butt like he was supposed to, but like I said, he was kind of mad. So he slapped me a little bit too hard by mistake, and my nose popped out like that and it's been that way ever since."

"Uh uh! You made that up!"

"Did I? Are you sure about that?"

"I get in trouble sometimes and I get spanked on my butt, but my nose never did that."

"It's a pretty rare thing," Buz told him. "But that's what happened."

Bobby looked toward Weber and Robyn, seeking some confirmation or denial of the story in their faces. But they were giving nothing away."

"Anyway," the sheriff said, "everything is okay and you're going to be just fine, Mrs. Pelszynski. Deputy Carelton here will be on duty until 2 AM, and when the shift changes, Deputy Wingate and Deputy Northcutt will be on. Everybody knows to come by here on a regular basis. And like I said, if you have any problems at all, you call us. Okay?"

"Okay," she said, but Weber could hear a bit of reticence in her voice. He retrieved his handcuffs and they bade them all good night before leaving.

On the drive home, Robyn said, "I hate to see somebody that scared over this kind of nonsense. Stupid kids doing stuff like this. Why, Jimmy?"

"I guess it could be worse," he told her. "Teenagers down in the city are getting high and shooting each other or ripping off people's houses."

"Not every kid in the city does that stuff."

"You're right. And not every kid up here is running around playing ninja. Just one, or maybe two if we can believe the story about two of them sword fighting on the school playground."

"It doesn't matter if it's one or two, it's still too many," Robyn said.

They arrived at their house, which had been newly built on the same property where Weber's family home had once stood before an arsonist burned it to the ground. When they went inside, Weber stood for a moment in the kitchen, looking like he had something on his mind.

"What's wrong, Jimmy?"

"Nothing's wrong. I was just wondering about something."

"What's that?"

"Well, Parks and me are about the same size, but you're a lot smaller than Marsha."

"Yeah. So what?"

"So how sturdy do you think this kitchen table is?"

Chapter 7

"This whole thing is outrageous, Your Honor. It's police brutality! Abuse of power! What kind of police department do you have up here when an innocent young woman minding her own business and out for a ride with friends can be pepper sprayed and then pulled from a car and handcuffed face down in the dirt? And then to lock her in a cell overnight like a common criminal? Someone is going to pay for this terrible miscarriage of justice!"

The man's name was Daniel Richardson, but with his thousand dollar suit, his razor cut silver hair, the gold framed half glasses perched low on his nose, and his imperious manner, Weber had mentally identified the attorney as Dapper Dan and he already had no use for the man.

"My client is innocent of all of these charges," the attorney continued in a haranguing tone of voice, "and her family will be bringing a lawsuit against the Sheriff's Department and the Town of Big Lake for unlawful arrest, police brutality, and unlawful detainment."

"Your Honor, as the dashboard and body cam videos clearly prove, Sheriff Weber made a lawful traffic stop because the driver was speeding," said town attorney Bob Bennett. "And as you can hear and see quite plainly on those videos, the defendant, Miss Pendhill, who was a passenger in the car and not involved in the interaction between the sheriff and the car's driver, was argumentative right from the start. When Deputy Fuchette attempted to remove her from the vehicle, after Miss Pendhill refused a lawful order to do so more than once, she tried to slap Deputy Fuchette not once, but twice, and then she pulled her foot back like she was going to kick Deputy Fuchette. Only then was pepper spray deployed as a last resort to protect both the defendant and Deputy Fuchette from injury."

"That's all a lie. My client did no such thing."

"We've all seen the same video, Counselor," Judge Harold Ryman said. "What I saw was what Sheriff Weber and Deputy Fuchette have in their incident reports and what they have both testified to here this morning."

"Those videos are irrelevant," the attorney said, waving his hand dismissively as if to brush them away. "In fact, they are inadmissible because my client did not give permission to be recorded. They are a violation of her right to privacy."

"That's nonsense, Your Honor," Bennett said. "Both dash cameras and body cameras are common tools of law enforcement and legal precedent has established that a defendant has no right to privacy when it comes to being filmed in the course of an officer's duty."

Daniel Richardson slammed his fist down on the table and said, "I object!"

"What is it you object to, sir? Mr. Bennett is simply establishing legal precedent for the admission of these videos into this hearing," Judge Ryman said.

Bob Bennett leaned toward Weber and said just loud enough to be heard, "There's an old saying among attorneys. When the law is on your side, pound the law. When the facts are on your side, pound the facts. If neither one are on your side, pound the table."

"Even if the videos are admissible, which I still intend to dispute, there is no question in my mind that both Sheriff Weber and Deputy Fuchette overreacted right from the start. There was no reason that this routine traffic stop should have escalated to this point."

"Now, that's something we can agree on, Mr. Richardson," the judge responded. "After looking at the videos more than once, it is obvious that there is absolutely no reason this had to happen except that all four young women in that car were rude and disrespectful to Sheriff Weber right from the start."

"Since when do we pepper spray and arrest people for being rude and disrespectful in this country, Your Honor?"

The judge scowled at the interruption. "Excuse me, Mr. Richardson, I'm talking."

The attorney sat back down.

"It's also crystal-clear to me that your client did in fact refuse Deputy Fuchette's lawful orders and that she assaulted Deputy Fuchette when she attempted to remove her from the vehicle, and that she resisted arrest. Unless you have something real to add to the discussion, I believe we're done here."

"This is nothing more than a kangaroo court. This doesn't end here, Judge Ryman. Not by a long shot. I'm giving you notice that I intend to name you as a party to every lawsuit I will be filing in this matter."

The judge was an easy-going man and prone to give young people the benefit of the doubt whenever he could. But he was no pushover and he did not suffer fools well. By threatening to include him in any frivolous lawsuits he might be filing, Richardson had stepped over the line.

"We're done here. Miss Pendhill, please stand."

The defendant and her attorney got to their feet and the judge said, "In view of the videos we have seen and the testimony of the arresting officers, I find you guilty of assault on a police officer and resisting arrest. Assaulting a police officer is something we don't take lightly in Arizona. It is a Class 5 felony and the penalty can include a two year prison sentence, a fine, or both. That means having a felony criminal record that can follow you the rest of your life."

Weber heard the young woman's mother gasp from where she was seated behind him.

"Now, normally in a case like this I tend to be somewhat lenient with a young defendant like yourself. However, you don't seem to have any remorse whatsoever for your actions yesterday."

The woman behind him was sobbing and the young woman standing before the judge bowed her head and wiped tears away.

Weber wasn't sure if that was just for show, or if the reality of just how much trouble she was in was finally hitting home.

"Do you have anything to say before I pass sentence, Miss Pendhill?"

"I just want to…"

"Don't say a word," her attorney interrupted. "This is all bluff, Coleen. They're just trying to intimidate you."

"That's enough, Daniel," the woman's mother said from behind Weber. "We all saw the videos of how Coleen was acting. That wasn't the way she told me it happened. It's obvious to me that these officers tried everything they could to avoid taking it to that level and she left them no choice. And now you're just making it worse."

"I'm doing the job you hired me to do, Ellen."

"If that's the best you can do, you're fired!"

The defendant turned toward her mother and said, "You're taking their side against your own daughter? Nice, Mom!"

Judge Ryman rapped his gavel and said, "Okay, enough. I will not have another outburst like that in this courtroom. Do you understand me?"

"Your Honor, with all due respect…"

"I said you're fired, Daniel. That's it, not another word."

The judge rapped his gavel again, then said, "Miss Pendhill, do you wish to continue to have Mr. Richardson representing you?"

"I don't know. I don't know what to say."

The defendant's mother got up and came forward. "Can I say something, Your Honor?"

"No, ma'am, you can't," the judge said.

"But I'm her mother!"

"Yes, ma'am, I understand that. But your daughter is over 18 and she has legal representation."

"Not unless she plans to figure out some way to pay him herself. Because I'm the one who pays the bills, and I'm the one that hired him, and now I have fired him."

The judge sighed and turned to the defendant once more. "Miss Pendhill, I'll ask you one more time, do you wish to have Mr. Richardson continue representing you?"

"I said I don't know what to do," she snapped, balling her hands into fists and shaking them at her side "Just shut up and give me a minute to think!"

From the glowering look the judge gave the young woman, Weber could tell that she had stepped over the same line her attorney had.

"Young lady, I will remind you that you're in a court of law," Judge Ryman said. "You might want to check your attitude."

"God, why doesn't everybody just shut up for a minute?"

The judge raised his hands palms up and gave Weber and Bob Bennett a perplexed look. "Did I whisper?" Then he turned to the defendant and said, "Miss Pendhill, you are skating on very thin ice with me. I'm going to declare a five minute recess. I suggest you take that time to consult with your attorney, if he is still your attorney, and your mother. And when I bring this court back into session, I expect a show of respect not only for this bench, but for the arresting officers involved in this case."

"You mean your Nazi thugs," Coleen said.

"Oh, you are so close to being held in contempt," the judge said. "If I were you, I would be quiet and take advantage of the time I'm giving you to compose yourself and talk to your people here. Then we will continue. And I am warning you right now, one more outburst from you and you are going back to a cell and you are going to sit there until you realize the error of your ways."

Without giving her a chance to respond, he rapped his gavel, stood up, and went through the door into his chambers.

While Coleen, her mother, and her attorney went into a huddle, Bob Bennett shook his head and leaned toward Weber and Robyn and said. "That little girl needs to learn to keep her mouth shut. Did you see the look on Judge Ryman's face when she told him to shut up?"

"It was the same way with her yesterday," Weber said. "All she had to do was keep her mouth shut and I'd have probably given the driver a warning and sent them on their way. Instead, she talked herself into handcuffs. A night in jail obviously didn't do a thing for her attitude, did it?"

"No, it didn't, Robyn," Bennett said. "And if she doesn't watch herself she's going to be spending a lot more days in a cell."

Raised voices from across the room got their attention and they turned to the trio.

"Coleen you need to settle down right now. All you're doing is digging a deeper hole for yourself."

"Shut up, Mom! I'm not a little girl anymore. You can't tell me what to do."

"As long as you live in my house and I pay the bills, I'll tell you what to do."

"I am so sick and tired of hearing about how I live in your house and I have to follow your rules. I'm done. You can stick your rules in your ass!" And with that, Coleen Pendhill started for the door.

"Hold on there," Robyn said, stepping in front of her to block the way. "Where do you think you're going?"

"Anywhere but here, bitch. Get out of my way."

"I don't think so," Robyn told her. "Now turn around and march yourself back up to the front of the room where you belong."

"Go to hell!"

"I'm not going to tell you again. Get back up there with your mom and your attorney."

"I said get out of my way!" And with that Coleen Pendhill made one more mistake in a long series of mistakes she had made since she came to Big Lake. She shoved Robyn with both hands, forcing the deputy a step backward. In what seemed to be no more than a second later, she found herself facedown on the floor of the courtroom with Robyn on top of her, forcing her arms backward.

"Put your hands behind you and stop resisting!"

Coleen cursed and struggled, turning her head and trying to bite Robyn on the arm. Robyn Fuchette may have been a petite woman, but she was nobody's pushover. And she had tangled with enough drunken cowboys, flatlanders who came up to the mountains to party and raise hell, and other lawbreakers of both genders to be intimidated by a spoiled rich girl who had no respect for the law or anyone else. She grabbed Coleen by the back of the head and pushed her face forcefully into the carpeted floor.

"Stop resisting!"

Weber ran to her assistance, and between the two of them they quickly got her hands cuffed behind her and the sheriff jerked her to her feet.

"You're never going to learn anything, are you?"

Coleen, her nose bleeding from her face plant on the floor, cursed again and spat in his face. The sheriff's natural reaction was to want to punch her, but years of training and experience came into play and instead he just swept her feet out from under her with one of his and put her back down on the floor. Then he put one knee in the middle of her back to keep her there.

"I've got her. Go out to your car and get a spit hood and hobbles," he told Robyn.

She left the courtroom while Coleen continued to struggle. Meanwhile her mother was screaming at her to stop fighting and Dapper Dan Richardson stood to the side, watching the melee with distaste, his arms folded across his chest.

Robyn was back in a moment and it didn't take much longer than that to slip flexible hobbles around the defendant's feet and attach them to her handcuffs. Then they rolled her to her side and placed the spit hood over her head.

Meanwhile, Judge Ryman had returned to his courtroom and seemed to be shocked by what he was seeing taking place in front of him for a moment. He rapped his gavel sharply.

"Enough already! Sheriff Weber, Deputy Fuchette, get this person out of my courtroom."

"Objection, Your Honor!"

"Shut up, Daniel," Coleen's mother said. "I told you, you're fired."

"I'm just looking out for…"

The judge slammed his gavel down so hard that the handle broke right at the head, the heavy wood clattering to the floor in front of the bench.

"Sheriff Weber, get this courtroom under control right now! You two," he said, pointing at the woman's mother and attorney, "take your quarrel outside. This is a courtroom, not some sleazy daytime talk show. Sheriff, check back with me in 48 hours. At that time, if Miss Pendhill can conduct herself as an adult, we will resume. If she gives you any more trouble, I will tack another 48 hours onto it. This hearing is adjourned."

He raised the handle of his gavel as if to rap it again, then realized there was nothing left of it and threw the handle down in disgust and left the courtroom.

Chapter 8

"Wow, what a circus," Robyn said a half hour later. Paramedics had been called to assess the prisoner's bloody nose after Robyn and Deputy Northcutt had taken Coleen back to her cell and removed the handcuffs, hobbles, and spit hood. "I don't think I've ever seen the judge so pissed off."

"That girl's got a way of pissing people off, that's for sure," Weber told her, then asked, "Did she settle down at all?"

"Not much. According to her, you and the judge, and Jordan and the paramedics are all douche bags."

"Really? What are you two, sorority sisters or something?"

Robyn sighed and shook her head. "No, according to her I just need a good douche."

Mary Caitlin laughed in spite of herself and said, "I just love tourist season."

"If they're in season, why can't we shoot them? What's the bag limit, anyway?"

Mary slapped Weber on the arm with the back of her hand and said, "It's attitudes like that that make people call you a douche bag."

"Maybe so," the sheriff agreed. "But what about Jordan? He's a mellow young fellow."

"I saw what you did there," Mary said, pointing at Weber and smiling.

"Does Jordan even know what a douche bag is? Or what it's for?"

The young deputy's face reddened at Dolan Reed's question.

"Give him a break. I don't think they even make those things anymore," Mary said. "Everything is disposable these days, right, Robyn?"

"Can we talk about something else?"

"Yeah, can we, please?"

Weber laughed at his wife and his deputy's discomfort. "Moving right along, what else is happening, Mary?"

"Well, let's see. Dolan took a call for an abandoned car on Brandywine Way. Reporting party said it had been parked in her neighbor's driveway for three days and she knows that they are out of town this week. Plate and VIN came up as stolen out of Holbrook."

"What did you find out there, Dolan?"

"Keys were still in the ignition, Jimmy. I talked to all the people in the neighborhood. Some of them remember seeing the car, but nobody remembers seeing anybody getting in or out of it. I checked the house, it's Walden and Betty LaSalle's place, and everything is secure there."

"That's only a block from Main Street," the sheriff said. "Whoever parked and left it at the LaSalle place probably walked over there. Not much chance of finding out who did it."

"Probably not," Dolan said.

The dispatcher had taken a call and handed the slip to Mary, who looked at it and said, "Here we go again."

"What's up?"

"Kallie Jo just called. She said she was out behind the store putting some trash in the dumpster and she saw the ninja."

"You're kidding?"

"Nope, she's said it wasn't more than a couple of minutes ago."

"Let's go see if we can find this clown," Weber said, heading for the door.

~~~***~~~

"It was the strangest thing, Sheriff Jimmy. I went out to dump the trash and I felt like somebody was lookin' at me. You know that feeling ya get when ya'll feel like someone's spyin' on you? Well, that's exactly how I was feelin.' And I know that feelin'. Yes, sir, I do. There was this boy back home, Bobby Lee Bosarge, well, his name was Bobby Lee, but everybody called him B.B., that's for Bobby and Bosarge."

"Yeah, I got that," Weber replied.

"Yeah, well B.B., he had himself kind of crush on me. I think he started likin' me way back about when we was in the fifth grade. 'Course, he never said anything about it, bein' a shy boy and all that. But we'd be out on the playground at recess and I'd look up and he'd be starin' at me. Or we'd be on the bus goin' home and it just felt like his eyes was borin' a hole right there in the back of my head. If I turned to look, B.B. would real quick like look the other way or drop his head. And he did that all through high school. Yes, sir, he did! At first it was kinda cute, I guess. But then it got kinda creepy, if you know what I mean. It ain't like B.B. was ugly or nothin' like that. No, sir, he was a fine lookin' boy. Fact is, all those Bosarge boys was handsome. My cousin Irene, she married Abraham Bosarge. Now, he weren't one of B.B.'s brothers. I think he was his cousin. Yeah, that's right, 'cause Stumpy Bosarge was B.B.'s daddy, and Abraham's daddy was Carlton, which made him B.B.'s uncle. I mean, it made Carlton B.B.'s uncle, not Abraham. That would make them cousins."

All this was said in a rapid fire monologue that always left Weber wondering how such a tiny woman had the lung capacity to get so many words out at once without stopping to breathe. He had learned a long time ago that when Kallie Jo Wingate started talking, the best thing to do was just nod his head and let his eyes glaze over. Sometimes that worked, but other times, like now, he needed the information she would eventually get around to telling him. So while Kallie Jo tried to explain that the reason B.B.'s daddy was called Stumpy was because he was short and bowlegged, which made him look totally different than his three

47

brothers, Carlton, Leon, and Burt, who all three were tall drinks a' water, Weber interrupted her and asked, "So what happened?"

"With B.B.? Nothin' happened. All through school that boy would just stare at me everywhere I went. I got used to it and usually it didn't bother me none. Well, it did that one time when I came out of the outhouse and saw him standing there in those trees behind our place, starin' at me. I mean, it weren't like he could see what I was doin' inside there, but even so, a girl needs her privacy when she is doin' her business, if you know what I mean. That time I was goin' to go over there and confront him and tell B.B. he needed to either ask me out proper or quit spyin' on me all the time. But as soon as he saw me he turned tail and run."

"Kallie Jo, stop," Weber said, holding up his hands as if he could block the flow of words coming from her. "Tell me about the ninja."

"Who? Oh yeah, the ninja. I'm sorry, Sheriff Jimmy, you know me. I get to talkin' and sometimes I lose track and before you know it I've done went and rattled on all afternoon. My mama is like that, too. Now, bless her heart. I do love my mama, but that woman can talk. One time Daddy said she could talk the whiskers right off of an old house cat. And I believe it was true, yes, sir, I do."

"The ninja, Kallie Jo. All I want to hear about right now is the ninja."

"Oh, that's right. Like I was sayin' before, I came out to throw some trash in the dumpster and I felt like someone was lookin' at me. Don't know why, I just felt it. And when I closed the lid on the dumpster I looked and there he was."

"The ninja?"

"Yes, sir, who else would I be talkin' about?"

Weber was afraid of that can of worms because most the time he had no idea what or who Kallie Jo was talking about, so instead he just said, "Yeah, the ninja. Where was he when you saw him?"

"Right over there, next to the lumber shed."

"And what happened when you saw him? Did he say anything or do anything?"

"No, sir. He just looked at me and then he pulled himself a B.B."

"What? He pulled a B.B.?"

"Yes, sir. He done just like B.B. did that time back home when I come out of the outhouse and saw him standin' there. He just turned around and ran away."

"How long ago was this?"

"I don't honestly know, Sheriff Jimmy, but it weren't long. 'Cause I knew all about the ninja, everybody in town's been talkin' about it. So I came right inside and I called you. Well, I didn't call you, I called Dispatch. Should I have called you directly?"

"No, that's fine," Weber assured her. He walked over to the shed, which was actually a long corrugated metal lean-to that housed racks with different sizes of lumber. There were no footprints or anything to indicate that the mysterious ninja or anybody else had been there, though he didn't expect to find any in the crushed gravel of the lumberyard. But Weber was sure that if Kallie Joe said she had seen him, he was there. Deputy Archer Wingate's mail order bride, a pretty thing from down around Waycross, Georgia, might talk a lot, but she wasn't given to making things up or exaggeration. If she said she saw a ninja standing next to the lumber lean-to, he was sure there had been one there.

"Okay, thanks for letting us know, Kallie Jo. If you see anything suspicious, you call right away."

"I will, I promise."

Weber started to walk back to his car and she asked, "Why would he do that anyway, Sheriff Jimmy?"

"It's hard to say. We think it's just some kid dressing up and acting goofy."

"Oh yeah, that. Probably so. But I was talkin' 'bout B.B. I mean, why would he spy on me like that all the time and never say a word?"

"I guess he was just shy," Weber said, shrugging his shoulders.

"Well, he weren't so shy it didn't keep him from watchin' me go in the outhouse! Do you know that after that, every time I had to go out there I looked all around first, just to make sure he weren't out there no more. It's hard to concentrate on what you're doin' in there when you're wonderin' who's outside!"

"Yeah, I imagine it would be," the sheriff agreed. "Let me see if I can help find this idiot." He started to walk away, then decided that he might want to clarify his last statement. So he turned back to Kallie Joe and said, "I mean the ninja, not B.B."

Chapter 9

Weber and his deputies drove up and down every street within a mile of the hardware store, peering into backyards and getting out to check on anything that looked the least bit suspicious. But once again they saw no sign of the elusive ninja. Back at the office, Weber studied the large map of the town that was attached to a corkboard backing on a wall.

"Mary, do you have some of those little plastic pins you use?"

"Yeah, what do you have in mind?"

"Let's see if we can find a pattern here."

Using the reports they had of the ninja sightings, Weber pushed a pin into the map at each location and stepped back to study it. Standing beside him, Mary asked, "What are you seeing, Jimmy?"

"I'm seeing a pattern, and I'm seeing something totally off the pattern."

"What do you mean?"

"See, this was the first sighting," Weber said, putting his finger on a pin. "Hazel Fuller said she saw the ninja late at night near her garage. We didn't take her seriously because, well, because it was Hazel. Then, two days later Imogene Buckley saw somebody all dressed in black with a hood or mask peeking in her bedroom window. The next sighting was the people from Tucson Friday night, over here on Foxglove Lane. And then Burl and Sharon Pierce said they saw two ninjas fighting with swords at the playground of the middle school, here. Next was when Clyde

Gardner saw a ninja on Appaloosa Trail. Then we had the attack on Doug Mullins over here on Providence Road. The next day Sonia Bristow said she was washing the breakfast dishes and looked out and saw somebody dressed like a ninja running through her backyard.

"Actually, she just said it was somebody in black pajamas with a hood over their head."

"Close enough."

Weber pointed to another pin. "That same day we had a call from a summer visitor saying that a ninja, and that was the term she used when she called it in, was just outside the tree line at her neighbor's backyard on Larkspur Lane. Then here," Weber said, indicating another pin, "Beatrice Kettleman saw the ninja on Flickertail Road yesterday, and the same day the Pelszynski woman and her kids saw him at their cabin on Redbird Road. And then Wes Manchester showed us his trail cam videos from his place on Whippoorwill Way, which is almost directly behind the Pelszynski cabin. And today Kallie Jo saw him at the hardware store." The sheriff stepped back and studied the map, and then asked, "What does this tell us?"

"I don't know. You tell me," Chad said.

"I see it," Mary said. "At least, I think so."

"What am I missing?"

"All of these are in a cluster, more or less, Chad. All except for these two," Mary said pointing at two separate pins. "All of them are right here in town, except for the sighting at Imogene Buckley's place and the attack on Doug Mullins."

"You're right," Chad said nodding his head. "All of these are really close together except those two. The rest of these, they're within what, a mile of each other? But these two," he said, indicating the Buckley and Mullens incidents, "they're both over here, a noticeable distance away. Why did the pattern change with those two?"

"I don't know," Weber said. "There has to be a reason."

"People tend to stay in their comfort zone if they can," Robyn said. "We're assuming a kid is doing this, or kids, since that one reported sighting said there were two of them. A kid doing something he shouldn't be doing isn't going to travel too far from a place he knows."

"And," Chad added, "there's the logistics of it all. Does this kid have a car or access to one? Because the Buckley and Mullens sightings are a good two or three miles from where everything else is taking place. How did he get there?"

"Even though they're not right in town where everything else was happening, I thought nothing of walking a couple of miles to do something when I was a kid," Weber said.

"Yeah, I know, you walked 20 miles uphill in the snow every morning to go to school and 20 more miles uphill to go home," Robyn said.

"And I was barefoot!"

"It doesn't matter what you did when you were growing up," Chad said. "Today's kids won't put down their videogame controllers and get off the couch long enough to walk across the room if they can avoid it."

"Who said Jimmy ever grew up, Chad?"

He chuckled at Robyn's comment, then said, "Okay, I think the greater question is, why these two out here? I guess I can understand someone peeking in Imogene Buckley's window. She's a good looking woman. But why would a kid walk that far to do that?"

"Maybe some student who has a crush on her?"

"I guess that's possible," Weber said. "I know they damn sure didn't have teachers that looked that good when I was in school."

"Maybe it was somebody with a crush like Robyn says. But that still doesn't explain going after Doug Mullins with a sword."

"No, it doesn't, Chad."

"Except for the kids sword fighting or whatever they were doing at the school, there hasn't been any hint of violence except for the thing with Doug Mullins," Weber said. "Anytime you see a break in a pattern, a change of some kind, you have to ask yourself why. Okay, so maybe some kid hopped up on testosterone has the hots for his teacher and goes by her window and gets lucky and sees her getting undressed. But why attack Doug Mullins?"

"That's the one that doesn't make any sense," Chad replied. "I've known Doug forever. He's a nice guy and I can't remember anybody ever having a bad word to say about him. Can you?"

"Nope."

"Me, either," Mary said. "Him or Tracy either one. They're both good people."

"Then do we assume it was a random attack?"

"You know what happens when we assume," Mary said. "You make an ass of you and me."

"Any suggestions of what we do next, guys?"

"I guess my first suggestion is you go back to school and take a lesson in anatomy," Mary told Weber. "Of the three of us standing here with you, only one of us is a guy."

"I don't know whether or not Jimmy needs a lesson in anatomy, but rumor has it that young Mr. Dan Wright may be studying that subject with a certain good-looking schoolteacher these days," Chad said.

"What do you mean?"

"The way I hear it, he's been very diligent about making sure Imogene Buckley isn't bothered anymore."

"Really? Well, he's a good looking man and she's a good looking woman, and they're both young and not attached," the sheriff said. "More power to them."

Mary looked at him quizzically and said, "You're getting soft and romantic ever since you and Robyn got hitched. Way to go, girl!" She raised her hand and gave Robyn a high-five.

Weber looked at Chad and said, "For the record, that whole getting soft thing..."

His deputy grinned and said, "Never believed it for a minute, boss."

The telephone rang again and a moment later dispatcher Kate Copley said, "Sheriff, I've got Doug Mullins on the phone. He says someone just tried to kill him again!"

~~~***~~~

54

Three police cars sped towards the Mullins' home, sirens wailing. Sliding to a stop in front of the house, Robyn and Chad exited their units and ran around both sides of the building with their weapons drawn, ready to confront anybody they found on the property. Weber, with his Kimber .45 semi-automatic pistol in his hand, went to the door and raised his hand to knock, but stopped when he saw what was embedded in the wooden door.

The door opened about three inches and then stopped, held in place by a safety chain.

"Hang on, Sheriff. The door closed again and a moment later a very shaken Doug Mullins opened it.

"Are you injured, Doug?"

The man shook his head, but his face was pale and his teeth were chattering.

"Let's get you inside so you can sit down."

Weber followed him into the tidy house and Mullens sank down into his recliner.

"What the hell happened, Doug?"

"It's crazy. It's flat ass crazy."

"Take a deep breath. There you go. Take another one."

Robyn and Chad came through the door, and when Weber looked up at them, they shook their heads to indicate they had not found anybody.

"I was in my office and the doorbell rang. I didn't think anything of it, so I just opened it. The son of a bitch was standing right there."

"Could you tell who it was?"

"No, just somebody dressed up like a freaking ninja. As soon as I saw him, I started to slam the door shut and he threw that thing at me!"

Chad studied the item, then pulled his phone from his pocket and took several pictures before pulling on latex gloves and pulling it out of the door. He held out his hand to show it to Weber and Robyn.

"What the hell is that thing, anyway?"

"It's a throwing star," Weber told Mullins, examining the five pointed weapon in Chad's hand. "From what I've been able to read about ninjas, it's apparently part of their standard arsenal."

"Why is this happening to me, Sheriff? What the hell did I ever do to anybody to deserve this?"

"I don't know, Doug. Like I told you before, there's been somebody running around town playing ninja. Several people have reported seeing him, but you're the only one who's been attacked."

"Well, that makes me feel a lot better!"

"Did this person say anything to you at all when you opened the door, Doug?"

"No. Nothing at all."

"Did you see what direction he went?"

"No. I was so scared all I wanted to do was put as much distance between him and me as I could. I wasn't sure if he was going to try to kick the door in or if I should run out the back door, or just call you guys."

"You did the right thing," Weber assured him. "If you would've run outside, he might have gone around the back and been there waiting for you. In a situation like this, never leave a safe sanctuary where you have locked doors between you and whoever is out there." The sheriff didn't mention the possibility there might be more than one person playing ninja in Big Lake.

There was the sound of a car door slamming outside and Tracy Mullins burst through the door.

"Doug, are you okay? What happened?"

"He tried to kill me again, Tracy."

"What? Who tried to kill you?"

"That crazy ninja."

"No way!"

She turned to Weber and he nodded his head as Chad held out the throwing star for her to see.

"What happened?"

"Apparently, somebody rang the doorbell, and when your husband opened the door, someone dressed like a ninja was standing out there and threw this at him," Weber said.

"Oh, honey! Are you all right?"

She leaned over the recliner and hugged her husband tightly. Weber could hear Doug sobbing and Tracy murmured comforting words to him. They gave him a moment to compose himself, and then Tracy turned to the sheriff and asked, "Why is this happening? Why my husband? Doug doesn't have an enemy in the world."

"I don't know, Tracy. I really don't," Weber admitted. "This started out as kid stuff, somebody dressed up like a ninja running through people's backyards and things like that. And we had a couple reports of this character being a Peeping Tom, looking in people's windows. But nobody has been attacked or threatened except for Doug. We're as mystified as you are as to why he's being singled out."

"Well, you have to do something! Doug has a bad heart, he can't handle this kind of stress."

"I promise you, we're trying to get to the bottom of it. Can either of you think of anybody at all that might be upset with Doug for any reason? Maybe a customer who didn't like a fencing job he did, or a former employee? Anybody at all?"

Doug shook his head, but after a moment his wife asked, "What about Marvin Harris? Do you think he would do something this crazy?"

"Marvin? No way," her husband said, shaking his head dismissively.

Weber knew Marvin Harris. He also owned a fencing company and was in competition with Mullins. Marvin had always seemed like a decent guy to him.

"Have you two had any conflicts?"

"Not really," Doug said. "I mean, we bid on a lot of the same jobs, and sometimes I get them and sometimes he gets them. But we've always gotten along."

"What about the Rhino? He was pretty upset about that," Tracy said.

"Honey, that was months ago, and it all worked out."

"What's a rhino and what are we talking about?"

"It's a tool for driving fenceposts," Doug said. "We borrowed one from Marvin and the guy who was working for me lost it. At least he said he lost it. I kind of think he sold it to somebody."

"And Marvin Harris was upset about that?"

"Yeah, but like I said, we worked it out."

"You worked it out, but not before Marvin said he was going to kick your ass," his wife said, and then turned to the sheriff and said, "You need to talk to him. Maybe he's behind all of this!"

Chapter 10

"Are you kidding me? Doug Mullins thinks I tried to kill him?"

Weber had talked to a lot of suspects about a lot of crimes over the years and was pretty good at reading body language. From the incredulous look on Marvin Harris' face and the tone of his voice, he seemed genuinely surprised that he would be accused of the attacks on his competitor.

"Nobody's saying you did anything like that," the sheriff assured him. "Like I said, his wife mentioned something about there being some hard feelings between the two of you about some tool that got lost or something."

"A tool?"

"I think she called it a rhino."

"Oh, that? Yeah, I guess I was a little pissed, but it was not that big of a deal. And I damn sure wouldn't try to hurt somebody over something like that. Especially not Doug Mullins. He's a good man, Jimmy."

"I'm afraid I don't even know what a rhino is," Weber admitted. "Can you clue me in about what happened there?"

"A Rhino is a gas powered post driver. A while back Doug called me and said his was on the blink and he was in the middle of a job and asked if he could borrow mine. I said sure and he came and got it. It went by a week or so, maybe two, and I had a job coming up and I needed it. I called Doug and asked when he would be finished with it. He said he thought he had already returned it, and I told him no. He said he would get it right over to me, and then I didn't hear anything else for two or three days, so I called him again. He said that it had been returned and I told him it hadn't been, and we went around and around about that for a little bit. But we worked it out and got past it. It really wasn't that big of a deal."

"According to Tracy Mullins, you threatened to kick Doug's ass."

"What? No way!"

"That's what she said."

"I'd never say that! Shoot, Doug and I may be competitors, but we've always gotten along great. Sometimes I need to borrow some material or a tool from him and there's no problem and the same way on my end of things. There's plenty of business to go around, what with all the building that's going on here these days."

"If you two get along so well, why was there the hassle over the Rhino tool?"

"Like I said, I needed it for a job. And it's not something you can just run down to the hardware store and buy. They cost a couple grand and you have to go through a supplier that carries them. So yeah, I didn't appreciate the downtime on the job and I didn't want to lose a tool that cost that much money. But again, we worked it out."

"And just how did you go about working it out?"

"Apparently Doug told this kid he had working for him to return it, and the kid didn't. So, when Doug told me they had brought it back and I told him no, we both maybe got a little hot under the collar. Doug said something like he wouldn't lie to me, and I told him I wouldn't lie to him either, but he was wrong when he said they had returned it. It took him another week or so to scrape up the money, but he bought me a brand-new one. I told him my Rhino was a couple of years old and he didn't have to buy a brand-new one, but that's what he did. He told me that he had fired the guy he had working for him because he was pretty sure he had stolen it instead of bringing it back to me."

"But you never said you were going to kick his ass?"

"No, Jimmy! I don't think I've ever told anybody that in my life. And especially not somebody like Doug, not with all the problems he's got going on."

"Problems? What problems are we talking about, Marvin?"

"You didn't know?"

"I guess not. What problems?"

Even though there were only two of them in the back of the shop, Marvin looked around to make sure nobody was listening, and then said, "Doug Mullins is dying."

~~~***~~~

"The doctors tell me I've got probably a year, maybe eighteen months left, if I'm lucky. I'm hoping to stretch it out to two years."

"I'm so sorry, Doug. I had no idea," Weber said.

"It is what it is, Sheriff. We all start dying the day we're born. Some of us get more time than others before we do it."

"Can I ask what the problem is?"

"It's his heart," Tracy said. "It's been going bad for a long time now. It started out with shortness of breath and some chest pains, but the last year it's gotten worse."

"Isn't there something they can do?"

Doug shook his head. "Not unless you've got an extra million dollars laying around you can loan me. Running a small business like we are, we can't afford health insurance. And you can't put a heart transplant on a credit card."

"You can't get some kind of insurance to help you with the costs?"

"It's a pre-existing condition. No insurance company is going to take on a client that's going to cost them a fortune. They're in business to make money, just like I am."

Weber wasn't sure he could be so nonchalant about something that serious, but Doug Mullins seemed to have made his peace with the way things were.

"So, I just keep doing my thing every day, and I will for as long as I can."

"Doing his thing," his wife said, shaking her head. "I keep telling him he needs to slow down, not to keep pushing so hard. But he won't listen to me."

"Somebody's got to pay the bills," Doug replied. "You know I've got a plan, honey."

She looked at Weber and shook her head again. "His plan is to work as hard as he can for as long as he can and put every penny he can away in the bank so that I'll have something to live on once he's gone. I keep telling him the only thing I want is time with him, but he's a stubborn man."

Doug looked away, not meeting the sheriff's eyes. "Honey, Sheriff Weber doesn't need to hear about our problems. I'm sure he's got plenty of his own just keeping people in this town doing what's right."

"Well, he's not doing a very good job of it when you've got some crazy person trying to kill you, Doug!"

"We're trying to get to the bottom of this," Weber replied. "I know this must be terrifying. Especially on top of everything else you guys are dealing with. But I promise you, we're going to find whoever it is doing this."

"When? When are you going to do that, Sheriff? The day of my husband's funeral after this maniac kills him? That's if he doesn't have a heart attack the next time this ninja bastard comes after him!"

"Honey, stop. The sheriff and his people are doing everything they can."

Weber noticed the man's face had taken on a gray tinge and his breathing seem to be somewhat labored. "Are you okay, Doug?"

"I think I need a pill."

His wife quickly ran into the other room and came back almost immediately with a small white pill. Doug opened his mouth and she placed it under his tongue. He closed his eyes and sat for a couple of moments, then nodded his head.

"Are you okay, Doug?"

"Yeah, honey. It's letting up."

"Do you need us to call an ambulance?"

The man shook his head and said, "No thanks, Sheriff. I'll be okay. I just need a minute."

"Do you see what he's going through? This stuff that's happening is going to kill him before his heart does," Tracy said. "You've got to do something, Sheriff."

There were tears in her eyes and Weber wanted to reach out and hold her, to give her some comfort and reassurance that they were not all alone in the world. But that wasn't professional, and he knew that the best thing he could do to help them would be to find whoever was harassing her husband.

"You mentioned some employee that was supposed to return that tool to Marvin Harris. The Rhino. You told me you think this employee may have sold it and claimed it was lost."

"Yeah, it wasn't the first time things came up missing around him. I tried to give him the benefit of the doubt, but after that... I just couldn't afford another expense like that, Sheriff. So, I let him go."

"Who was this guy, Doug?"

"Fellow by the name of Mercer. J.T. Mercer. Do you know him?"

Weber definitely knew who John Thomas Mercer was. A local bully who had used his size to intimidate anyone smaller than himself all through school, J.T. had grown to be a hulking man who still liked to push people around. Weber figured he must be somewhere in his mid to late 20s by now. He was surprised to hear that J.T. had held any kind of job, let alone one that required as much physical exertion as installing fences. In his experience, J.T. lived off a series of girlfriends, spending his days sleeping off night-long drinking binges or running around with his two henchmen, Bobby Christensen and Rick Lyons, looking for trouble.

"Yeah, I know J.T. How long did he work for you?"

"Not long. Maybe three weeks or so."

"Which was too long," Tracy said. "I told you the day you hired him that it was a mistake."

"Why do you say that?"

"Why? I'll tell you why, Sheriff. He was lazy, he's obviously a thief, and he tried to put the make on me right here in my own house. That's why!"

Chapter 11

Weber was surprised not to find J.T. Mercer at the Antler Inn. The big lout had been having an on-again off-again affair with Margo Prestwick, the bar's heavyset blonde owner, even though she was several years older than him. Housed in a square cinder block building situated two miles outside of Big Lake on the road to Round Valley, the bar attracted a rough crowd and Weber's deputies responded to the establishment on a regular basis to break up fights between its patrons.

Margo was behind the bar watching a soap opera on the fuzzy screen of the TV and didn't look up as Weber and Coop came through the door. The air was heavy with cigarette smoke and the smell of stale beer. Three men sat at the bar nursing their beers, two of them together and one further away by himself.

"How are you today, Margo?"

She glanced at Weber out of the corner of her eye and then back at the TV, where some incredibly handsome man who Weber figured could only be gay was telling an equally beautiful woman how much he loved her in spite of the fact that he had had an affair with her best friend. Weber didn't know how they handled that kind of situation on television, but in Big Lake it was the kind of thing that could get you killed. Or at least beaten within an inch of your life.

"What? You're just going to ignore me?"

She turned to him and the look on her face wasn't friendly. Then again, it never was.

"It's kind of like ignoring a nasty fart," Margo said. "You can't make it go away, all you can do is hold your breath and try to ignore it."

"Well, if you hold your breath that long, you're probably going to pass out," Weber told her. "I'm looking for J.T."

"Who?"

"Your boyfriend, J.T. Mercer. You might remember him, a big guy with tattoos all over his arms, the IQ of a chipmunk, and the personality of a badger."

"Haven't seen him."

She was looking back at the TV again, so Weber used the back of his hand to sweep an empty beer glass some departed customer had left from the top of the bar onto the floor, where it crashed and shattered.

"What the hell are you doing, Weber?"

"Oh, I'm sorry. Just trying to get your attention."

"I told you I haven't seen J.T."

"Let's be more specific. You haven't seen him today, or you haven't seen him this week, or you've never seen him since when?"

"It's been a while."

"What? Did he find somebody new to shack up with?"

"I wouldn't know."

"Help me out here, Margo. I just need to talk to him."

"Help you? Why should I do that? What have you ever done for me?"

Weber could have mentioned all of the times his deputies had responded to calls at the bar, breaking up drunken brawls before her customers could destroy the place completely. Or he could have mentioned the time a sniper was shooting the place up with a high-powered rifle and he had risked his life to stop the attack. But he knew that Margo had selective memory. So instead, he walked down the bar to where the two men were sitting and said, "Fellas, I need you to stand up and put your hands on the top of the bar. You too, mister," he told the third man, who'd been sitting apart from the others. "Come over here and put your hands on the bar."

"What the hell are you doing? They're not doing anything wrong," Margo said as Weber started to pat the men down.

"Just looking out for you, Margo. If J.T.'s not around to keep you safe from the kind of people you have coming in here, somebody has to do it."

"Leave them alone!"

"Nope, I'm going to frisk them and everybody else that comes through the door until you can remember where I might find J.T."

"That's illegal. That's harassment."

"Really? Sir, do you feel harassed?"

The man Weber was patting down didn't know how to respond, so he shook his head.

"See. These gentlemen want to be safe, too. You guys appreciate me looking out for your best interest, don't you?"

All three men nodded their heads, not sure what was going on but not wanting to be involved in it any more than they already were. When he was done searching them, finding nothing, Weber said, "I appreciate your cooperation, guys. Now if you could do me one more thing, finish your beers and go someplace else. There's a felony police investigation going on here and I wouldn't want you to get underfoot."

All three men quickly headed for the exit, not bothering with their unfinished drinks.

"Are you crazy? You can't run my customers away like that!"

Weber looked toward the door and said, "Apparently, I can."

"I'll call the mayor!"

"You do that. Now, you do know that Chet Wingate's not the mayor anymore, right? You need to call Kirby Templeton at his pharmacy. He's filling in for now."

"Look, I told you I don't know where J.T. is."

"Why don't I believe you, Margo?"

"I hate you, Weber."

"That must be why I didn't get a Christmas card from you this year. I thought it just got lost in the mail."

Weber reached out his hand, preparing to knock another beer glass onto the floor, pausing to look at Margo questioningly.

"Okay, enough already! Last I heard, J.T. was living with Vicki Spradlin."

"Vicki? The girl with the blonde mohawk?"

"That was last year's look. This year it's pink."

"Well now, isn't that festive? Do you know where Vicki and J.T. are living?"

"They were at her mother's house for a while. But I think they got kicked out. That's all I know, honest."

"How about Bobby Christensen and Rick Lyons? Have you seen them around lately?"

"Not since me and J.T. broke up. You know those three are like peas in a pod. You find one, you'll find the other two."

"Now see, that wasn't so hard, was it?"

"You owe me for that glass you broke."

"Do I?" Weber flipped his hand and knocked the other one to the floor, it shattering like the first. "Tell you what, Margo. Just put them on my tab."

She was cussing him when he walked out the door.

~~~***~~~

"Yeah, I kicked them out a month ago," Dorothy Spradlin said around the cigarette dangling from her mouth. "What did they do now?"

"I just need to talk to J.T., that's all," Weber told her.

The woman wrinkled her face in disgust at the sound of her daughter's boyfriend's name. At least Weber thought she had wrinkled her face. Years of hard drinking and heavy smoking had left it as lined and rutted as a dirt road in the rainy season. She took a long drag off the cigarette and removed it from her mouth, exhaling in a cloud of smoke and bad breath that caught him off guard and made his stomach turn.

"Well, whatever you think he's up to, he probably did it. And I wouldn't be surprised if that daughter of mine wasn't involved, too."

"Why do you say that, Mrs. Spradlin?"

"Because she's just as worthless as he is. I thought when she got knocked up, she might start settling down a little bit. But I was wrong."

"She's pregnant?"

"Yeah, looks like she's shoplifting a pumpkin."

Weber had had enough experience with Vicki Spradlin to know that shoplifting wasn't above her. More than once she had been arrested for stealing everything from beer and cigarettes to frozen pizzas.

"Do you know where they're living at these days?"

"Last I heard it was some trailer over behind Randy Laird's garage someplace. In that little trailer park on the street behind the garage. But knowing them, they probably got kicked out of there already."

"Why do you say that?"

"Because all they do is drink and party and play their music loud, and they never paid me a nickel while they were staying here. I don't figure they'd be any different someplace else."

"Okay. Thank you for your time," the sheriff said.

He started back to his car when the woman said, "You tell Vicki I plan to get custody of that kid of hers once it's born." She paused to cough, then spit a glob of something greenish onto the ground next to her porch. "That girl ain't fit to be a mother. I don't want my grandkid growing up in that environment."

Another fit of coughing overtook her, and Weber didn't wait for it to pass before getting in his Explorer and driving away.

Knowing J.T.'s propensity toward violence, Weber had taken Coop with him when he went to the Antler Inn. When they pulled into the Coyote Wells trailer park they paused at the entrance, wondering which of the eight or ten rundown mobile homes J.T. and Vicki were living in, assuming they had not already been evicted, like her mother had said might be possible.

A young woman with a crying baby on her hip opened the door of the first trailer when they knocked, a waft of foul air hitting them in the face. She told them she had only lived there for a week and didn't know any of her neighbors. When they described J.T. and Vicki, she shook her head. "Sorry, I don't pay much attention to what's going on outside the door here. I got enough to keep me busy between this one and tryin' to get my old man out of bed and to work in the morning."

They didn't do any better at the second mobile home, but at the third one an old man wearing a dingy sleeveless T-shirt and loose fitting blue boxer shorts nodded his head. "Yeah, they live right across the street there. The green and white place. I don't know what they done now, but I hope you take both of their asses to jail."

"Why is that?"

"Why? I'll tell you why." The man leaned forward on his cane and said, "Because they're terrible neighbors, that's why! Always got the music playing' full blast and comin' and goin' at all hours of the day and night. And I know that son of a bitch stole my trollin' motor. I had it sittin' right here in the porch and I saw him eyin' it, and the next day it was gone."

"A trolling motor? Did you make a report of it being stolen, sir?"

"What for? Damn thing wasn't worth more than thirty or forty bucks. Not like you guys are goin' to spend a lot of time looking for it."

"What makes you think your neighbor stole it, sir?"

The old man looked at Coop like he was crazy and replied, "Because he's a thief, that's why! He was over here tryin' to sell me a power saw. Only wanted $10 for it. But what the hell am I goin' to do with a power saw?"

"And you thought the saw was stolen?"

"Damn straight. Who sells a brand-new power saw still in the box for $10?"

"Thank you for your time," Weber told him. "If we happen to turn up your trolling motor, we'll let you know."

"Yeah? Well, I ain't goin' to hold my breath."

Chapter 12

A rusted old Chevy S-10 Blazer that had seen better days 100,000 miles earlier was parked in front of the trailer, but nobody answered when they knocked on the door. Weber wasn't sure if that was because of the loud music playing inside, because the mobile occupants were asleep, or if they were just ignoring him. Either way, he wasn't going to be discouraged that easily. While his first knock on the door had been polite, the second time he went with the cop knock, pounding on the flimsy door with the side of his closed fist hard enough to rattle the whole trailer. He did it a second time and thought he heard someone moving about inside. He stepped back, with his hand on his holstered pistol.

The door opened and Vicki Spradlin looked out, her face puffy from sleep. Weber noted that her mother was right, the young woman's grungy T-shirt was stretched tight over her bulging belly. Margo had also been right. Her hair, shaved on both sides of her head, leaving only a three or four inch high strip running from back to front across the top, was some kind of bright pink.

"What do you want?"

"I need to talk to J.T."

"He ain't here."

"Isn't that his car parked right there?"

"Yeah, but he ain't here."

"Are you sure about that? You wouldn't lie to me, would you, Vicki?"

"Why would I lie to you, Sheriff?"

"I don't know. Habit, maybe?"

Before she could reply, he heard J.T. yelling from inside, "Who the hell's pounding on the door, Vicki?"

"He's not here? Really?"

Vicki sighed and stepped aside and Weber went inside. To call the trailer filthy would have been an understatement. Dirty clothes, empty beer bottles and cans, and fast food wrappers littered the floor and a coffee table that was covered with a dirty yellow blanket. He could see at least three cats and could smell a litter box that had been neglected for a long time. Coop followed him inside as J.T. called again, asking Vicki what the hell was going on. They followed the sound of his voice down a short hallway, stepping over a black cat that was nursing three kittens and past a disgusting bathroom to the lone bedroom in the back of the trailer. J.T. was sprawled out on the bed, naked and obviously hung over.

"Get up, J.T. We need to have a talk."

He peered at them with bleary eyes and asked, "What the hell are you guys doing here? I ain't done nothing wrong."

"I said get up and get dressed. Otherwise I'll drag your naked ass out and throw you in the back of the car and we can talk at the office. Which is it going to be?"

J.T. sighed and sat up in bed, rubbing his eyes and scratching his balls.

"Whatever you think I did, you've got the wrong guy."

"Just get dressed," Weber ordered.

He pulled on a pair of jeans that looked like they had not been washed since the day they left Walmart and led the way down the hall, where he flopped down on the couch next to a gray tabby cat. The cat looked at him balefully and got up, moving to the far end of the couch where it laid back down.

Coop turned off the stereo and J.T. said, "Vicki, make me a cup of coffee."

She went in the kitchen, not offering their visitors anything. Not that Coop or Weber would have ingested anything that came out of that place. Breathing the fetid air was bad enough.

"Okay, what the hell's this all about?"

"Have you been playing ninja lately, J.T.?"

"What? I don't know what the hell you're talking about. Ninja?"

"Yeah, you know. Black pajamas, a hood over your face. A ninja."

"Why in the hell would I do that?"

"That's what we're trying to figure out," Weber told him.

"No, man, I ain't been playing ninja."

"Where were you earlier today?"

"Nowhere. I haven't been outside since the day before yesterday."

"Are you sure about that?"

"Ask my old lady."

Vicki had returned, stirring instant coffee in a cup that obviously had contained something else before that.

"He's telling you the truth. We both been here all along. What's this about, anyway?"

"Tell me about Doug Mullins, J.T."

"Who? Never heard of him."

Weber pulled his handcuffs from the pouch on his belt and said, "Okay, if that's the way you want to do it, that's fine with me. Stand up, turn around, and put your hands behind your back."

"For what? I didn't do nothing wrong."

"Come on, J.T., we both know you just being born was wrong. I know you worked for Mullins, and you just gave me false information when you said you'd never heard of him. That's a crime. So we'll have this conversation down at the jail."

"Oh, come on, man. This is bullshit. Yeah, I know Doug. So what?"

"I heard you worked for him for a while and that you got fired. Tell me about it."

"There's nothing to tell. He's a dick."

"Why do you say that?"

73

"Because he is."

"Why did he fire you?"

"I don't know. He just told me he didn't need me anymore."

"Could it be because of the tools that came up missing?"

"Is this what this is about? Because I lost a pair of pliers or something?"

"Maybe because you ripped off a Rhino and told Mullins you returned it to Marvin Harris?"

"That's bullshit, man. I took that thing right back to him, just like Doug told me to."

"So Harris is lying about not getting it back?"

"I don't know what he's saying, I just know that I took it back."

"Maybe it's not about .the tools going missing," Weber suggested. "Maybe he fired you for making a pass at his wife."

"Are you kidding me? That didn't happen."

"That's not the way I hear it."

"Wait a minute. You hit on your boss's wife? We were together when you were working for Doug Mullins," Vicki said.

"I didn't hit on nobody! She was the one coming on to me. I told her I wasn't interested. That I had a good woman."

"Do you really expect anybody to believe that, J.T.?"

"I don't care if you believe it or not," Sheriff. "She's the one that grabbed me by the dick, right there in the living room of their house while Doug was in the office writing my paycheck."

"And when did this happen?"

"I don't know, a couple days before he fired me. I guess she told him a bunch a shit that wasn't true because she was afraid I'd say something about what she did."

Given J.T.'s reputation as a liar, a thief, a bully and a horndog, Weber wasn't believing a word he said. And though he didn't know Tracy Mullins all that well, he couldn't see her throwing herself at somebody like J.T., or any other man, for that matter. All he had ever seen or heard between Tracy and her husband was total devotion to each other.

"Somebody has made two attempts on Doug Mullins' life, J.T. Do you know anything about that?"

"Wait. Somebody tried to kill Doug? And you think I did it?" J.T. shook his head vehemently. "No way. No freaking way."

"You said you were here all day, is that right."

"Yeah, man. I haven't been anywhere. Neither one of us have."

"You wouldn't have a ninja costume laying around here anywhere, would you J.T.?"

"It's not Halloween, why would I have a costume?"

"How about a sword? Or maybe some throwing stars?"

"You're welcome to look around. I ain't got nothing like that."

"So, just to be clear, you're giving us your permission to search this place?"

"Yeah, go ahead. I don't care."

With J.T. and Vicki sitting on the couch, they did just that. They found enough empty beer cans to melt down and make a rowboat, along with a tattered stack of adult magazines, clothes that had never seen a washing machine and probably never would, a compound bow and some arrows, and assorted trash. But nothing that would implicate J.T. in the attacks on his former employer. Weber thanked him for his time and they left. As they closed the door behind them, he and Coop could hear J.T. and Vicki arguing about what had happened between him and Tracy Mullins.

"What do you think?"

Weber put his seatbelt on and said, "Those two are about as disgusting a pair of individuals as I've seen in a long time. How can anybody live like that?"

"I just feel sorry for the kid when it's born," Coop said. "They choose to live that way. The baby doesn't have any say in the matter."

"Do you think J.T. had anything to do with what's been happening around here?"

"He may have something to do with it, but he's not the one running around in a ninja costume. He's too big, he doesn't fit the description. And his girlfriend is too pregnant. I'm sure somebody would have mentioned that."

"Could he be putting somebody up to it?"

"That's a good question," Weber said. "I wish I had an answer for it."

He put the Explorer in gear and drove away from the sad little trailer park.

Chapter 13

Weber was on the back deck slathering barbecue sauce on chicken wings when the door opened and Robyn walked out with his phone in her hand, saying, "It's Dispatch. There's some hassle going on between J.T. Mercer and his girlfriend. Neighbors called it in and three units responded. But it's getting ugly."

Weber took the phone and asked, "What do you need, Judy?"

"Sorry to bother you at home, Sheriff, but Buz said he really needs you out at the Coyote Wells trailer park."

"What, three deputies can't take down J.T.?"

"J.T. isn't the problem this time."

"What do you mean?"

"Apparently his girlfriend is holding a big butcher knife to his throat and swears she's going to cut his head off if you don't come there."

The sheriff looked at his chicken and sighed. He wondered what his life would be like if he had chosen some other profession. Then again, what would he have done? He couldn't see himself working in an office, shackled to a desk all day long, and being a truck driver staring out a windshield for mile after mile would have been boring. He had long since dismissed the idea of being a schoolteacher or clerking in a retail store. People who worked those kinds of jobs might have better hours and probably were not subject to being called out at any time of the day or night, but he was pretty sure they didn't have as much fun as he did. Then again, they probably got to cook something on the grill and eat it without being interrupted.

"Tell Buz I'm on the way," he said, turning off the grill.

~~~***~~~

There was a small crowd of people standing in the middle of the trailer park's single road when Weber pulled in and he had to blip the siren to get them to move out of the way. He parked behind Dolan Reed's unit and got out. Buz and Archer were standing on the ground at the bottom of the steps leading up to the trailer and Dolan was at the open doorway.

"What's going on?"

"Neighbor said J.T. and his girlfriend had been fighting all afternoon and it kept getting louder and louder," Buz said. "Somebody finally called it in and Archer was the first unit on the scene. He said when he got here the door was open and the girlfriend was holding a big old knife to J.T.'s throat and it looked like she had slashed him across the arm. She told him to back off or she would kill him. Dolan and I tried to talk her down, but she wasn't listening. She kept saying she wanted to talk to you. We thought about using a Taser on her, but with her being pregnant and everything, we didn't think that was a very good idea."

Weber hadn't bothered to put on a uniform, he was dressed in a button front shirt and Levi's, with his pistol and handcuffs tucked into his belt. Dolan saw him and said to the couple in the trailer, "All right, Sheriff Weber's here. Now put down the knife, Vicki."

"No! I want the sheriff right here, inside with me. Otherwise I'm gonna cut this son of a bitch's head off and throw it at you."

"Just take it easy, Vicki. Nobody has to get hurt here."

"Oh, somebody's going to get hurt all right! Somebody's going to get hurt real bad."

"Let me talk to her," Weber said.

There wasn't room for both of them on the small wooden steps, and as rickety as they were, Weber did not think they would hold the weight of two people anyway. So Dolan came down and Weber took his place. What he saw inside the shabby trailer made him forget all about barbecued chicken. The place had looked bad before, but now it was even worse. The coffee table had been turned over, the stand that held the stereo had collapsed, and the blanket that once covered the threadbare couch was bunched up on the floor. But what really got his attention was the sight of J.T. Mercer and his girlfriend.

J.T. was face down on the floor and Vicki was sitting on top of him, one hand wrapped into his greasy long hair, pulling his head back, and the other holding a twelve inch knife to his throat. There was blood over both of them and Weber could see a deep cut on the man's left arm.

"Vicki, put the knife down. Do it now!"

"I'm going to kill this cheating asshole. I'm going to kill him and then I'm gonna cut his cheatin' dick off and shove it up his ass."

"Do something, Sheriff. This bitch is crazy!"

Vicki pulled sharply on her boyfriend's hair, and said, "Call me a bitch again and I'll scalp you, you cheating prick."

"Ouch! Do something before she kills me, Sheriff."

Weber stepped cautiously into the room, keeping his hands open in front of him, palms forward. "Come on, Vicki. He's not worth it."

"He put a baby in my belly and then he's cheating on me with somebody else!"

"I told you, I never cheated on you!"

"That's not what your boss's wife said. Why would she lie about that?"

"I swear to God, nothing happened between us."

"Vicki, put the knife down and we'll work this out."

"No. I've put up with him laying on his ass all day long and not working. I've put up with him shoving me around when he gets pissed off about something. But this time he went too far."

"Vicki, for all I know maybe J.T. is right. Maybe Tracy Mullins made the whole thing up. Or maybe she did hit on him, just like he said."

"You don't believe that for a minute, do you, Sheriff?"

No, Weber really didn't, but he wasn't going to tell her that.

"Who knows? I wasn't there, and neither were you."

"It wouldn't be the first time he's cheated on me. Yeah, J.T., I know all about you and Margo in the back room of the Antler. I heard all about it. Why would you screw that fat pig when you've got me at home, anytime you want? Is it because I'm fat and pregnant? She's fatter than me. So why, J.T.? Tell me why."

"Jesus Christ, Vicki, that was six months ago. I didn't even know you were pregnant at the time. Or if it was even mine."

"Even yours? How dare you say I was screwing around behind your back? You're the one who does that," Vicki screamed, twisting his hair viciously and drawing a loud yelp from J.T.

"Shoot the knife out of her hand or something before she kills me," J.T. pleaded.

"This isn't television or the movies," Weber said. "It doesn't work that way."

"Well do something. I'm about to die here!"

As serious as the situation was, Weber still couldn't help but feel some amusement that the big bully who had pushed people around all of his life, intimidating them with his size and his reputation, was now dominated by a pregnant girl half his size who had obviously taken enough of his crap. But he couldn't just stand there and allow her to kill a man. Not that it would be any loss to the world.

The problem was, he couldn't figure out how to handle what was happening. Dolan was right, they did not want to use a Taser on a pregnant woman, and he was afraid if they tried to pepper spray her and take the knife away by force, somebody was going to get hurt even worse than J.T. had already been cut. The only alternative was to try to talk her down. The problem was that Weber knew from experience that when somebody was that worked up, reasoning with them was often impossible.

"Vicki, I want you to think about your baby. That little person growing inside of you needs his mother and his father. I know J.T. is a piece of work, and in any other situation I might just turn around and walk away and let you do what you need to do. But that's not fair to the baby and it's not fair to you."

"I love him, Sheriff! I love him and he cheated on me."

"I never cheated. I keep telling you…"

"Shut your lying mouth," the distraught woman shouted, twisting his hair even harder.

"Yeah, J.T. Just shut up," Weber said. "Every time you open your mouth you make it worse."

"Why, Sheriff? Why would he keep cheating on me? I know I'm as big as a cow, but we can still do it. And I do other things for him, too. It's not like he doesn't get off at home. So why is he out there cheating on me?"

"I didn't…"

"Shut up, J.T.," Weber said again. "Vicki, let's be honest. You knew J.T. was no prize when you got involved with him. What did you expect?"

"I thought I could change him," she cried.

"Guys like him, they don't change. I think you know that, deep down inside, don't you?"

"What more can I do? What's wrong with me that he would cheat on me like this?"

J.T. started to open his mouth to deny his infidelity one more time, but as if expecting it, Vicki twisted his hair again and pushed the knife even tighter against his throat. Weber could see a small trickle of blood at one spot and wondered if he was going to witness her executing the father of her child. In any other situation, they could have gone hands-on and taken her down or resorted to one of the nonlethal tools at their disposal. He didn't really give a damn about J.T. Mercer or Vicki. Both of them were losers who had been involved in one problem after another, thorns in the side to law enforcement and to the good people of Big Lake since they were kids. But Coop had been right earlier when he said that their unborn child didn't deserve to be a victim of its parents' many shortcomings.

"Honey, there's nothing wrong with you. Not a thing. You're pretty and you're smart, and it's too bad this idiot is too dumb to see that. You could do a whole lot better than him. To be honest with you, I don't know what you see in him. It's not like he's good looking, and he can't hold a job. Not to mention the fact that he treats you like crap and shoves you around. If I was your father

81

instead of the Sheriff, I'd probably tell you that he deserves exactly what you're doing and be done with it. But I can't do that, and I can't let you kill him. So, what are we going to do?"

"I don't know," she sobbed. "I love him so much, but he treats me so mean. I don't know what to do!"

"Well, for starters how about you put the knife down? Then we can figure the rest of it out."

"No! He has to pay for what he did!"

"I get that," Weber told her. "And you're right, he does. But you shouldn't be punished for the things he's done wrong. If you cut him again, that's what's going to happen. You're going to go to jail and you're never going to get to hold your baby. It will go to your mother and that will be it. Is that what you want?"

She didn't answer, so Weber played his trump card. "Vicki, if you kill him or hurt him any worse than he already is, your mother will be the one raising your baby. She'll be the one feeding it and hearing it say its first words and calling her Mama. It will be her seeing it taking its first steps. Do you want her to have all of that instead of you?"

"No! That woman ain't fit to raise anything. Look how I turned out. I don't want her anywhere near my baby."

"Well, that's what's going to happen if this gets any worse."

"No." she said, shaking her head. "No, I don't want anybody raising my baby but me."

"Okay then, we need to end this right here and right now."

"I just don't know what to do," she sobbed.

"Why don't you tell me what you do want to happen, Vicki."

"I just want…" she stopped and took a deep breath, then said, "I just want him to love me."

"He does love you, Vicki. The problem is he's too stupid and too immature to show you that in the right way. He's still a little boy inside who only wants what he wants and doesn't care about anybody else."

"But why? Why ain't I enough for him? Why does he go cheating on me with some skank like Margo Prestwick? Why is he hitting on his boss's wife?"

"It's like I said, he's like a little kid in a toy store who wants everything he sees."

"I just want him to grow up and be a man."

"I know you do, Vicki," Weber said. "But if you kill him, he can't do that, right?" The sheriff didn't really believe that J.T. would ever grow up. He had seen enough men like him in their 40s and 50s and even 60s who still acted like teenagers. Slicked back hair, sleeveless T-shirts and black jeans, holding onto a youth that had long since disappeared. But he couldn't tell Vicki that, not while she was holding that knife to J.T.'s throat.

"What do I do, Sheriff?"

"The first thing is, you put the knife down. Nothing can happen until you put the knife down."

"Am I going to jail?"

"I won't lie to you, Vicki. The law on domestic violence in Arizona says that if the police respond, the aggressor has to go to jail. But that's not the end of the world. You're not going to prison, and with you being as far along as you are in your pregnancy, I know that Judge Ryman is not going to keep you locked up. You'll get a fine and some community service maybe, that's about it."

"They won't take my baby away from me?"

"No, ma'am. Not if you put the knife down right now and we get J.T. some medical attention. That looks like a pretty nasty cut on his arm."

Weber thought it was going to work. He thought he had been able to make Vicki listen to reason. And it might have worked. She pulled the knife away from his neck and started to let go of it when J.T. had to open his damn mouth.

"You're damn right it's a nasty cut. You need to lock this crazy bitch up forever! I don't want my kid anywhere around her."

Vicki screamed in rage and raised the bloody knife high, ready to plunge it into his back. Weber had slowly been working his way further into the room as they talked, and when it looked like J.T.'s death was imminent, he leapt forward, wrapping both hands around her wrist and twisting, trying to force her to release the weapon. Dolan and Buz rushed inside, and between the three of them, they managed to pull Vicki off of J.T., being as careful as they could to prevent any injury to her or her baby.

As soon as the weight was off of his back, J.T. rolled away and sat up. Weber saw him looking toward the door, seeking an escape route, and warned, "Don't try it, J.T.! I've got an officer outside and he will shoot you if you come out the door all covered in blood like that."

Weber doubted Archer could react quickly enough to do anything, and if he did actually try to shoot anybody, he would most likely blow one of his own toes off. Fortunately for everybody concerned, the warning was enough to convince J.T. to stay put.

With Vicki handcuffed, Dolan pushed the key on his portable radio and told the dispatcher to send an ambulance to their location.

Chapter 14

Just as Weber had predicted, when they took Vicki before the judge the next morning, he took note of her pregnancy and was reluctant to give her any jail time. Instead, he fined her $1,500 and sentenced her to 80 hours of community service. J.T., with a bandage on his arm and a band aid on his neck, was there to pay the fine and the couple walked out of the courthouse arm in arm cooing words of love to each other. The sheriff had seen the same scenario play out time after time with couples like J.T. and Vicki and he had no doubt that they would repeat the scenario again. Hopefully without weapons or bloodshed the next time around.

Two hours later he was back at the office dutifully going through a week's backlog of paperwork under Mary's watchful eye when the dispatcher came to his office door and said, "Sheriff, there's been a shooting at Norton's Auto Parts."

"Oh, shit. What did Todd do now?"

"I don't know," the dispatcher said. "He's the one that was shot."

"It was the craziest thing. I was standing at the counter going through the mail when I looked up and this goddamn ninja was standing there. I never even heard him come in. He was like a damn ghost!"

"A ninja?"

"Yeah, a ninja. Just like the one that's been running around town that everybody is talking about."

"And the ninja shot you?"

"Yes! Hurts like a son of a bitch!"

"Can you give me a description of this ninja?"

"He was all dressed in black with some kind of mask or hood over his face."

"Could you see the color of his eyes?"

"No. If I did, I don't remember."

"Was he tall or short, slender or stocky?"

"He was a big son of a bitch!"

"Big like Deputy Wright here?" Weber asked, referring to the former college football player.

"Yeah, about his size."

Weber looked at the man's left hand, which was dripping blood onto the floor in spite of the red shop towel wrapped around it. Taking it in his own hand as gently as he could, he removed the improvised bandage and inspected the wound. What had once been the tip of Norton's index finger was now no more than a pulpy red mush, and the tip of his middle finger was hanging by just a few sinews of flesh. Norton winced and moaned as the sheriff turned his hand over, then let it go.

He heard a siren yelping outside, and a moment later paramedics Rusty Heinz and Pat Price came through the door. As they began assessing the victim's wounds, Weber got on his portable radio and told the dispatcher that he wanted every available deputy on the street looking for someone dressed like a ninja, and added that they should exercise extreme caution if they spotted the suspect, who was to be considered armed and dangerous.

"How bad is it?"

"The tip of the one finger is pretty much gone and the other one's just hanging on by a few threads. So you're going to lose those," Rusty, a stocky bald man with a goatee and a silver hoop in his left ear said. "But the good news is, you're not going to die."

"You are going to need to go to the hospital in Show Low, though," Pat Price added. "This isn't something our little Medical Center's gonna be able to handle."

While they were bandaging the man's hand, Weber said, "Walk me through the whole thing from when it started to when it ended, Todd."

"I told you. I was standing right here at the counter and I looked up and this ninja asshole was standing there. Didn't say a word, just shot me."

Looking at the blood on the floor, it was easy to determine where the man had been standing when the attack took place. Weber pointed at it and asked, "So you were standing right there?"

"Yeah, right there."

Being careful not to step on the blood, Weber moved into that position and asked, "And the ninja was there, right across from you, or further back in the store?"

"No. He was standing right there across from me. I could have reached out and touched him!"

"Did he say anything at all, Todd?"

"I just told you, he didn't say a word. He just shot me."

"Coop, go around to that side of the counter," Weber asked his deputy, then turned to Norton. "You were standing here and he was standing about there where Deputy Cooper is, right?"

"Yeah."

"And you looked up and he was pointing a gun at you?"

"That's what I said."

"And what did you do? Did you raise your hands? Did you say anything to him?"

"I thought it was a robbery, so I raised my hands. I think I told him to take whatever he wanted or something like that. I don't remember my exact words."

"And he didn't reply at all? He just shot you."

"Yeah, for the third time, he just shot me! You guys need to find that prick and lock him up. And when you do, do me a favor and let me spend a few minutes in a cell with him."

Ignoring Norton's last comment, Weber asked, "What happened after he shot you? Did he take any money or anything?"

"No, that was the crazy thing. He didn't rob me. He just shot me and turned around and walked out the door."

"Walked or ran out, Todd?"

"Christ, I don't know. I just got shot, it wasn't like I was trying to remember everything about it. I was just glad he left without shooting me again to finish the job."

"What kind of gun was it, Todd. Any idea?"

"It looked like a .22 or .25 automatic from what I could see."

Weber nodded his head and stepped away while the paramedics worked on the wounded man's hand. Cooper caught his eye and subtly pointed his head away from the counter. Weber joined him, Dan Wright, and Dolan a few steps away.

Coop asked in a low voice, "Are you buying any of this?"

"As big a jerk as Todd is, I'm surprised someone didn't shoot him years ago," Dolan replied.

At barely five feet tall, Norton had always had a bad case of little man's syndrome and walked around with a chip on his shoulder. Weber couldn't begin to count the number of times he had heard reports of Norton starting fights with men that weighed twice as much as he did and stood head and shoulders above him.

"I don't disagree with you about that," Coop said, "but I don't think that's what happened here."

"Neither do I," Weber agreed. "I don't know much about ninjas, but I've never heard of one of them using a gun before."

"Me, either," Coop said. "And every report we've had says the ninja is smaller, about the size of a teenager. Not nearly as big as Dan."

"I guess if a guy was pointing a gun at me, he'd seem pretty big," Dan suggested.

"That may be true," Coop admitted, "but the position of the wound is all wrong, too."

"Yeah, I picked up on that," Weber told him. "Let's go have a talk with Todd and see what he has to say."

"We can take you to Show Low in the ambulance if you want, or you can have somebody drive you there," Rusty was telling the patient. "But you shouldn't be driving on your own."

"I'm not going to bleed to death, am I?"

"No, but once they get done working on you you're gonna be pretty doped up and in no condition to drive home."

"Excuse me," Weber said, interrupting. "Todd, I want to get the sequence of things that happened right for the report, okay?"

"What more do you want me to tell you, Sheriff? I was standing there, the ninja walked in and was standing there on the other side of the counter and he shot me and walked out. That's all there was to it."

"You said he walked out, but a couple of minutes ago you said you didn't remember if he walked or ran away. Which was it?"

"How the hell should I know? When you get shot, you don't have time to take notes on everything that's happening around you."

"Fair enough," Weber acknowledged. "Let's go through it one more time, okay?"

He resumed his position behind the counter and had Coop stand on the other side of the counter from him.

"So you're standing here and you look up and the ninja is there pointing a gun at you, right?"

"Yeah."

"And you raised your hands like this?" Weber held his hands palms forward at shoulder height.

"Yeah, I raised my hands. I already told you that."

"And you were holding them like I am mine? Like anybody would in your position."

"Yeah. How many times do we have to go over this? I'm hurting like hell."

"I understand," Weber told him. "I just need to get the facts straight while they're still fresh in your memory."

"Trust me, I ain't forgetting this anytime soon!"

"I don't doubt that," Weber said, then asked, "He shot you while your hands were up in the air? You didn't try to reach for the gun or anything like that? You didn't make any aggressive moves toward him?"

"Hell no! When someone's pointing a gun at me, I'm not going to do something stupid and get myself shot. What kind of fool do you think I am?"

"That's what I'm trying to figure out," Weber said.

"What the hell do you mean by that, Sheriff?"

"Where's the gun, Todd?"

"Gun? What gun?"

"The gun you got shot with. Where is it?"

"How the hell do I know? I guess the ninja took it with him."

Weber looked the little man in the eye and said, "Let's stop the bullshit, Todd. What really happened?"

"I told you what happened. The son of a bitch came in and shot me and left!"

"I don't think so."

"What? You think I'm lying? The next thing you're going to say is I shot myself."

"Did you, Todd?"

"Did I what?"

"Did you shoot yourself?"

"Hell no!"

"Are you sure about that?"

"Of course I'm sure. What kind of fool do you think I am?"

It was the second time the surly little man had asked him that question and Weber could have listed many ways in which he considered Todd Norton to be a fool, but he didn't feel like elaborating.

"The story you're telling me doesn't jive with your wounds."

"What do you mean by that?"

"From the look of your fingers, I can tell the bullet came in from the thumb side and through the top of your index finger and then your middle finger. If you were standing facing the counter with your hands up at your sides like this," Weber said, holding up his hands again, "your palms are facing the guy and your fingers are upright. The bullet would have hit the flat part of your finger, the part facing the shooter. Your wound is a classic example of

90

what happens when someone shoots himself in the hand by accident."

"That's bullshit, Sheriff. It happened just the way I said it did."

"No, it didn't."

"You can believe what you want. That's what happened."

Weber squatted down behind the counter and began pulling ledgers and boxes off the shelves.

"What the hell are you doing? You can't do that."

"I'm looking for the gun, Todd. How about you save us both some time and trouble and tell me where it's at."

"I told you, the ninja took it with him."

"You keep telling that story," Weber said. "All you're doing is digging your grave deeper."

"What grave? What the hell you talking about?"

"First of all, you have no business with a gun. After you shot Three-Bob Davis' drone when we were searching for that missing kid, Judge Ryman put you on two years probation and said you couldn't own any firearms during that time. And filing a false police report is also illegal. Every time you open your mouth, you're making it worse for yourself."

"That's bullshit. I don't have a gun and I didn't shoot myself."

"I think you did."

"And I think you're full of shit, Sheriff. Why aren't you doing your job and looking for the maniac that shot me instead of standing here trying to make me look like the bad guy?"

Running his hand behind a line of parts catalogs under the counter, Weber felt something hard and smiled to himself as he pulled out the little .25 FIE Titan semiautomatic pistol. He grinned at Norton and said, "Bingo."

"I never saw that gun before in my life!"

Weber removed the magazine from the pistol and pulled the slide back to eject a round of ammunition. He then smelled the barrel. "It's been fired pretty recently. What do you think, Coop?"

He passed the handgun to his deputy, who sniffed the barrel and said, "No question about it."

While they were talking, Dolan was prowling around behind the counter and bent down in a corner and picked up something.

91

He turned to show Weber the empty shell casing in his gloved hand.

"This kind of seals the deal, Jimmy. A pistol's going to eject the empty casing to the right. If the shooter was on the other side of the counter where Todd here says he was, it would be over in that direction. But it's not, it's over here."

"I don't know what you assholes are trying to do, but it's not working," the store owner said stubbornly. "What the hell is wrong with you guys? Someone comes in my store and attacks me and you're trying to blame me? That's bullshit. That's total bullshit!"

It took another ten minutes of searching before they found the copper jacketed bullet, which had lodged itself in a wall after tearing through Todd Norton's fingers.

"So, we've got the nature of your wounds, which indicates you weren't shot in the way you said you were. We've got the spent brass over here behind the counter. We've got the gun, and we've got the bullet that went over there instead of behind the counter somewhere if it had been fired from where you said, Todd. And I'm pretty sure when we run ballistics on the gun, and check it and the shell casings for fingerprints, we're going to find yours. How about you start telling the truth? Because I can tell you already what happened, just based on this evidence. You started to chamber a round, and when you pulled back the slide and let it go you probably had your finger on the trigger. It went off and you got shot. But instead of admitting you're a dumb ass who has no business with a gun even if the judge hadn't told you not to have one, you had to make up this big story and waste a bunch of time for myself and my deputies."

"I told you, that's not the way it happened," Norton insisted belligerently.

"Well, here's what I'm going to do," the sheriff told him. "I'm going to have Dolan here take you to Show Low and get you treated. And when he brings you back, I'm going to lock you up and we'll let Judge Ryman decide who's right and who's wrong. How about that?"

92

"I'm a taxpayer in this town. I pay your salary and I don't appreciate being treated like this when I'm the victim," Norton shouted.

"You know the old saying, Todd. Tell it to the judge, because nobody else is listening," Weber told him, shaking his head. "Deputy Reed, please place this man under arrest for filing a false police report and read him his rights. Then take him to Show Low for treatment. After that, you know what to do with him."

Chapter 15

"Can you believe that idiot? Not only is he so stupid that he shoots himself, but he concocts some wild ass story like that and expects us to believe it?"

"What can I say, Coop? Everybody is crazy about this ninja crap going on. I guess Todd just figured that was a good way to cover his ass."

The ambulance crew had left to return to their base at the Medical Center, Dolan was on his way to Show Low with the injured man, and they were locking up the store behind them. A crowd had gathered on the sidewalk, and Weber could hear people talking about how the ninja had struck again. Somebody said it was time to put an end to that nonsense before someone got hurt worse, and somebody else said if they saw the ninja, they were going to shoot first and ask questions later. Weber knew how dangerous that kind of talk could be and decided to try to stop it before it got out of hand.

"Okay, people, listen up! This incident had nothing to do with the ninja that people have reported seeing around town."

"That's not what I heard," Joanne Galbreath said. "Todd told my husband Gary that a ninja shot him. He should know who did it, shouldn't he?"

"A preliminary investigation has shown that the information your husband was told is not correct," the sheriff said.

"Well, if it wasn't the ninja, who was it? Probably one of those damn flatlanders up here raising hell all high on dope," Harley Willits said.

"This is still an open investigation, so I can't go into details," Weber replied. "But we believe this was an accidental shooting."

"What? No ninja? That's not what I heard!"

"I don't care what you heard, Arnold."

"He didn't hear shit," Harley sneered, shaking his head. "This damn fool is just about stone deaf."

"I hear enough to know you need a good ass kicking," Arnold replied. The two old men were brothers-in-law who were always at war with each other over something silly. Yet they hung around together, went fishing together, and drank beer at the brewpub together, snipping at each other and arguing all the while. More than once they had come to blows and deputies had to break up their battles, but the crusty curmudgeons never seemed to hold a grudge against each other. Weber suspected that was because neither one wanted to waste time fretting about past sins when they both knew the other guy would commit brand-new ones the next day.

"Okay, enough! You two, take your business elsewhere because you've got none here. Come on, people, move along."

As the crowd dispersed, Coop said, "The scary thing is, if we don't find out who this ninja fool is before too long, I think somebody will get shot, Jimmy. People are scared. And scared people do dumb things when they think they're protecting themselves and their family."

"I hear what you're saying, Coop. Believe me, I think it's only a matter of time before something bad happens."

~~~***~~~

"Where's your boss?"

"I don't have a boss," Margie Shores, the combination receptionist and office manager at the *Big Lake Herald* newspaper told Weber. "In case you didn't know it, I'm a woman of independent means."

"I never knew that about you. So, you just hang out here, why?"

"Because once in a while a good-looking guy like you walks in and makes my day," the big woman said. "And I can't believe you're standing on that side of the counter instead of coming over here and giving me a hug."

Weber and Margie had been friends forever, classmates dating back to their grade school days. In high school she had helped him squeak through chemistry and geometry with barely passing grades, and in turn, Weber had teased her mercilessly, been her date for the Junior Prom, and had been the one who set Margie up with his friend Keith Shores. Wedding bells had followed soon after graduation, and the young couple had settled into a quiet life in Big Lake.

Twelve years later, as a deputy sheriff under Pete Caitlin, it had been Weber's sad duty to bring the news to Margie that Keith had died when his logging truck rolled over on a narrow mountain road and crushed him. Margie had never remarried, turning herself instead to her work at the newspaper and raising her young daughter, Jennifer. Jennifer, like her mother, was a round girl with merry brown eyes and a curly mop of dark hair. Now a teenager, she worked part-time at the Arby's, occasionally helped out at the newspaper, and excelled on the high school's debate team.

Weber went behind the counter and hugged his old friend. When they broke the embrace, Margie patted his stomach and said, "Married life must agree with you. Are you happy, Jimmy?"

"I am, Margie," he told her. "I really am."

"Then I'm happy for you."

"Thank you. Where would I find Paul?"

Margie stuck out her bottom lip in an exaggerated pout. "You'd rather talk to him than me. I mean, aside from man boobs, what's he got that I don't have?"

"You have man boobs, Margie?"

"Man boobs, girl boobs, whale boobs. All three and more. Want to see?"

"It's not that I don't want to," Weber assured her. "But if I did I wouldn't be able to control myself. Besides which, if I didn't die of a heart attack when I saw them, Robyn would probably kill me."

"What? That pretty little wife of yours never learned to share her toys?"

"What can I say? She was an only child."

"Well, if you're not going to have your way with me, go find Paul and bother him. He's hanging out in back."

"Just like that, you're done with me?"

"Move along, buster. There might be some other hunk coming through the door any minute now and I don't want you to get in the way. I'd hate to trample you into a big ugly stain on the carpet, but I would."

Weber laughed and walked past her and through the big main room that contained desks and a pair of light tables. Paul Lewis, the newspaper's owner and publisher, wasn't in his office, but Weber found him in the press room. And Margie had been right, he was indeed hanging around. Hanging upside down, to be exact.

"What the hell are you doing, Paul? And what is that thing?"

The portly newspaper publisher was suspended upside down by his heels on some sort of device that made the sheriff wonder what kind of weird bondage games his friends Paul and Margie were up to.

"Hey, how you doing, Jimmy?"

"I'm okay, Paul, but I'm not too sure about you right now."

Chuckling, Paul grabbed the curved frame of the device and pulled himself upright with an audible grunt.

"You've never seen one of these? It's called a Teeter inversion table. They advertise them on TV all the time."

"What's it supposed to do?"

"It stretches your back to relieve muscle pain, helps with circulation, all kinds of good stuff. Want to try it?"

"No, thanks. One of us looking like a piñata is enough. When did you get that thing, and more importantly, why?"

"Well, since my diet isn't working out the way I had hoped, I decided to forget that and just try to get taller. What do you think? Is it working?"

Weber and the newspaper publisher had been friends since they were little boys, and the good-natured little round man never took himself seriously. But Weber knew that in spite of his self-deprecating humor, Paul was an intelligent and warmhearted person who had never had an enemy in the world.

"Let's just say you're going to have to do some more stretching to get the job done, okay?"

"The way I figure it, Jimmy, with all this extra flesh I've got, if I hang off this thing long enough, I'll be seven feet tall, and halfway skinny. It's a simple case of taking eighteen inches off my waist and redistributing it elsewhere." He leaned over with some difficulty and released the cups holding his ankles and stepped outside of the inversion table's frame.

"Hey, if it keeps you out of trouble, that's all I care about," Weber told him.

"So, what brings you here besides your innate need to heckle a man who's only trying to better himself?"

"Well, since you're too busy hanging out here to do your job, I have to do mine and yours both. Did you hear what happened at the auto parts store this morning?"

"We got a call that said Todd Norton got into an argument with somebody and they punched him out or something. As often as Todd shoots his mouth off at people, I'm surprised it hasn't happened sooner."

"Actually, it was more than that. Todd wasn't shooting his mouth off, he was busy shooting himself in the hand."

"No kidding? How the hell did he manage that?"

"Well, let me tell you a story," Weber replied.

"How about you hold that story and we'll go down to the ButterCup and you can tell me over lunch?"

"Are you buying?"

"I was thinking we'd go Dutch."

"I'm thinking too much blood has gone to your head and you're not thinking at all, Paul. I bring you a juicy story for the front page and you won't even buy me lunch?"

"I think that's illegal, isn't it? Abuse of power or something like that."

"Probably."

"Okay, but if I ever know something important, I'm not going to tell you unless I get something out of it, too."

"Paul, Paul, Paul. You have never known anything worth listening to as long as I've known you."

His friend frowned and said, "Now that hurts, Jimmy. That cuts me to the bone."

"Shit, Paul, your bones are buried so deep that it would take a chainsaw to get to them."

"Oh yeah? Well when I'm seven feet tall, you won't be such a smart ass, will you?"

"Time will tell, buddy," the sheriff said. "Let's go eat."

Chapter 16

The lunch crowd at the ButterCup Café was abuzz with excitement over news of the shooting. Before they even made it to their table, three people had asked the sheriff how Todd Norton was doing and what had happened to him. Weber overheard three or four others saying something to the effect of if they encountered the ninja, they were going to shoot him on sight. The sheriff wanted to tell them that kind of talk was foolish and dangerous, but he knew he would be wasting his time. People were frightened, and frightened people say crazy things. He hoped they would stick to talking and not make rash decisions like Coop had speculated. Rash decisions that could result in tragedy. He could only hope that they caught whoever was parading around town in the ninja costume and put a stop to the nonsense before something bad happened.

"Don't even need to see the menu," Paul said, holding his hand up when the waitress came to their table. "I'll have the special."

Weber was tempted to ask how his friend knew what the special was without looking at the menu, but he figured Paul made it his business to know things like that ahead of time. He himself didn't, so he asked.

"Open face roast beef sandwich, mashed potatoes, and corn," Gail Lowry, the waitress replied.

"I'll have it, too," he told her, then nodded at Big Lake's interim mayor, Kirby Templeton, as he approached their table.

"You guys got room for a third person there?"

"Have a seat, Kirby. You know the rules. Keep your fingers away from Paul's mouth, and if he reaches for something on your plate just back up so you don't get injured in his feeding frenzy."

If the newspaperman took offense to the sheriff's comments, he didn't show it. He simply nodded at Kirby and took a long drink of iced tea.

"You don't have to take that crap from this guy, Paul," Kirby said with a smile. "He is a public servant, after all. If you want to file a complaint with the Town Council, I'll certainly be your witness."

"I thought we were done having jerks for mayors when Chet Wingate retired," Weber said.

"Hey, I'm only filling in for a little while. Come election time, I'm done," Kirby replied.

"Say it ain't so," Paul said. "You're the best thing that ever happened to this town or the Town Council, Kirby."

"I agreed to fill the position until election time, but that's it."

"As far as I know, nobody has said anything about running against you."

"They won't be running against me. I don't want the job."

"Well, you know what they say, Kirby. Some are born great and others have greatness thrust upon them."

"If I wasn't such a devout man, I would tell you to thrust this." Kirby replied, then turned to Weber. "So, what the heck happened at Todd Norton's place today?"

"According to him, a ninja as big as a football tackle walked in the store and shot him and walked out without saying a word," Weber told him.

"But that's not the way it happened?"

"No. All the evidence shows that Todd was fooling around with a pistol and shot himself."

"And you're pretty sure that's the way it happened?"

"Yes, sir. There's no doubt in my mind about that at all."

102

The waitress brought their orders and looked at the mayor, who shook his head. "Just some lemonade for me, please, Ms. Lowry."

When she went away to fill his order, Kirby shook his head and said, "Well, Todd's always been a bit of a jerk, hasn't he?"

"That's an understatement."

"I hope you're going to charge him with something, Jimmy. Not only did he waste a lot of time and resources, he's got this town even more on edge than it was before with this ninja stuff."

"Yeah, he's getting charged with filing a false police report. And since the judge told him he couldn't have any firearms in his possession during his two year probation for that stunt shooting down Three-Bob's drone, I imagine he's going to be up a creek without a paddle."

"Couldn't happen to a nicer guy if you ask me," Paul said. "Every damn time I go to see him to try to sell him an ad, I have to listen to thirty minutes of him pissing and moaning about how the town's gone to hell in a handbasket and how bad the flatlanders are, and a dozen more things that upset him that day. Then, after all that, he usually doesn't want an ad anyway. Says he doesn't need it because he is the only auto parts store in town."

"Yeah, well that's about to change," Kirby said.

"Really? The O'Reilly Auto Parts is really going in?"

"Sure looks like it. The Town Council sent a letter notifying them that their zoning variance was approved two weeks ago, and according to what I heard today, they've signed the contract on the parcel of land where they are going to build."

"That's great news, Kirby."

"That depends on who you talk to. We both know there are some diehards around here who hate all the changes in the last few years. If they had their way, we'd still be a one horse town and the tourists would never hear of us."

"You can't stop progress."

"No," Kirby agreed. "And I wouldn't want to. I'm all for growth, as long as it's managed. But let's face it, gentlemen, we've had a lot of growth around here in a very short time. It's been hard for infrastructure to keep pace with it. I mean, look out there right now," Kirby said waving his hand toward the street. "A few years ago, you might not see a dozen cars parked the whole length of Main Street, even in the middle of the day, like now. These days, we have our own version of gridlock, and parking spaces are scarce as hen's teeth. And I know your office has seen a big upswing in calls, Jimmy."

"No doubt about that," Weber said. "But at least with you as mayor and the changes on the Town Council, we're getting the funding we need to get the job done."

"I never understood why Chet Wingate was so stingy with the Town's money," Kirby said, referring to his predecessor in the mayor's office. "There was a time when we had to budget carefully, but between the ski lodge and all the new building going on, plus the new businesses, it's created a tax windfall for us. I mean, it's not like we've got money to burn, but I think we're doing a pretty good job of keeping up with things and planning ahead these days."

"And that's exactly why you need to make it official and run for mayor," Paul said, tapping his finger on the table to emphasize his point. "We need to keep the momentum going in a positive direction. I really think we can have controlled growth that benefits the town but still preserves something of its character for the long-term."

"Well, you've certainly got my vote," Gail said, setting his glass of lemonade in front of Kirby. "You're doing a good job. And I have to say that with Chet Wingate and Adam Hirsch gone, the Council seems to be taking a new direction."

"Thank you, Ms. Lowry. We're trying," Kirby told the waitress.

"Well, now, you keep it up. We appreciate your efforts," she said, patting him on the shoulder as she moved away to greet a couple who were just taking seats nearby.

"You see? The people want you, and the town needs you, Kirby. Or should I just call you Mr. Mayor?"

"You can call me anything you want, as long as it's not too late for dinner. But let's not get carried away with this election stuff, okay? Like I said before, I agreed to fill in temporarily, but I really don't want the job full-time. I've got enough on my hands running the pharmacy and with life in general. Haven't you ever wanted to just stop and smell the roses, Paul?"

"Don't tempt him with something like that," Weber said. "The next thing you know, he'd be eating the damn roses and trying to talk with thorns sticking out of his lips."

"Okay, moving on, is there anything new that is real about this ninja case, Jimmy? Because there are so many rumors floating around town that I'm getting a dozen calls a day from citizens asking me when we are going to put a stop to it."

"We're working on it," Weber told him. "And for what it's worth, we're getting three times as many calls at the Sheriff's Office with people asking the same thing, or else reporting every squirrel and stray dog they see as the ninja. Seriously, we had one this morning from a lady who saw a big old black Lab wandering down the road and she called to report it as the ninja. Jordan Northcutt put a rope around its neck and brought it back to her yard and showed her it was just an old mutt, but as far as she was concerned, it was the ninja in some kind of crazy disguise. She swore she saw it walking upright right before he got there."

"Well, Hazel Fuller can't live forever," Paul observed. "It's good to know we've got somebody waiting in the wings to replace her. And speaking of replacing somebody," Paul continued, turning to Kirby, "how about if I put something in the paper just asking for public opinion on you continuing in the mayor's job? Sort of an informal poll. Let's see what people have to say about it."

"Can I borrow your gun, Jimmy? I need to shut this guy up before he gets me drafted into a job I really don't want."

Before Weber could reply, his cell phone rang with the tone reserved for the dispatcher. He pulled it from his pocket and pushed the button to take the call.

"Sheriff, you need to get over to Randy Laird's garage. Doug Mullins was in an accident and Randy says it looks like somebody tried to kill him."

Chapter 17

"I don't know what the hell happened," Doug Mullins said. "I was driving into town and I came to that steep hill by the Baptist Church and started to slow down, and all of a sudden I didn't have any brakes!"

Weber looked at the mangled front end of the man's pickup truck, it's bumper, grill, and hood caved in.

"What did you hit?"

"A telephone pole right there at the curb at the bottom of the hill. I kept hitting the brakes and the pedal went all the way to the floor. I tried to shift to a lower gear, but I was going too fast and by the time I got there I couldn't make the curve."

Noting his pale skin and the bandage on the man's forehead, Weber asked if he was injured.

"I banged my head pretty good against the steering wheel, or maybe it was the airbag. I'm not sure which. But it's nothing serious."

"You said something looks suspicious about the accident, Randy?"

"Yeah, Jimmy," the mechanic said. "Whenever I hear something about brakes failing, I always check the fluid reservoir first thing. The one on this truck was dry."

"When's the last time you checked your fluid, Doug?"

"I don't know, Sheriff. I do my own routine maintenance, oil changes, things like that. But I can't really tell you when the last time I checked it was."

"What about the brakes themselves? What kind of shape were they in?"

"The brakes are good," Randy said. "He was in here last Fall and I put new brakes and shocks on all the way around."

"So what happened today to cause the accident?"

"Fluid has to go somewhere," Randy said. "It's a closed system. Usually when you have a brake fluid leak there's a pinhole in a brake line or something like that somewhere. Possibly even a loose connection. And the brake pedal gets weaker when you push on it. But when you have a sudden loss of fluid like this, there's a reason for it, and it's not a simple leak. Here, scoot under the truck on this creeper and you'll see what I mean."

Weber laid down on the flat four wheeled dolly and slid under the truck, Randy laying on his back and joining him.

"See there," the mechanic said, pointing at a severed steel brake line with is pen light. "Something like that doesn't just break on its own. There's no rust on it, it looks like it's in good shape, and the breaking point right there? Take a close look, Jimmy. See how even it is almost all the way through except the very top there? Somebody took a saw and cut this line almost all the way through. How far do you live from that hill, Doug? Maybe a mile or so at the most?"

"Yeah, about that."

"And you didn't stop anyplace when you left the house before the accident?"

"No. No place."

"The way I see it, he probably didn't have to use his brakes at all until he got to Freeman's Hill," Randy said. "Then when he stepped on the brakes going down the hill, the pressure was enough to sever the brake line the rest of the way and poof, Doug is whipping down that hill like a bat out of hell."

"Can you take both ends of that brake line off for me? I need it for evidence," Weber said.

"No problem. I just wanted you to see this before I did anything else."

They scooted out from under the truck and stood up. As he bent down to pick up some loose change and the key ring that had fallen out of his pockets, Weber said, "Man, I'm sure glad you're okay, Doug. This could have turned out really bad."

"Who's doing this to me, Sheriff? I don't have an enemy in the world. Why me?"

"I wish I had an answer for you, Doug. I really do. We're going to find who is doing this. I promise you."

The three men turned at the sound of a car skidding to a stop on the garage's concrete parking apron. A distraught Tracy Mullins jumped out of her white Honda Accord, rushing to her husband's side.

"Oh my God, Doug! Are you okay?"

"I'm fine honey," he assured her.

"You're not fine! If you were fine, you wouldn't have a big bandage on your head!"

"It looks worse than it is," her husband said.

"Oh, honey, what happened? Did you black out or something?"

"No, the brakes went out and I hit a telephone pole. It could have been worse."

"It could've been a lot worse," Randy Laird said. "You're a lucky man, Doug."

"Lucky? You call this lucky? First that crazy ninja tried to kill him twice, and now this? That doesn't sound very lucky to me," Tracy replied acidly, then quickly apologized for her tone of voice. "I'm sorry, Randy. I'm just so scared. I didn't mean to take it out on you."

"Don't worry about it," the mechanic said. "I don't blame you one bit. You folks have enough on your plate already without all of this."

"Randy here doesn't think it was an accident," Doug told her.

"Not an accident? What do you mean?"

"It would appear that somebody tampered with the brake lines on your husband's truck," Weber said.

"What? Wait a minute. Somebody cut the brake line?"

"It looks that way to me," Randy said.

"No way! This just can't be happening." Tracy put her head down and massaged her forehead with her fingers, trying to process the news.

"Tracy, did you hear anybody or see anybody around the house that didn't belong there last night or this morning?"

"No, Sheriff. I left the house somewhere around 10 o'clock and I didn't notice anything. And believe me, with all that's been happening, I'm being extra alert."

"No strange cars, nobody on foot?"

She shook her head, then turned to her husband and gently caressed his cheek. "I'm so sorry it took me so long to get here, honey. I was on my way to Pinetop for my dentist appointment this morning and you know how bad the cell phone service is between here and there. As soon as I got within range of a tower and my phone beeped to show a message, I checked it. When I heard your voicemail, I turned around and headed right back. Do you need to go to the Medical Center to get checked out?"

"No, I'm fine, babe. The paramedics cleaned up my head and put this bandage on it."

"But what about a concussion or something like that?"

"I'm fine," he assured her.

"How is your chest feeling? Any pain?"

"I had a couple bad twitches when it first happened, but I'm okay now."

"I still think we need to get you checked out. Please, just to make me feel better?"

"You're such a worrywart," he told her.

"Maybe so, but I'm going to keep right on being a worrywart. Somebody has to look out for you because you won't do it for yourself."

Weber's phone rang and he answered it. "Yeah, Buz, what's up?"

"I went and checked the driveway at the Mullins' place and then followed the path Doug would've taken coming into town. There's a couple of little drops of what appears to be brake fluid in the driveway and a little trail, just some spots along the way. But just past the top of the hill, right where someone normally would step on the brake, there's a lot more fluid and you can see it all the way down the hill to where he slammed into the telephone pole."

"Okay. Any witnesses to the accident?"

"Myron Bock said he was mowing his grass when Doug went flying past his place, and he said the first thing he thought was that whoever the fool was behind the wheel was going to wind up taking out a telephone pole when he got to the curve at the bottom of the hill. He said he lost control of his car on the ice going down that hill two winters ago and wrecked it. And he said he wasn't going as fast as Doug was."

"Anything else?"

"Judy Pope was the first person on the scene. She was going the other way and saw the whole accident. She stopped and said that Doug appeared to be stunned, but he was awake. She called the office and said we needed an ambulance and a wrecker out there. I was the first unit on the scene and Robyn was right behind me. She directed traffic while I assessed Doug and conducted the investigation."

"Okay. Good job. Thanks, Buz."

"One other thing, Jimmy."

"What's that?"

"When Randy got to the accident scene and was putting Doug's truck on the hook, he pointed out the brake line to me. So I went back to the house and did a closer search. I collected what looks to be some fine metal flakes on the driveway right about where Doug parks his truck. Debris consistent with a brake line that's been sawed in half."

"Good work," Weber said. His attention was pulled from the phone call when he heard Tracy shouting, calling her husband's name.

He turned his head and saw that Doug was teetering on his feet. Randy grabbed him as his knees started to buckle and held him up. With Weber's assistance, they eased him down onto his back. Looking at the man's pallid skin, Weber keyed the microphone on his radio and told the dispatcher to send an ambulance to the garage. It seemed like what Doug Mullins at first thought was no more than a bump on the head might be much more serious.

Chapter 18

"He's going to be okay," Doctor Priya Patel said an hour later, after examining Doug Mullins and running an EKG and other tests. "Fortunately, it wasn't another heart attack. It was basically a stress reaction to the accident."

"Do we need to take him to the big hospital in Show Low, or maybe fly him to Phoenix or Tucson?"

Dr. Patel took Tracy's hands in hers and said, "Mrs. Mullins, I assure you that's not necessary. Your husband is resting comfortably, and he's going to be fine. I would like to keep him here overnight for observation, though, just as a precaution."

Observing how Big Lake's newest doctor remained professional while comforting the worried woman, Weber couldn't help but think that she was a valuable asset to the community. A short, mocha skinned and somewhat squat woman with dark features and amazingly white teeth, she had excelled in medical school and came to Big Lake as a single mother because she wanted to raise her son in a small town away from the crime and pollution she had seen in the big city. Nobody knew much about her husband, though there were rumors that he had died just as she was finishing her internship. She had quickly gained a reputation at work for her gentleness and kindness with her patients and their families, for getting along well with the rest of the Medical Center's staff, and because she was an excellent doctor. Weber made a mental note that he and Robyn should invite Dr. Patel and her son to dinner sometime.

"Can I see him now?"

"Sure," the doctor said, "follow me."

Weber tagged along and stood in the back of the little examination room while Tracy almost threw herself on her husband, sobbing.

"I love you so much."

Maybe it was because of the tubes going in and out of him and the oxygen cannula looped around his ears and resting inside his nostrils, along with the hospital gown he was wearing, but Doug Mullins looked smaller and weaker to the sheriff. But that didn't stop him from smiling and patting his wife's head to comfort her.

"I love you, too, babe. Don't worry, this is just another little speedbump. I'm fine and things will get back to normal here any day now."

She pulled away slightly and held his face in both hers, shaking her head. "Is it ever going to be normal again, Doug?"

"It's okay. Everything's okay."

"I just want you home. I want you home, and I want you well again. I want you to stop working so hard and to take care of yourself, Doug. I'm not ready to lose you yet!"

"I'm not going anywhere," he promised.

Dr. Patel busied herself checking the monitors hooked up to her patient, and then said, "Mr. Mullins, everything looks fine, but I want to keep you overnight for observation. Would that be okay with you?"

"Uh, do I really have to stay, Doc? You said everything looks fine, right?"

"Yes, I did. But I would just feel more comfortable if you stayed the night."

"To be honest with you, I'd feel more comfortable at home."

"Honey, if the doctor thinks you need to stay here…"

"I'm going to be okay, Tracy. Really, I just want to get home."

The doctor looked at him skeptically, then at Weber and shrugged her shoulders. "Of course, I can't force you to stay. But with your existing heart problems…"

114

"I don't mean to be disrespectful, Doctor Patel, but really, I just want to go home."

"It's about the money, right? You're worried about the hospital bill, aren't you, Doug?"

"We've got enough bills to deal with already, Tracy. We don't need to add more to the pile. And everybody knows you don't get any rest in the hospital anyway. They wake you up every couple of hours to check your pulse and ask you if you're sleeping well. Trust me, I'll get a lot more rest at home."

"If I let you go home, will you promise me that you'll go right to bed and stay there until tomorrow?"

Doug held out his hand, the middle three fingers extended and thumb holding the little finger. "Scout's honor, Doc."

Doctor Patel folded her arms across her chest and looked at him. "That means you stay in bed and you rest. You don't lay there and do paperwork. You don't start planning your next projects. You don't worry about anything. You rest, that's it."

"You have my word," he promised her.

"All right then. I don't like it, but you're an adult. But please, Mr. Mullins, you are not a well man and this latest incident has only exacerbated your problems. Slow down and take it easy, at least for a few days, okay?"

"I got no choice," Doug told her. "My truck's totaled and I can't get any work done until I figure out how to pay for another one."

The doctor looked at Tracy and said, "I'm counting on you to try to keep him off his feet for a day or so, okay?"

"Oh, trust me, Doctor, he's going to stay in bed if I have to borrow the sheriff's handcuffs to keep him there!"

"Now, now, Tracy. These people don't want to hear about our sex life," Doug teased his wife, with a wink at Weber.

Doctor Patel smiled and said, "And with that, I'll have the nurse come in and disconnect all of this equipment and let you get dressed. I'll see you in a few minutes."

Weber followed her out of the room and touched her shoulder when they were out of hearing.

"Seriously, Doctor, how is he?"

"You know I can't discuss a patient's case without their permission, Sheriff. But I will say this. Mr. Mullins has been burning the candle at both ends for way too long."

"I know he's got a bad ticker and things don't look good."

"No, they don't," the doctor said, shaking her head with a sigh. "I came here because I wanted the slower pace of small-town life. The thing I didn't expect was that in a small town my patients aren't just faces who come through and get treated and are gone in a few days. They're my neighbors. I see them at the store, they teach my son at school, we work together on projects and committees. I know you must run across the same thing all the time. At least I'm an outsider. You have known most of these people all of your life. How do you do it, Sheriff? How do you keep that professional distance when you're dealing with someone you have broken bread with? Someone you consider a friend?"

"It's a fine line to walk," Weber told her. "I'll be honest with you, Doc. Sometimes it's not easy. I've had to handcuff guys I hung around with in high school. Just a little while ago I was visiting with a good friend I've known forever, and I was the one who had to tell her that her husband had been killed in an accident."

"So what's the secret, Sheriff? How do you do it? How do you keep from hiding in a closet sometimes and crying?"

"To be honest with you, Doctor, I've been in that closet more than once."

She looked at him with sad dark eyes and said, "Me, too, Sheriff Weber. Me, too."

~~~***~~~

"We need to figure out what the hell is happening in this town," Weber told his deputies at a hastily called meeting later that afternoon. "Where did all this ninja nonsense come from to start with? And how did Doug Mullins, of all people, become the target for this idiot?"

"You don't watch much TV, do you, Jimmy?"

"No, not if I can avoid it."

116

"Maybe you should once in a while," FBI agent Larry Parks, who was sitting in on the meeting, said. "Ninjas seem to be the big thing this week. For the last couple of weeks lately."

"Why?"

"One of the cable channels out of Phoenix was running a ninja marathon a week or so ago. Something like five days of ninja movies and ninja TV shows."

"What, like *Kung Fu*?"

"Actually, kung fu is Chinese and refers to pretty much any kind of Chinese martial arts. Ninjas are Japanese. In old-time feudal Japan they were like mercenaries."

"Like samurais?"

"Not exactly. Samurais, who the Japanese actually call bushi, considered ninjas to be dishonorable thugs, not deserving of the warrior code and not worthy of the honor being a samurai carried with it."

"How do you know all this crap, Parks? I never know if you're really that smart or if you're just bullshitting everybody all the time."

"Hey, I'm not just another pretty face! I know stuff."

"If you say so. Anyway, you're saying because of a bunch of stupid movies on TV, we've got somebody running around here pretending to be a ninja?"

"It's not just the TV thing," Parks said. "There's been a thing going around to different places in the Southwest putting on ninja demonstrations and a big ninja convention, from want of a better word. They had one in Tucson three weeks ago and then last week it was in Mesa. I think there's going to be another one in Flagstaff pretty soon. They have ninja fighting demonstrations, actors who play ninjas on TV and in the movies on hand to meet and greet fans. It's quite an event."

"Why?"

"Why does anybody do anything, Jimmy? The promoters make big bucks and a lot of nerds dream of being warriors show up dressed like it's Halloween and get to pretend their fantasy is real."

"Kind of like a comic con?"

117

"Pretty much, Jordan," Parks replied.

"I hesitate to ask this. I really do," Weber said. "But what's a comic con?"

"Man, you really do need to spend some time watching TV," Parks told him. "Comic con stands for comic convention. They have them all over the country."

"I don't find anything comical about this shit," Weber said. "If it keeps up, somebody's going to get killed."

"Not comic like standup comedians, Jimmy. Like comic book heroes."

"Okay. I don't believe half the crap you tell me, Parks, but I can see you reading a lot of comic books. That suits your mentality."

"That's right, I'm a superhero. They call me Dongman."

"In your dreams," Robyn said, shaking her head.

"No, in *your* dreams," Parks replied with an exaggerated leer.

"Moving right along, I don't give a rat's ass what's causing some nerd to run around here playing ninja, or maybe more than one, since we've had at least one sighting of it being more than one person. What I care about is how do we put a stop to it?"

There was silence in the room for a moment, and then Coop said, "I don't know what else we can do, Boss. We've got people working overtime, we're spending a lot of time on the streets looking for anything suspicious, and we're talking to everybody we can to try to get information out of them. Everybody seems to know about the ninja, or ninjas, whichever it is. But nobody knows who it is."

"The thing I keep asking myself is, why Doug Mullins? What singled him out for this kind of attention?"

"I wish I had an answer for that, Mary," Weber said. "That part doesn't make any sense at all."

"I've known Doug all my life. He's a good guy who never bothered anybody," Buz said. "It makes no sense at all."

"The incidents with the sword and the throwing star, they were crazy enough, but at least they are kind of ninja related," Dan Wright said. "But this thing today, with the cut brake line? That's as bizarre as Todd Norton claiming a ninja shot him."

"Speaking of Todd, what's up with that dumb ass?"

"Dolan called a few minutes ago," Mary said. "He said they are wrapping things up at the hospital and they will be heading back this way before too long. He also asked if it would be okay with you if he shoots Todd somewhere along the way and feeds him to the bear and coyotes because he's tired of hearing him bitch. He's still sticking to his story about the ninja shooting him and claiming that we're setting him up."

"Yeah, right. Because we've got nothing else to do with our time," Chad said, shaking his head. "That man was born with a piss poor attitude and it's gotten worse every day of his life. I wonder what makes a man that way. I knew his mom and dad, and they were decent people."

"So is his sister. You couldn't ask for a better woman," Mary said.

"Who is his sister?"

"You don't know, Jimmy?"

"No, I guess I don't."

Everybody knew that Mary had the scoop on everything that was happening in town and everybody there. She had an incredible memory and knew who was married to who, their often-complex family lineage, who had been in trouble with the law in the past, and who was struggling to get by in the town's often shaky economy. She never gossiped, but there wasn't much that happened in Big Lake or its environs that she didn't know about.

"You're kidding me? You don't know?"

"Hell, Mary, I didn't even know the difference between a ninja and a samurai. How do you expect me to know who's kinfolk to who in this town?"

"Tracy."

"Who?"

"Tracy. Tracy Mullins. Doug Mullins' wife is Todd Norton's sister. How did you not know that?"

Chapter 19

"Everybody in town is talking about this crazy ninja stuff," Marsha said that evening as they sat down at a table at the Ming House Chinese restaurant. "I had a lady in the shop today who insisted it's a plot by the Communists to take over America. She said she read all about it in one of those tabloid newspapers at the supermarket checkout. Ninja sleeper cells or something like that all over the country just waiting for the secret message to go to war."

"Lord knows that's where I get my news," Parks told her.

"I didn't say it was true, I just repeated what she said. She's not the first person I've heard talking about it. Mavis Detweiler said she's afraid to let her dog out in the yard to do its business because she's afraid the ninja will attack it."

"I wish you wouldn't talk about that while we're in a Chinese restaurant. Now I'm hungry for poodles and noodles," Parks said, earning himself an elbow jab in the ribs from his girlfriend.

"I know what you're talking about," Weber said. "I can't begin to count the number of calls we've had from people claiming they saw the ninja."

"Were any of them real?"

"Who knows? None of the deputies who responded have seen anything or any evidence of someone being there. Maybe the people calling really saw something, or maybe their imaginations are running wild. Either way, it's a waste of time and resources and we're not getting anywhere. And after that bullshit with Todd Norton claiming a ninja shot him, it's only getting worse. I'm afraid that if we don't put a stop to it, somebody's going to get scared and kill the neighbor kid when he comes around offering to mow the grass."

"That's for sure," Robyn said. "Lester McCrea flagged me down today and wanted my help pulling the slide back on a rusty old .45 pistol that looked like it hasn't been out of a box since he brought it back from Korea. He's like 90 years old and so frail he couldn't rack a round into the chamber, but he's ready to defend himself and his wife from the ninja."

"I hope to hell you didn't do it," Weber said.

"I acted like I tried and couldn't do it either. Told him it's probably rusted shut."

"It's crazy, but it shows you the thinking around town these days," Parks said.

Marsha changed the subject, asking, "How's Doug Mullins doing? I heard he was in an accident."

"Not good, Marsha. He collapsed after today's incident and the doctor wanted to keep him overnight for observation, but he wouldn't do it. Insisted on going home."

"Those folks have got their hands full. I was talking to Tracy the other day and the poor woman looks like she's about to have a nervous breakdown. She said Doug just won't slow down even with all the problems he's got. He's obsessed with putting money away and making sure she'll have something after he's gone."

"I can't imagine what that must be like for either one of them," Robyn said. "Knowing the person you love is going to die. How do you deal with that on a day-to-day basis? And for him? Most people facing what he is facing would want to just sit down and enjoy the time they have left."

Parks was looking at the menu and asked, "What the hell is tofu?"

"It's bean curd," Marsha told him. "Try it, you'll like it."

"No, thanks. I'm not that adventurous. I'll stick with the shrimp fried rice."

"You have the same thing every time we come here."

"What can I say, babe? I'm a creature of habit."

"Why don't you mix things up and try something new once in a while?"

"Don't even go there, Marsha," Parks told her. "When I asked you that same question the other night, you called me a pervert."

"Shut up," she replied, "I have a reputation to protect and that kind of talk might make people start thinking I'm normal."

"Yes, ma'am." Parks said, nodding his head meekly.

"Well now, I guess we know who wears the pants in your relationship," Weber observed with a grin.

"It's been my experience that relationships work best when no one wears pants," Marsha told him.

The waitress came to take their orders, and when she left the table three men who looked to be in their early twenties sitting at another table called her over. Weber observed one of them grinning lasciviously at his buddies when he pointed at something on the menu. When the young waitress bent over to look at what he was indicating, he casually put his hand on her rear end. She stiffened and moved away quickly, giving him a dirty look, which drew laughter from all three men.

"Hey, come back, I have more questions," said the man, a beefy fellow who looked like he spent a lot of time working out in the gym.

The waitress went through the double doors in the kitchen and a moment later the older Asian woman who owned the restaurant came out and marched up to the table. "You go now. You go and you no come back. No touch girls like that," she said sternly.

The big guy put his hands together in front of his face and bowed, then said in a high falsetto voice, "It's okay, mama-san. I got lots of love to go around." And with that, he patted the woman's bottom.

She pushed his hand away and said something in Chinese, and the three men laughed at her anger.

"Hey, get the other one and bring her back, we'll have ourselves a party," said another man at the table, this one a broad shouldered, shaven headed hulk with an evil grin on his face.

"Well, that's enough of that nonsense," Weber said with a sigh, pushing his chair back and standing up.

"Need any help, Jimmy?"

"Have you seen the size of those three? Of course he's going to need help," Marsha said.

Parks looked at Robyn and asked, "Well, girl, what are you doing just sitting there? Go stand by your man!"

"I got this," Weber said.

He walked across the room to the table and said, "You boys need to learn some manners. I don't know how they do things where you come from, but we don't treat people that way here in Big Lake."

"Who are you, Goober? Mind your own business."

"I think it's time for you fellows to leave."

"I think if you don't go back and sit down and mind your own business, I'm going to kick your ass," said the original offender.

His buddy with a shaved head smirked and said, "Watch out, Nate. This guy thinks he's some kind of hero. I don't know about you, but I'm so scared I'm about to piss my pants."

"I'm not going to tell you guys again. Get up and get out of here, right now."

"Who died and left you in charge?"

"Actually, nobody died yet," Weber said. Then he reached into the back pocket of his jeans and pulled out his badge case and opened it up to show them the gold star inside. "But the Town Council did put me in charge of dealing with jerks like you. So, what's it going to be? We can do this the easy way, or we can do it the hard way."

Most people back down when they realize the person they are confronting is a police officer. But these three were just high enough on testosterone and ego not to have that much common sense.

"The way I see it," Nate said, "badge no badge, there are still three of us and one of you, cowboy. I kind of like those odds. How about you?"

Parks and Robyn were on their feet and moved up on either side of Weber.

124

"What's this, your crew?"

"This pretty lady next to me is Deputy Robyn Fuchette," Weber said. "And this guy? He's FBI Special Agent Larry Parks. So yeah, no matter how big and buff you guys think you are, my crew is better."

"What's that little girl going to do? Why should I be afraid of her?"

Robyn pulled the hem of her T-shirt up enough to show her badge and .40 Glock Model 27 pistol and said sweetly, "I've got PMS and a handgun, mister. You damn sure better be afraid."

"Hey guys, chill out," said the third man at the table, who except for laughing earlier had been quiet up until then. "We don't need any trouble."

"You should listen to your friend," Weber said. "He's the only one of the three of you who seems to have any sense."

"Nah, I don't think so. You and I both know you guys aren't going to shoot us, and Little Miss Muffet there doesn't impress me at all, gun or no gun. So take your best shot, pig. What's the worst that could happen?"

"Well, let's see," Weber said. "The worst that could happen is that you'd kick our asses."

"You got that straight."

"Yeah, and then every deputy and every lawman in this part of the country would descend on you, and all you would see is a whirlwind of nightsticks and boots as you hit the ground. And when they get done stomping you, which would take them a while because they enjoy that kind of thing, they would haul your asses to jail. You'd be charged not only with assaulting police officers, but with assaulting a federal officer, too. The FBI frowns on that big time. If you're lucky, you will only do four or five years. But it's going to be a rough four or five years, because as big and tough as you guys think you are, you're going to meet some cons that will look at you and see a bunch of soft gym rats. They're going to beat you to a bloody pulp before they shiv you. Or, they might decide to make you the cellblock bitches. Trust me, you'd be better off being beaten and stabbed. So, the choice is up to you, boys. You can walk out on your own and end this right here, or you can do something stupid and see how it plays out. But I have to tell you one thing. You were wrong when you said we wouldn't shoot you. Deputy Fuchette here is not a big woman, but she's an excellent shot. And no jury in the world would have a problem with her blowing your asses away, seeing as you're three times her size."

The third man at the table, the one who had urged his friends to calm down, said, "Listen, we don't want any trouble. We're just up here for a few days to have some fun."

"That's fine," Weber told him. "I've got no problem with that as long as your fun doesn't involve putting your hands on other people or doing anything else stupid. We like folks to come here and enjoy themselves. But when you step over the line, you need to remember the old saying, come on vacation, leave on probation."

Weber wasn't sure if the first man was going to listen to reason or if he was going to try something foolish. It could go either way. But after a long minute his body relaxed and he said, "Screw this bullshit. Let's go someplace we can get a beer, guys."

Weber watched them as they went out the door, then Parks said, "Well, that could have gone either way."

"Let's be glad it went the way it did," Weber told him. "Those are some big sons of bitches and I wasn't looking forward to tangling with them."

They went back to their table and the older woman said, "Thank you, Sheriff," bowing her head, then turned to Robyn and Parks and repeated her expression of gratitude. "Tonight dinner on me for all of you."

"That's not necessary, Mrs. Liu. We were just doing our jobs."

"Those not good men."

"No, ma'am, they're not," Weber told her. "Hopefully that's the last we'll see of them and they'll stay out of trouble the rest of the time they're here in town."

While the sheriff would get his wish in one respect, since they would not see those three again, that was still plenty of trouble coming to Big Lake.

Chapter 20

On her second appearance before Judge Ryman, it was obvious that Coleen Pendhill's extended time behind bars seemed to have given her a change of attitude. She appeared contrite, answering the judge's questions with "Yes, sir" and "No, sir" and keeping her head bowed.

"Miss Pendhill, I notice that your attorney is not here today."

The girl's mother shook her head. "No, sir, he's not. He is no longer representing Coleen."

"Do you wish to retain other counsel before we proceed? That's your right, Miss Pendhill."

"No, sir."

When asked how she pled to the charges against her, she said "Guilty" and the judge asked her if she had anything to say before he passed sentence.

"Just that I'm very sorry for what I did," she replied, then turned to Weber and Robyn and said, "I apologize for the way I behaved. I was totally out of line and there is no excuse for what I did. I promise I'll never do anything like that again."

Judge Ryman studied her for a long moment, as if trying to discern whether she really meant what she said or if it was all an act. Finally, he seemed to make up his mind. "Miss Pendhill, I understand you are a student at Arizona State University. Is that so?"

"Yes, sir," she replied, nodding her head.

"What are you majoring in?"

"I haven't chosen a major yet, sir. I was thinking about law school, or maybe education. I haven't really made up my mind yet."

"That's fair enough," the judge said. "To be honest with you, I don't know what I want to be when I grow up yet, either."

She smiled weakly.

"Here's the thing, Miss Pendhill. A criminal conviction, especially one for assaulting a police officer, means all that goes down the drain. The competition is pretty stiff to get into law school as it is, and a black mark on your record like that? No way. And what school system is going to hire someone with a felony conviction? Do you understand how serious this is?"

She wiped tears from her eyes and nodded her head. "Yes, sir, I do. I really messed up and I know that."

The judge looked at Weber and Robyn and said, "What do you think, Sheriff? Deputy Fuchette? You were the victims here, more or less."

Weber looked at Robyn, who said, "Your Honor, we've all been young and done things that we regret. There's no question that Miss Pendhill was way out of line the other day, and again when she was in here for her first appearance before you. But I really don't want to see her life ruined by one incident."

"Fair enough, Deputy. Sheriff Weber, what say you?"

"Miss Pendhill made a series of foolish choices, Your Honor. No question about that. But I agree with Deputy Fuchette. Maybe she can take something away from this; a learning experience that will make her a better person in the future."

The judge folded his arms across his chest and looked at the defendant. "You said that you were thinking about law school?"

"Yes, sir."

"You know, Miss Pendhill, attorneys are just like any other profession. There are good ones and there are bad ones, and I've seen my share of both, believe me. I'm not saying that Mr. Richardson is a bad attorney, but he certainly didn't help your case in this courtroom."

"No, sir, he didn't."

"Sometimes we learn from our experiences, and sometimes we can learn by the examples other people set for us, both good and bad."

"Yes, sir."

"Sheriff Weber and Deputy Fuchette have been more than gracious, I think you'd have to agree with that, wouldn't you?"

"Yes, sir, I do. And I appreciate it very much," she said, turning to the sheriff and deputy. "After the way I acted, I didn't deserve that."

"Here's what I'm going to do," Judge Ryman said. "I'm fining you $5,000. And I'm sentencing you to 500 hours of community service. I have some connections down in the Valley, and I'm going to arrange for that community service to be working with the Public Defender's Office in Maricopa County. They may have you doing everything from emptying the wastebaskets in the offices to assisting with paperwork. Whatever they need done. You will have an opportunity to see how the legal system works and maybe get an idea as to whether or not that's something you want to pursue with your life. As for the fine, I'm going to suspend it on the condition that you fulfill your community service obligation without any problems, and that you stay out of trouble for the next two years. If you do all of that and I get good reports back about you, you come see me then and I'll expunge this whole thing. You won't have a record. It will be like it never happened. Is that fair enough?"

She was crying and nodded her head. "Yes, sir. Thank you, sir."

"But be forewarned, young lady," the judge said sternly, pointing his finger at her, "If you mess up again, if I hear of you getting into any trouble of any kind, I don't care what it is, you and I will be meeting again. And I promise you, you're not going to like the way that turns out. Do you understand me?"

"Yes, sir, I do."

"One other thing, Miss Pendhill. I want you to apologize to your mother for how snotty you were to her the first time you were in here. I see a lot of young people in this courtroom, but it's not very often their parents show up with them. And when they do, more often than not they try to excuse their kid's behavior. Your mother set an example for you, just like your attorney did. The only difference is, by her example she was showing you that you need to stand up on your hind legs and take responsibility for your actions. Mrs. Pendhill, I compliment you for that."

Wiping her eyes, Coleen turned to her mother and said, "I'm so sorry, Mom."

"All right then," Judge Ryman said. "We're done here. Do not let me down, Miss Pendhill."

He rapped his gavel and stood up, leaving the courtroom through the door behind the bench.

~~~***~~~

When they walked out of the courtroom, Coleen and her mother approached them.

"We just want to apologize again, and thank you for what you did in there," the older woman said.

"Yes, thank you," Coleen added. "I'm really not that person that you saw the other day. I really don't know what got into me. My boyfriend and I broke up last week and I was in a bad mood, and my friends thought it would be fun to get away for a few days to make me feel better. But that didn't work out very well."

"Things happen sometimes," Weber said extending his hand to shake both the mother and the daughter's. "You're a smart girl and you've got a lot going for you, not the least of which is a mother who really cares. The judge was right, more often than I want to think about, parents right away think we're the bad guys just for doing our job. You've got a good role model there."

"Yes, I do."

"Good luck to you, Coleen," Robyn said, also shaking their hands. "Take care."

They watched them get in their car and drive away, and then Robyn said, "I'm technically off duty today, Jimmy. But since I'm in uniform anyway, how about I cruise around town a little bit. I might get lucky and spot this ninja."

"Or, you could go home and dress in something a little less bulky than your uniform, and I could come home for lunch and we could both get lucky."

"Or," Robyn said, counteroffering, "I could go home and spend the day vacuuming and washing windows and be so tired that when you came home this evening, all you could do is rub my feet."

"Just your feet, huh?"

"It's a big house with a lot of windows, Jimmy. A girl would get really tired doing all of that."

"On the other hand…"

She bumped him with her hip and said, "How about you go do your thing and I'll go do my thing."

"Or we could do each other's things," Weber said hopefully.

"I'll see you at home tonight," Robyn said, looking around to be sure no one was watching before kissing him lightly on the lips and getting into her patrol car.

~~~***~~~

Weber checked in with Dispatch on the radio, and when they told him nothing much was going on, he decided to drive by the Mullins house and see how Doug was doing. He was surprised to see a Dodge pickup with the Harris Fence Company logo painted on the doors. Tracy answered his knock and stepped back to let him in. Doug was sitting in his recliner in the living room, looking a bit better than he had the day before.

"I'm sorry, I didn't know you had company," the sheriff said. "I just wanted to see how you were feeling today, Doug."

"No company. Marvin heard about what happened yesterday and brought one of his pickups by and told me to use it as long as I needed it," Doug said.

"That was damn nice of him."

"He even told me to take the magnetic signs off my truck and put them on his."

Weber was impressed. He had always respected Marvin Harris, but that respect increased greatly hearing how he was willing to reach out his hand to help a competitor.

"You're not going to do anything for the next couple of days," Tracy said. "You're going to follow doctor's orders and just take it easy for a while."

"Honey, stop worrying all the time. I'm fine."

"No, you're not, Doug. You need to start taking better care of yourself."

Doug shook his head and smiled at Weber. "What can I say, Sheriff? My wife is the ultimate mother hen."

"You're a lucky man to have her."

Doug looked at his wife with loving eyes and said, "Don't I know it. She can have any man she wants, and to be honest with you, I don't know why she settled for me."

"I did not *settle*, Doug Mullins," Tracy said. "I've got the best man in the world. I just want to keep you around for as long as I can."

"Hey, what's this we heard about Tracy's brother getting shot and going to jail?"

"To be honest with you, Tracy, I didn't know Todd was your brother," Weber admitted.

"He's a brother in name only," she replied bitterly. "We don't have anything to do with him."

"Really? I'm sorry to hear that."

"I'm not," Tracy said. "Todd has been a jerk since the day he was born. Do you know that when our dad died, he went to the house the day after the funeral and cleared out the garage? Took all of his tools, even the lawnmower! I guess he figured that with Daddy dead, the grass would just stop growing. So until Mom passed on, Doug went over every week and mowed the grass and did whatever else she needed done. Todd was always too busy running his business to care about her. But as soon as she was gone, he was right there wanting everything he could get his hands on. He even called a real estate agent and had a For Sale sign up in the yard within two days. Didn't even talk to me about it. And when

132

the place sold, he tried to cheat me out of what I had coming from the estate."

"So, the two of you don't get along very well?"

"We don't get along at all, Sheriff. But it's not just because of that. Like I said, Todd was always a jerk. He never had time for our parents, even though they bankrolled his store when he was first starting out. He never paid them back a dime, never went by to visit with them unless he wanted something from them. But the final straw was when him and Jessica were getting divorced. Me and her, we always got along real well, even before her and Todd got together. That girl put up with so much crap from him over the years, I'm surprised she stuck it out as long as she did. One time, after she moved out, he saw us having lunch at the Frontier Café and came totally unglued. He came up to the table and called me a traitor and ordered me not to ever speak to her again. He caused a big scene and the manager threw him out of the place. That night he showed up here at the house and was calling Jessica all kinds of filthy names and saying she was trying to take him for everything he had. He told me if he ever saw me even talking to her again, he was going to kick my butt. Well, he said it a little more graphic than that, but you know what I mean."

"Wow. I knew Todd could be difficult, but I never knew he was that far off in left field."

"Let me put it to you this way, Sheriff. You know Doug and you know what a nice guy he is. He doesn't have an enemy in the world and I've never seen him argue with anybody about anything. But that night he ordered Todd off our property and warned him not to ever come back. Told him if he ever did, he was going to be sorry."

Weber had been exposed to a lot of family drama in his years on the job, and he knew how bad things could get between people who shared the same blood. Especially when there was a death in the family and money to be had from an estate, no matter how large or small it was. He was just sorry that a nice couple like Doug and Tracy Mullins had to put up with aggravation from somebody like Todd Norton.

"Well, if it's any consolation to you, he's our headache right now. He'll go to see the judge tomorrow sometime, and we'll see how that goes."

Chapter 21

Weber was driving back to the office when he passed by an elderly couple on the sidewalk halfway up the same hill where Doug Mullins had his accident. The man, who had a fringe of white hair around his bald head, was trying to push a motorized wheelchair uphill and not having much luck with it. Weber pulled to the side of the road and asked, "It looks like you folks have a problem. Need any help?"

"Darn battery up and gave out," Bill Starkey said, wiping sweat from his forehead with the back of his hand. "I thought I could push Shirley the rest of the way home, but either this hill has gotten steeper over the years or else I've gotten older. When I was 16, I could run up and down hills all day long and never break a sweat. But at 88, it's not that easy anymore."

"It's probably the hill," Weber said, getting out of his Explorer. "I notice the hills are getting a lot steeper myself. How you doing, Miss Shirley?"

"I'd feel a lot better if I was home," the woman replied, holding a liver spotted hand up to shield her eyes as she replied.

"Well, let's see if we can get you there. If I help you, can you get into my car?"

"Yes, I can walk a little bit, I just get shaky. That's what happens when you get old, Sheriff. Your whole body starts to fall apart on you."

135

With her husband helping, they got her to the Explorer and Weber opened the back door so she could get in.

"I've never been in a police car before," she said, looking around at the radio, the shotgun mounted on a rack attached to the dashboard, and all the other equipment.

"Well, the good news is, you get to get back out of it at home," Weber told her. "Most folks who wind up back there end up spending a night in jail."

She laughed and said, "Never been there, either. And I hope I never will be."

"Oh, it's not all that bad," the sheriff assured her. "You get three hot meals and a nice cot to sleep on. You be surprised how many people we've got standing in line waiting their turn to be our guest."

"I think I'd just as soon be at home, if it's all the same to you."

"That's fine, ma'am. Let's get you there."

He loaded the wheelchair into the back end of the SUV and her husband climbed in the front seat beside him, and he drove them home, which was less than a half-mile from where they were. Weber helped the woman into the house, accepting her offer of a glass of lemonade. While she was filling the glasses, he helped her husband push the wheelchair up the ramp into the house and plugged it in, noting the green light that indicated the battery was charging.

The house was a small bungalow, its furnishings outdated but neat as a pin.

"Here you go, Sheriff," Shirley said, bringing a tray with three glasses of lemonade on it to the living room, her hands so shaky that some spilled. Weber quickly took the tray from her so she could sit down, and then perched on a couch with a crocheted afghan covering the back. Weber remembered his mother having a similar afghan on the family couch when he was growing up. He wondered if every house in that time period had one. He did not see a television in the living room, but there was an old piano whose yellowed keys and worn wood indicated it had seen a lot of use over the years. A book of sheet music on the piano's music rack, the page opened to the notes and words to *In The Good Old*

Summertime. Weber couldn't remember the last time he had heard that old song.

"Who plays the piano?"

"Oh, I play at it, but that's about the best I can say," Shirley replied.

"Don't listen to her, Sheriff. She can tickle the ivories with the best of them," her husband told him.

"Now Bill, don't exaggerate," Shirley said modestly, but her beaming face showed that she appreciated the compliment. She gave her husband a smile that reflected the many years of love they had shared between them. Weber remembered the close relationship that his own parents had shared and wondered if they would be just as loving to each other in their old age if an accident hadn't taken their lives way too soon. He was sure they would have been.

He was tempted to ask her to play it for him, but he figured the old woman had had enough activity for one day. It was a warm day and the lemonade went down well. As Weber drank, he looked at her husband, who was still very red-faced.

"Are you okay, Bill?"

"Yeah, just need to catch my breath. This gettin' old stuff ain't for sissies, Sheriff."

"No, it's not. Listen, do you have a cell phone."

"I do," his wife said. "Bill don't want nothing to do with any of this new stuff. If he had his way, we'd still have those old phones that you have to turn the crank on hanging on the wall."

Weber took a business card from his pocket and wrote his cell phone number on the back before giving it to her husband. "The next time you guys have a problem like this, or anything at all, you give me a call. Don't be trying to push something up that hill like that."

"We hate to bother anybody," Bill said.

"It's no bother," the sheriff assured him, touching the badge pinned to his shirt. "You see what it says right here? To Serve And Protect. It says the same thing on the side of my car. Our job isn't just running around locking people up. We're here to help anytime you need something."

"Well that's mighty kind of you, Sheriff. It truly is."

"I'm serious," Weber told him. "I would much rather give you a ride someplace when you're stuck than have to call the ambulance to give you a ride to the hospital."

"Speaking of hospitals, how is Doug Mullins doing? We heard about his wreck."

"He got a nasty bump on his forehead, but he's okay."

"He's such a nice man," Shirley said. "Do you know that he came over here and built that ramp out front so I can get in and out of the house when my legs gave out? Just took it upon himself to do that. And then he wouldn't take any money for his time or the stuff he used to make it."

"He is a good man," Weber agreed.

"It's a shame what's happening to him," Bill said.

Weber wasn't sure if he meant the man's health problems or the ninja attacks and did not want to say something out of line, so he simply nodded his head and said, "Yes, it is."

"Do you know who I think is behind all of what's happening to him?"

"Now Bill," his wife gently chided, "don't be telling stories out of school. Just because you think something don't make it real."

"I know that, but I still think Todd's behind it."

"Todd? Todd Norton?"

"Yeah, him."

"What makes you think Todd would have anything to do with what's been happening around here?"

"Because the man's a first-class A-hole, that's why!"

"Bill, watch your language."

"I didn't say anything bad, honey. And I imagine the Sheriff's heard a lot worse."

Indeed, Weber had, but right now he was more interested in hearing what the old man had to say about Todd Norton and his relationship with his brother-in-law.

"No question about it, Todd can be difficult," Weber said. "But do you really think he would do anything to hurt Doug Mullins? Why would he do that?"

"Why does anybody do anything, Sheriff? It usually comes down to money, and sometimes sheer cussedness. I don't know if Todd stands to gain anything if something happens to Doug, but he's mean enough and ornery enough to do anything. I know there's been bad blood between him and Doug and Tracy ever since their folks died. Todd had it in his head that he could sell their place and pocket all the money, but Tracy dug in her heels and told him that wasn't going to happen. She's a good, decent woman, but she went and got herself a lawyer and saw to it that not only did the proceeds from selling the house get split right down the middle, she also got a court order that the money that Todd owed his folks came out of his half! He didn't like that. No sir, he didn't like that at all!"

"No, I don't imagine he would," Weber said. His mind was reeling with the new information about the relationship between Todd Norton and his sister and brother-in-law and he missed it when Shirley asked him a question.

"Sheriff? Are you okay?"

"Oh, sorry. Yes, ma'am, I'm fine. What was it you were saying?"

"I asked if you wanted some more lemonade. I've got a whole pitcher full in the refrigerator."

"No, ma'am. Thank you. It's delicious, but I need to get back to work." He stood up and shook Bill's hand and nodded at Shirley. "Remember what I said, if you need anything at all, you give me a call. Okay?"

"We will surely do that," the old man replied. "Thanks again, Sheriff."

Weber got back in the Explorer and looked at the house for a moment, making a mental note to himself to check up on its elderly occupants now and then to see if they needed anything.

Chapter 22

"You think Tod Norton is the ninja?"

"I don't know, Mary. I know there have been problems between him and the Mullins. And he is about the right size."

"Yeah, I know about the estate and all that mess," Mary said.

Weber was not surprised by that in the least. He sometimes wished there was some way to install a USB port in the side of Mary's head and download all of the information about the town she had in there.

"What do you think, Mary? Could he be our guy?"

"I don't know," she admitted. "We keep thinking it's some kind of kid prank, but would a kid be attacking somebody with a sword or those metal stars like the one that got stuck in Doug's door? Not to mention cutting his brake line? Why would a kid do that?"

"Personally, I think we're dealing with two different things," Coop said. "I think there is a kid or kids running around playing ninja. But the other stuff? There's an adult behind that."

"I guess anything's possible," Weber said. "But if that's the case, it still comes down to the same question. Why Doug Mullins? And when we look at it from that perspective, Todd is the only person we know who has a grudge against Doug."

"So, what do we do about it?"

"I guess we go have a chat with him," Weber said, pushing his chair back and standing up, then leading the way down the hall to the cellblock.

~~~***~~~

Todd Norton was sitting on the bunk in his cell and looked up when they approached.

"It's about damn time. Let me out of this place!"

"You're not going anywhere until you see the judge," Weber told him.

"Well then, take me to see him!"

"Here's the thing," Weber said, "Judge Ryman works on his schedule, not yours. We can hold you up to 72 hours, so you might as well get used to your accommodations."

"This whole thing is bullshit, Sheriff! I told you what happened, and when I tell the judge he's going to let me go. And when he does I'm gonna to sue you and everybody else involved in this bullshit. I'm sitting here losing business and my reputation is being ruined when I was the victim!"

"We read you your rights when we arrested you. Do you remember that, Todd?"

"Yeah, so what?"

"I've got some questions I need to ask you. So I'm going to read them to you again, just in case you forgot"

"Whatever."

Weber read him his Miranda rights and the prisoner acknowledged that he understood them.

"Okay, tell me about what's been going on between you and your sister and Doug Mullins."

"What? Nothing's going on. I haven't talked to that bitch or the asshole she's married to for over a year."

"That's a bit harsh, don't you think? Calling your sister a bitch like that."

"I've got good reason," Norton said.

"Yeah, I heard there was some problem with an inheritance or something like that."

142

"You're damn right there was! They beat me out of what I had coming to me when our mother died."

Weber had no interest in getting involved in the family dynamics of who was right and who was wrong, so instead he said, "That must have pissed you off."

"You're damn right it did. You'd be pissed off, too, if it was you it was happening to."

"How pissed off were you, Todd?"

"What do you mean?"

"I mean, how pissed off were you? Pissed off enough to want to hurt one of them?"

Norton's eyes narrowed and he asked, "What the hell are you gettin' at, Sheriff?"

"I'm just wondering if you were pissed off enough to try to hurt Doug or Tracy."

"Hurt them? I don't know what the hell you're talking about."

"Here's the thing, Todd. You know about someone coming after Doug with a sword, and then trying to assault him at his house, right?"

"Yeah, so what?"

"So, we keep looking at Doug and we can't find any reason for anybody to want to harm him. We can't find anybody who's got a motive for doing something that crazy. Well, nobody but you."

"Whoa, Sheriff," Norton said, holding up his hands like he was under some kind of attack. "If you think I had anything to do with that crazy ninja going after Doug, you're out of your mind!"

"Am I, Todd?"

"Yeah, you are. Why would I do something like that?"

"I don't know, Todd. You tell me."

"I'm not telling you shit because there's nothing to say. I don't know where you're coming up with this bullshit, but you're barking up the wrong tree."

"Am I, Todd?"

Norton pointed an angry finger at Weber and said, "I know what's going on here. You've got it in for me, Sheriff! First you helped that bitch I was married to take me for everything I owned

143

in our divorce, then you arrested me for shooting down that drone that was spying on me a while back. And now you're coming up with this crap. I can tell you right now, it's not gonna work!"

"Why would you think I have some kind of personal vendetta against you, Todd?"

"I don't know and I don't care. But you'll damn sure care when I sue your ass for everything you own."

"As far as you and your ex-wife, all I did was suggest she talk to an attorney. You and I both know you were trying to cheat her out of her fair share of your community property. And as for you shooting down Three-Bob's drone, I wasn't the one that told you to do something stupid like that."

"Yeah, right," Norton said. "And then you lock me up when I'm the victim, and come up with this shit about whatever happened to Doug Mullins. Well, it ain't gonna work. You're messing with the wrong man, Sheriff!"

"So, if I get a search warrant for your house, I'm not gonna find a ninja costume or sword?"

"You're not gonna find shit. First, because there's nothing to find, and second because the judge can't give you a search warrant in the first place. I know my rights. This is America!"

"So, what about cutting the brake line on Doug's pickup?"

"What? What the hell you talking about now?"

"Someone cut the brake line on Doug's truck and he was in an accident yesterday."

"Well, it wasn't me. I was busy getting shot and going to the hospital, and then sitting in a cell ever since you arrested me yesterday!"

"We suspect that whoever cut the brake line did it the night before. That was before you shot yourself and the rest of this stuff with you even started."

"How many times do I have to tell you? A goddamn ninja shot me! I didn't shoot myself, and I didn't try to hurt Doug with a sword or anything else, and I didn't cut his brake line."

Norton was shouting and his face was red, his hands balled into fists. Weber had no doubt that if the cell's bars were not separating them, the little man would have attacked him. For a moment he wished the bars weren't there.

"Come on, Todd. Stop the bullshit. You're the only person who has a reason to want to hurt Doug Mullins. You know it and I know it."

"You know those rights you read a while back? One of them is that I have right to an attorney and another is the right to remain silent. Until I get a lawyer, I'm not sayin' anything else to you."

"That's it, huh?"

"Yeah, that's it."

"Okay, have it your way," Weber said.

Norton sat back down on the bunk and glared at him. Weber looked at Coop, who shrugged his shoulders.

The two men turned and walked out of the cellblock.

"Come on, Sheriff. Asking for a warrant because you think Todd Norton might be this crazy ninja we keep hearing about is a bit of a stretch, don't you think?"

"Under normal circumstances, I would agree, Your Honor" Weber said. "But we both know how volatile Todd can be. We also know how vindictive he can be. Look at the way he treated his wife when they were getting divorced. He tried to get her fired from two different jobs when she stood up to him."

"Even so," Judge Ryman said. "I can't issue a warrant based upon a supposition like this. And while I don't disagree about Mr. Norton's personality, to me he seems like a take charge and get things done kind of guy who doesn't bother to think about what he is doing or the consequences. Could I see him going after Doug Mullins because he's mad about the inheritance thing? No question about it. But I think he would show up at his door and take a swing at him, not dress up like a cartoon character with some elaborate scheme like this."

"Well, I figured it was worth a try," Weber said, standing up.

"Hold on there," the judge said, raising his hand. "I told you I couldn't issue a warrant based on your suspicions that Mr. Norton might be the ninja. But if you were to ask me for a warrant to search his house for other firearms, based upon the pistol you found at his store, which is in direct violation of my court order from before, after he shot that drone down, that would be a different story. Now, let me caution you, Sheriff, the warrant would be for looking for firearms. Anything else you find incidental to the search might help you build a case for something else, but it wouldn't be directly admissible. Do you get my drift?"

Weber sat back in his chair and grinned. "Yes, sir. I guess I need to go have Mary type up a new warrant request, don't I?"

"I wouldn't begin to tell you your business, Sheriff Weber," the judge said. "But just so you know, my wife is having people over for dinner tonight and she wants me to get out of the office early so I can help her get things ready. I will only be here another hour or so."

"I'll see you in fifteen minutes," the sheriff told him.

Chapter 23

"Nothing at all," a frustrated Chad Summers said three hours later. "No guns, no ammo, no ninja swords, and the closest thing to a ninja costume we found are some black socks.

"I know Todd had a bunch of guns at one time," Weber said. "I wonder what happened to them."

"Last I heard, he stored them with Matt Wells over at the sporting goods store after that drone thing," Dolan Reed said.

Weber looked around the house. The walls are covered with a mixture of NASCAR memorabilia and the stuffed heads of half-dozen big game animals. The only reading material they found in the house was a stack of gun magazines in the master bathroom. A flat screen TV that was almost as wide as Todd Norton was tall was mounted on one wall. A stack of DVDs were on a small stand below the television. Weber sorted through them. There were several Best of NASCAR type videos, a couple of shoot 'em up, bang-bang action-adventure ones, but nothing at all related to ninjas. He wasn't ready to let go of the idea that Todd Norton might be responsible for the attacks on Doug Mullins, but there was nothing here to indicate his suspicions were justified.

"Okay, I guess this was a waste of time. We tried."

"So, what now, Jimmy?"

"I don't know, Buz. I guess we just keep plugging away at it. Sooner or later this ninja is going to turn up somewhere."

As if on cue, Deputy Archer Wingate's voice came over the radio. "Uhhh, Dispatch, I just passed someone dressed like a ninja driving a white car. I made a U-turn and I'm following them."

"Do you have a license plate yet?" the dispatcher asked.

Archer read off an Arizona license plate number and the dispatcher told him to stand by while she ran a check for wants or warrants.

Weber keyed his portable radio and asked, "Where are you, Archer?"

"I'm right behind the car, Sheriff."

Ignoring the laughter from the three deputies with him, Weber keyed the microphone again. "I met, where are you located?"

"Uh, right here in town, Jimmy."

Trying to remain patient, Weber said, "I know it's not a big town, Archer, but I really don't have time to drive up and down every street looking for you. Could you maybe give me some clue to exactly where you are in town?"

"Oh, yeah. I'm on Main Street in front of the bank."

The dispatcher came back to say that the vehicle was a 2018 Mitsubishi Outlander registered to somebody named Halima Fayad, with an address in Tempe, Arizona. There were no outstanding warrants showing for the vehicle or its registered owner.

"Stay behind them, I'm on the way," Weber ordered Archer. "Lock this place up, guys, while I go see what he's dug up."

~~~***~~~

It took less than three minutes to get to Main Street, where he quickly found Archer following the white car and it's two occupants.

Weber picked up the microphone clipped to his dashboard and said, "Light them up, Archer."

The light bar on top of Archer's cruiser went on and the Mitsubishi quickly pulled to the curb, with Archer stopped behind it. Weber pulled in front to block any attempt to escape and got out of his Explorer, walking up to the car's driver side window. As

148

soon as he saw the occupants, he knew that they had not found a ninja. The two women inside both raised their hands timidly and looked at the policemen.

"Good afternoon, ladies," Weber said. "I'm Sheriff Weber. Sorry to bother you, but can I see some identification, please?"

"Of course, officer," the driver said. "What did we do wrong?"

"At first glance you looked like someone we might be looking for," Weber said as the driver and passenger handed him their drivers licenses and passports. They identified the driver as Halima Fayad and her passenger as Saffiya Fayad, both with the same address in Mesa.

"I hope there is no problem," the driver said.

"No, ma'am. None at all," Weber assured her. "Like I said, my deputy thought you were somebody else. I apologize for the interruption to your day."

"We just came up to see the big pine trees," the passenger said. "I am Saffiya Fayad and this is my sister Halima. We are students at ASU."

"Yes, we don't see many pine trees down there, or at home," the driver added.

"Your passports say you are from Saudi Arabia. I guess you don't have a lot of forests there, do you?"

"No, sir. These trees are so big and smell so nice!"

"Most of the ones we have around here are called Ponderosa pines," Weber told her. "They are bigger around than a lot of pine trees."

"And snow? Someone told us you have snow here?"

"Yes, ma'am. In the wintertime we get a lot of it. In fact, there's a big ski lodge here in town. But it's the wrong time of year for that. Come back in winter and you'll see plenty of snow."

The sheriff handed them back their paperwork, tipped his hat, and said, "Again, ladies, I apologize for the interruption. Have a good day."

"Wait a moment, please," the driver said. Weber expected some question about racial profiling and would not blame them for asking it.

"The cowboy hat. Are you a cowboy sheriff, like in the movies? Do you ride a horse sometimes?"

Weber could tell the questions were sincere and he chuckled as he shook his head. "No, ma'am, I'm no cowboy. I was raised on a ranch here in town, but the last time I was on a horse I was in high school. These days I don't ride anything I can't put gas in."

The women laughed shyly from behind their hijabs as Weber nodded his head at them again. "You ladies have a nice day. Drive safe."

As they drove away he turned to Archer and said, "Those weren't ninjas, Archer. They are Muslim women and those things they're wearing are called hijabs. They are traditional head coverings for their faith."

"I'm sorry, Jimmy. I just saw the things on their heads and thought they were ninjas."

Weber was tempted to try to give his often difficult deputy a lesson in contemporary political correctness, but it was not something he was all that fond of himself. Besides, anytime Archer took the initiative to do something besides find a place to park and sleep while he was on duty was a good day as far as the sheriff was concerned.

"Don't sweat it, you did good."

Archer's face beamed with pride, and Weber didn't have the heart to mention the gravy stain on his uniform shirt. With Archer, baby steps were the most he could hope for.

As seemed to happen anytime there was a traffic stop, a small crowd of looky lous had formed on the sidewalk.

"Move along folks. Nothing's going on that you need to be here for."

As if not hearing or understanding his comment, an older man wearing a flannel shirt that stretched tightly over his potbelly in spite of the warm day asked, "What's going on, Jimmy? Were those the ninjas?"

"If they were the ninjas, we wouldn't be letting them drive away now, would we, Russ?"

"Looked more like Muslims to me," his pal Danny Shields said. "Don't know why you let them go, Sheriff. Everybody knows

150

they're here trying to make us follow that there Sharia law of theirs."

Shields and Russ Tucker were a couple of retirees with too much time on their hands who spent their days listening to cable news and talk radio. It had been a while since Weber had seen either one of them, but not long enough. The last time he had talked to the pair, they were convinced that the Russians were poisoning the water supply, which would explain why they had spent the whole day on the lake and not caught one fish. Weber suspected it was more likely that their loud conversation, both of them being half deaf, and their lack of skill as anglers that had accounted for their bad luck more than any government conspiracy.

"They're just a couple of college students up here sightseeing," the sheriff said.

"Well, I don't like it," Shields said, shaking his head. "No sir, I don't like it one bit. We let them get their foot in the door here in Big Lake and we'll never get rid of them. Look what they've done to California!"

"It wasn't the Muslims that ruined California," Russ told his friend. "No, sir. It was the Mexicans and the liberals that done that."

"Are you sure? I heard it was the Muslims."

Weber left them to debate current affairs and walked back to where Buz and Dolan, who had come to the scene after securing Todd Norton's house, were parked.

"False alarm."

"Damn, Jimmy, the first traffic stop Archer made this year and it was a false alarm? That sucks."

Weber pulled his phone out of his pocket and looked at it. "It's after five, guys, why don't you go ahead and go home. I'll see you in the morning. Get some rest."

At the time he said it, the sheriff didn't know how little rest he would be getting that night.

Chapter 24

The delicious smell of something baking greeted Weber when he walked in the door of his house half an hour later. He hung his hat on the rack next to the door and turned just as Robyn, wearing cut off jean shorts and a T-shirt, greeted him with a kiss.

"Something smells delicious."

"Homemade chicken pot pie. You liked it so much when we had dinner at Pete and Mary's last week that I asked her for the recipe," Robyn said.

"Well, if it tastes as good as it smells, I can't wait."

Robyn had never been much of a cook, something Weber knew was a result of the relationship she had always had with her mother. The few times he had eaten something Renée Fuchette had cooked, it had been delicious. Once, when he asked her why her mother had not passed any of her culinary skills down to her, Robyn had replied that Renée had tried, but was always so critical of everything she did that she had given up trying. "Even if she stood over me and watched every ingredient I put in and everything I did, she always made a point of telling me the finished meal was not as good as hers. It is always either too spicy or too bland or too burned or not done enough. I finally just quit trying. It was a constant hassle."

Weber, a lifelong bachelor, had always gotten by with TV dinners, frozen pizzas, or taking his meals at restaurants, so he had never complained. Now that they were married, Robyn had been

153

making an effort to learn to cook some of his favorite meals. And while her creations may not have been quite as good as her mother's, there was certainly nothing to complain about. He made a point to compliment her on every meal she served.

"I just put it in the oven, so it's going to be a little while yet," she told him. "Why don't you go ahead and jump in the shower."

"I'd rather stand here and hold you until it's done."

"I'd rather you take a shower," Robyn replied. "It's been a hot day and you're all sweaty."

"You could wash my back," Weber suggested.

"You're a big boy, Jimmy. I'm pretty sure you can wash your own back."

"I'm not sure I can."

"Who washed your back for you before we were together? Wait a minute. Don't answer that question. Parks was your roommate before we hooked up and I don't even want to know what you two had going on!"

"Now there's a thought that would put me right off my feed," Weber said.

"Go clean up," Robyn said, dancing playfully away when he reached for her again.

"So that's it, is it? The honeymoon's over already?"

"Never. But there's a time and place for everything."

"Well, this is our place, and there's no time like the present."

Robyn shook her head at him. "Honestly, Jimmy, sometimes I think that's all you ever think about."

"That's not true. I just spent a couple of hours going through Todd Norton's place with three deputies, and not once did I think about making whoopie with any of them."

"Well, that's good to know! Now go take your shower."

He went to their bedroom and took off his gun belt and set it on the dresser, then stripped off his uniform and threw it in the clothes hamper on his way into the bathroom. He was in the shower enjoying the feel of the water hitting his head and cascading down his body when he heard the sliding door open and Robyn stepped in with him. He started to say something but she put her finger on his lips.

"Shhh… give me the soap."

He handed it to her and she began rubbing it across his back, his bottom, and then his legs.

"Turn around."

He did and she proceeded to wash his chest and the rest of his body. Then she reached past him to put the soap on the tray and said, "We've got thirty minutes. Make them count."

~~~***~~~

Robyn's timing had been perfect, and by the time Weber came downstairs she was taking the pot pie out of the oven, its golden brown crust framing the mouthwatering filling bubbling in places where she had made slits to let the steam out.

"That is about the prettiest thing I've seen all day," he said as she bent over to close the oven door.

"Are you talking about my ass or the pot pie?"

"Okay, correction, those are the two prettiest things I've seen all day," he replied.

As she set the table, Robyn asked, "What happened with Todd Norton today? Did Judge Ryman throw the book at him?"

"The judge was feeling a bit irritated with Todd and all the trouble he's always causing," Weber told her. "So he said to let him sit in a cell and stew for another day to give us time to search his house and see what we can come up with."

"And did you find anything?"

"Nothing related to the ninja case, and no guns. It was pretty much a waste of time."

"Well, at least you tried," Robyn said.

The pot pie tasted even better than it looked, and after dinner he helped her wash the dishes. Then they retired to the living room. They watched a couple of sitcoms on the television, and then some kind of police drama that was so bad that they took turns making fun of all of the things the producers had gotten wrong, from a patrol officer crashing his squad car through the glass front of a supermarket to chase down the bad guy, to a gunfight at the end where the perpetrator fired nine rounds from his six shot revolver.

Later, in bed, they made love again, and when they finally rolled apart and were holding hands as they lay on their backs Robyn said, "You tell me, mister, is the honeymoon over?"

Weber laughed as he pulled her into his arms, her head upon his chest.

"Do you have any idea how much I love you, lady?"

"Do you love me, or is it the good cooking and the sex you love?"

"I don't know, maybe I should have a second helping before I answer that question."

"If you're talking about the pot pie, forget it," she told him. "Remember, you told me you were going to try to lose that five pounds you put on while we were out of town for our honeymoon. And if it's the sex you want another helping of, stop being greedy. Isn't twice in one day enough?"

"I could never get enough of that."

"I swear, Jimmy, sometimes I think you're hornier than a sixteen year old kid."

"What can I say? You have that effect on me."

"That's flattering," she told him. "But I hit my limit today, even if you haven't."

"Fair enough," Weber said, reaching for his phone on the nightstand.

"Who are you calling at this hour, Jimmy?"

"Nobody," he told her. "I'm setting the alarm for 12:03 to get a head start on tomorrow's lovemaking."

"I swear to God, Jimmy, I love you more than anything in the world, but if you wake me up in two hours to have sex, I'm going to shoot you."

"How about if I don't wake you up, and I cover you back up when I'm done?"

She kissed him and rolled over on her side and said, "Spoon me."

He did, and she said, "And no poking fun at me! Good night, Jimmy."

Chapter 25

The alarm on Weber's cell phone didn't go off at 12:03, but shortly after 2 AM the phone rang. Recognizing the ringtone and knowing that Dispatch wouldn't call him in the middle of the night unless there was reason for it, Weber was instantly awake and pushed the button to answer the call.

"What's going on, Judy?"

"Sorry to bother you, Jimmy, but Dan Wright just called and said he's in foot pursuit of the ninja."

"Where at?"

"2703 Ridgeview Drive."

"Ridgeview? Isn't that where Imogene Buckley lives?"

"That's the place," the dispatcher told him.

"Isn't Dan off duty tonight?"

"He is." Weber could hear the smile in the dispatcher's voice when she replied.

"Dan said they went through the backyard and into the woods behind the house and he wanted backup. Jordan and Tommy are working a rollover accident out at the Y or I would've called them."

"Okay, tell Dan I'm on my way."

He heard Robyn sit up in bed behind him and she asked, "What's happening?"

"Dan's chasing the ninja through the woods on foot."

157

He stood up and pulled clothes on and Robyn began getting dressed, too.

"You don't have to go, babe."

"As long as this ninja's been running around, if you think I'm gonna miss catching him, you're crazy!"

Four minutes later they were speeding toward town, the red and blue lights on top of Weber's Explorer lighting up the trees on both sides of the road. There was no need for the siren at that time of night, and it didn't take them long to get to Ridgeview Drive. They pulled up in front of Imogene's house, Weber noting that Dan's big Yamaha V-Star motorcycle was parked in the driveway next to Imogene's red Mazda CX-3. The porch light was on and Imogene came to the doorway.

"Dan's chasing him," she said.

From the way she was dressed in a short pink terrycloth robe, Weber suspected that he and Robyn were not the only ones whose night had been interrupted. With Robyn at his side, they walked around the house to the back yard and he keyed the button on his portable radio.

"Where are you at, Dan?"

"I'm east of the house in the trees. I've lost him."

Weber could hear the frustration in his deputy's voice.

"Description?"

"Just somebody dressed in black, Jimmy. I never got close enough to tell any more than that."

"Okay, we'll drive around to Modoc Road. If he's heading east he might come out there."

They got back in the Explorer and drove half a mile down to the nearest crossroad, then cruised slowly, using the spotlights to try to find the ninja. They saw a small group of cow elk, and a hundred yards further a fat porcupine waddled across the road in front of them, but that was it. They heard a whistle and Weber stepped on the brake. A couple of moments later, a bare chested Dan walked up to the side of the Explorer, breathing hard.

"Anything?"

"No," he said. "Little son of a bitch is fast, I'll give him that."

Weber pushed the button to unlock the rear doors and said, "Get in."

They drove around for another fifteen minutes, all three of them knowing it was a waste of time. Whoever Dan had been pursuing was long gone. Weber drove back to Imogene's house and parked in the driveway.

"So what happened?"

"We were..." Dan hesitated and Weber could tell he was uncomfortable. His girlfriend apparently didn't have his inhibitions.

"We were in bed. It's a pretty warm night and I don't have any air-conditioning, so I had the window open a little bit. I know that was dumb, especially after what happened before, but like I said, it was hot. I don't know if I heard anything or just something felt weird, but I looked over at the window and he was right there looking at us. Not six feet away! It startled me so much I screamed and then Dan jumped up and pulled on some clothes and took off after him."

Weber looked at his deputy, wearing just jeans and tennis shoes without socks and didn't say anything about the fact that he had obviously dressed in a hurry, and not completely.

"Did you see him too, Dan?"

"Just a glimpse before he took off running. By the time I got out in the backyard I could hear him crashing through the woods and I took off after him. But he had too much of a head start and I didn't have a snowball's chance in hell of catching up."

"Let's look around outside and see if we can find any footprints or anything like that," Weber said.

Using flashlights, the two men searched the yard, finding nothing.

"He would've been standing right here, outside this window," Dan said.

"Well, he's long gone now."

"I wish I would've caught the little bastard."

"We will," Weber assured him. "It's only a matter of time."

They started back toward the front of the house and Dan said, "Jimmy... I know this looks bad, but..."

159

"Hey, you two are adults and neither one of you are involved with anybody that I know of," Weber said, cutting him off. "You don't need to explain anything to me, Dan."

"She's a really nice girl. I know we've only been seeing each other for a little while, but…"

Weber put his hand on his deputy's arm and said, "It's okay, man. No judgments here. She seems like a nice lady and you're a great guy. I hope it works out for both of you."

"Thanks, Jimmy. I just don't want the guys at work to make a big thing about it."

"Come on, Dan. You grew up in a small town. You know that you can't fart here without everybody knowing about it before the air clears. And as for the rest of the guys, they're going to be just as happy for you as I am. So don't sweat it, okay?"

"Thanks, Jimmy."

Robyn and Imogene were talking when they went back into the house, and when she looked toward him to see if they had found anything, Weber shook his head.

"No luck."

"This is so creepy," Imogene said. "This is the second time this has happened. At least the second time that I know of. I feel like I need to keep all the doors and windows closed and locked and big heavy drapes over everything. I just feel so… so violated."

"I know it's not fun at all, Ms. Buckley," Weber told her. "I think that whoever is doing this is harmless. We keep thinking it's a kid. And we are going to find him, I promise."

"But what about the thing with the sword and all that? About that man that almost got chopped up? Do you think a kid did that? Because that doesn't sound harmless to me!"

"No, ma'am, we don't think it's the same person."

"Wait a minute. You think there's more than one ninja running around here?"

"We think it's a possibility. And we think the two things, the person peeking in windows and the other nonsense like tonight and the person who attacked Doug Mullins are totally unrelated."

"I'm not sure if that makes me feel better or worse."

"Look, Ms. Buckley…"

"Please, call me Imogene."

"All right, Imogene. I'll be honest with you. We don't know who is doing this. But I really do believe they are two separate cases, and I don't believe you're in any physical danger. To be honest with you, I think it's just a horny kid spying on a pretty lady."

She blushed slightly and Dan said, "I keep telling her, they didn't have schoolteachers that looked like her when I was in school, Jimmy."

Weber laughed and said, "No they didn't. Anyway, whoever it was isn't coming back tonight. Why don't you guys get back to whatever you were doing and we'll get out of here."

The amused look Robyn gave him told him that his words were not entirely appropriate, but neither Dan nor Imogene seem to notice his faux pas.

Back in the Explorer, heading home, Robyn said, "Do you really think it was just some horny kid peeping in the window, Jimmy?"

"Could you blame him?"

"What's this? Does my husband have some kind of hidden voyeuristic tendencies?"

Robyn had exhibited signs of jealousy in the past, although that seemed to be behind them. But Weber was never completely sure how to respond, never knowing if she was teasing him or was serious. She answered that question for him with a laugh.

"Oh come on, Jimmy. She's drop dead gorgeous."

"Is she? I didn't really notice."

"Bullshit. You'd have to be blind not to notice that. Hell, *I* noticed. If I was walking by the window and saw those two going at it, I'd probably be right there with the ninja watching."

"Now who's the voyeur?"

"Hey, even if I'm a woman, I can still appreciate a good looking girl. And face it, Dan's a bit of a hunk himself. Not that I ever noticed, mind you."

Weber looked at her smiling in the reflection of the dashboard lights and couldn't help laughing out loud. "You shameless hussy, you."

His eyes were only off the road for a second as he grinned, but that's all it took. The huge cow elk came out of nowhere and Robyn screamed as it suddenly filled the windshield. Weber turned his head back at the moment of impact, the Explorer's airbags activating and slamming them both in the face. Their seatbelts held them in place and it took several seconds for their heads to clear.

"Shit! Are you okay, baby?"

Robyn held a hand to her face and it came away with blood from her nose. "I think so. Are you?"

"Yeah, I think so."

"Call it in, will you? I'll go see how bad the damage is."

While she reached for the radio's microphone, Weber got out of the Explorer to check on the animal.

Chapter 26

"I don't know where it came from, Jimmy. One minute I was looking at the road and the next minute all I saw was elk."

"It's my fault, I should have been paying more attention to my driving.

The big animal had rolled off the hood and was struggling to get to its feet, but it's front and back legs on the left-hand side were both broken and sticking out at ugly angles.

"Son of a bitch," Weber said, angry at himself for his inattention, though he knew it could have happened to anyone. Motor vehicle collisions with elk and deer were common in that part of the country, and he was glad he had not been driving very fast or the two of them might have been as bad off as the elk, if not worse.

Robyn got out and joined him, saying, "Tommy and Jordan cleared the accident they were working and are on their way."

The elk thrashed on the pavement, squealing in agony. Weber knew the animal couldn't be saved and pulled his Kimber from his belt to put it out of its misery.

"Maybe you should look the other way, Robyn."

"It's okay, Jimmy. Just do it."

He stepped around the animal's head and put a 230 grain .45 jacketed hollow point bullet between its eyes. There was one quick spasm and then it was over.

Weber had grown up hunting in the mountains around Big Lake and had taken his share of big game animals, but it had been years since he had purchased a license or felt the need to do so. While he had no problem with sport hunting and knew it was an important part of wildlife management, as well as a long-standing tradition in the West, after he had been forced to shoot a teenage psychopath a few years earlier, he had lost any appetite for killing things.

"Why don't you call Dispatch back and have them get hold of Frenchy and see if he wants to come out here so we can salvage the meat." Weber said. "At least that way some good will come of it."

Jean Du Plessis was a French Canadian transplant to Big Lake who ran a food bank providing meals to the elderly and those who had fallen on hard times. Weber knew that protocol said that he should call Mark Santos, the Game and Fish officer assigned to the area, but he could not see any reason for waking the man up in the middle of the night to report the accident and the disposal of the meat as the law required. Whether he made the call now or later in the morning was not going to change anything. The elk was still dead.

Deputies Tommy Frost and Jordan Northcutt arrived at the same time, and with their help they dragged the elk off of the road. Weber knew that in the warm air the meat would spoil quickly, so using Jordan's folding Buck knife, he gutted the animal and propped its body cavity open with sticks to help it cool.

Looking at the Explorer he shook his head in regret. The grill was destroyed, the hood caved in the center where the animal had landed on it, and the windshield was a spiderweb of cracks. Radiator fluid had poured out onto the road's surface.

"Are you guys okay?"

"I am, except for being pissed at myself," Weber said. "Robyn, you've got blood on your face. Are you all right?"

"My nose was bleeding, but it's stopped now," she replied.

"Do you want me to run you to the Medical Center, or call the ambulance?"

"No, Jordan. I'm okay. Thanks, anyway."

Looking at the Explorer, Tommy said, "It could've been a lot worse."

"That's true," Weber said. "We were hauling ass when we went out the other direction earlier. I wasn't doing any more than 35 or 40 when I hit it."

"What was that all about? Dan chasing the ninja? Isn't he off duty?"

"Yeah, he was at Imogene Buckley's place and the little bastard was peeking in the window at them. Dan chased him through the woods, but he got away."

Jordan punched Tommy's arm lightly and said, "I told you so."

"Hey guys, don't give him any grief over it," Weber cautioned. "They're big kids, they can do what they want."

"Oh, I didn't mean anything bad by it, Sheriff. Dan's a great guy and I could tell he fell for her the first time he met her. I'm just glad she seems to feel the same way."

"What about the accident you guys were covering earlier? What was that all about?"

"Gary Owens and Jeff Bristol decided to have themselves a drag race," Tommy said. "Gary lost control and rolled his vehicle."

"Any injuries?"

"Looks like he's got a broken wrist. EMTs took him to the Medical Center. He was more afraid of what his dad was going to do to him when he found out he wrecked his brand-new pickup."

"I guess that's a lesson learned for him," Weber said.

"I doubt it," Tommy said. "This wasn't the first time and I doubt it will be the last for that kid."

They looked up when Randy Laird's tow truck came into sight. He pulled to a stop and got out.

"You guys are keeping me busy tonight, that's for sure."

"Sorry about that," Weber said.

"Shoot, Jimmy, if I wanted to work banker's hours, I'd be a banker."

He surveyed the front of the Explorer and said, "This is nothing. That will all buff right out."

At any other time Weber would have laughed at the joke, but he didn't feel much like laughing at the moment. Before he could reply, a black three-quarter ton four-wheel-drive Chevrolet pickup pulled up and stopped. A mountain of a man with curly black hair and a thick beard got out, along with a sleepy looking teenage boy who was a younger, smaller version of his father, minus the beard.

"How you doing, Frenchy?"

"Except for drugstore cowboys killing all the local wildlife in the middle of the night and making me come out and retrieve them, I'm good. How about you, Sheriff?"

"I've been better."

Frenchy looked at the battered Explorer and whistled. "Are you okay?"

"Yeah, just mad at myself," Weber said.

"Hey, Jimmy, shit happens. As long as you aren't hurt, that's all that matters."

"Try telling that to the Town Council when I explain how I wrecked my vehicle."

"At least you won't have Chet Wingate and Adam Hirsch to deal with," Tommy said.

"That's true," Weber agreed.

Ever since Chet Wingate had resigned as mayor and Councilman Adam Hirsch had been arrested for video stalking, distributing revenge porn, and sending obscene materials by electronic means, Big Lake's Town Council had been much easier to deal with. In the past, every Council meeting had been an ordeal of finger pointing and demands by the mayor that the Sheriff be reprimanded or fired for whatever kind of petty charge Chet Wingate could come up with, supported by Hirsch and Councilwoman Gretchen Smith-Abbot, the mayor's closest allies. These days Weber made an appearance, gave a brief report on the activities of the Sheriff's Department for the week, and answered any questions councilmembers might have. Still, he wasn't sure how they would react to the news he had wrecked his patrol unit.

They loaded the elk into the back of the Chevy pickup and Frenchy and his son took off for home, where they would butcher it in their garage and wrap the meat for distribution to those in need. With that chore out of the way, Randy hooked the Explorer to his tow truck and headed to town with it. By the time that was done, the sky was just beginning to show rosy hints of the new day to come to the east. Jordan gave Weber and Robyn a ride home, where they took showers and tried to catch an hour or two's sleep before going to work.

Chapter 27

Weber felt every bit of his age when he woke up the next morning, and then some. His eyes were gritty, his whole body ached from fatigue, and his mouth felt cottony and tasted like a skunk had spent the night in it. When he got out of bed, he felt soreness where the seat belt had grabbed him during the collision with the elk. He stepped into the shower and let the hot water cascade over him. Not for the first time in his career, he wondered what it would be like to have a job where he could call in sick on mornings like this.

The shower door slid open and Robyn stepped in. Weber noted the bruise across her shoulder and chest from the seatbelt the night before.

"You don't have to get up, honey," he told her.

"Shut up and hand me the soap." Robyn was definitely not a morning person.

There was none of the erotic playfulness of the evening before. They simply showered and got out and dried off. Weber could smell coffee from the kitchen, and he went in there and poured two cups for them, adding generous helpings of cream and sugar to Robyn's. When he got back to their bedroom, she was already putting her uniform on.

"Really, babe, you can take the morning off."

"I never took special favors when we were dating, Jimmy, and I'm damn sure not going to do it now that we're married."

"You are a stubborn woman. Do you know that?"

"It's one of the reasons you love me, right?"

"Let me count the ways," he said.

She took the coffee cup from him and sipped, nodding her head appreciatively.

"That helps."

Breakfast was a quick affair, Pop Tarts and coffee, and then they drove into town.

"How's it going, Crash?"

Weber expected the razzing and took it good-naturedly.

"Bite me, Mary."

"Now is that any way to be?"

"Hey, Jimmy," Dolan Reed said. "What's this I hear about you taking over Archer's job? Isn't he the one that usually wrecks cars around here?"

"You're a funny man, Dolan. Real funny."

Weber took the cup of coffee Mary handed him and went into his office and sat down at his desk, pulling the telephone closer to him. "Might as well get it over with," he said to himself.

His first call was to Kirby Templeton to report that he had wrecked his department vehicle. Once the interim mayor ascertained that he and Robyn were both uninjured, Kirby said, "As long as you guys are okay, that's all that matters. Cars can be fixed."

"I appreciate that, Kirby."

"Of course, you will have to give a report to the Town Council at tonight's meeting."

"Yeah, I know."

"Don't sweat it, Jimmy. Things are different now."

"Yeah, and I'm sure glad of that."

"Aren't we all, my friend."

Weber ended the call and then dialed Mark Santos. The game warden answered the phone and Weber told him what had happened the night before.

"Are you and Robyn okay?"

"We're fine. She got a little bit of a bloody nose from the airbag, but that's it."

"Well, let's be grateful for that," Santos said. "It could have been a lot worse. We've both covered more than one accident where there were serious injuries and even people killed when cars hit elk."

"I called Frenchy Du Plessis and had him come out and pick up the carcass," Weber said. "I know I should have called you first, but I figured you wouldn't want me to wake you up in the middle of the night."

"No problem, Jimmy. At least the meat will go to a good cause." There was a beep on the line and Santos said, "I've got another call coming in, Jimmy. Glad you and Robyn are okay. Catch you later."

Every Big Lake deputy was assigned a Department car, which they took home with them when they got off duty because in a small agency like theirs, they were always on call. The budget didn't include enough money for extra vehicles, but they did have two, a worn-out old Chevrolet Impala with close to 250,000 miles on the odometer, and a Ford LTD with slightly less mileage. Weber took the keys to both and went out to the parking lot, trying to decide which one he would drive until his unit was repaired.

"Hey, boss, how about I use one of these and you take my unit for now?"

"No, that's fine, Coop. I appreciate it, but I'll make do with one of these."

Weber was never a supervisor who demanded the best for himself and expected his deputies to get by with whatever was left over. It was one of the many reasons they were all so loyal to him. He tried the Impala first and only got a clicking noise when he turned the key. The weak battery wouldn't turn the engine over. Moving to the LTD, the seat sagged when he sat down, but when he turned the key it fired right up. The engine idled roughly for a while and then smoothed out somewhat. He drove to Schroeder's Body Shop, next door to Randy Laird's garage. Pat Schroder and his helper had already started working on the Explorer.

"I've got a radiator and new air bags in stock. But I'm going to have to order a new bumper, grill, hood, and windshield," Pat told him, wiping his hands on a red shop rag. "Probably going to take a few days to get everything in, Jimmy. But once the parts are here, I'll make it a priority."

"Thanks, Pat, I appreciate it."

Weber transferred his portable computer from the Explorer to the LTD, then opened the back end and took out the supplies he kept there and put them in the LTD's trunk. They included a first-aid kit, two blankets, a gallon of antifreeze, boxes of spare ammunition, a tear gas gun and four grenades for it, a six pack of bottled water, road flares and orange safety triangles, and two stuffed teddy bears to give to children who were traumatized by an accident or some other unfortunate event impacting their families. He had taken the Remington tactical shotgun from the Explorer the night before but couldn't get the locking rack in the front of the car to work, so he put the gun in the trunk with everything else.

"How are you and Robyn doing this morning after all that?"

"We're fine," Weber replied. "A bit sore from the airbags and seatbelts, but we came out of it better than the elk."

"Man, I'm sure glad you weren't going any faster than you were. Things could have turned out a lot worse."

"People keep telling me that," Weber said.

He looked across the storage yard the two businesses shared and saw a blue Nissan pickup truck, its roof caved in and one door hanging askew.

"Is that the truck that Gary Owens wrecked last night?"

"That's the one," Randy told him. "Fool kid is lucky to be alive. He swore he was only going 40, but we know that's a lie."

"What's this make? Three or four vehicles he's totaled?"

"This is the third one that I know of," Randy said. "I guess when your daddy's got a lot of money you can do that."

"His old man ought to take his drivers license away from him and make him walk until he's 30."

"I think if it was up to Richard, that's what would happen," Pat said. "But Gary is a mama's boy all the way, and mama won't let her precious little child want for anything."

"Her precious little child is going to wind up killing himself or somebody else at the rate he's going," Weber said.

"I don't doubt that for a minute," Randy agreed.

"I know that Tommy cited him for this latest accident. I'm going to have a word with Judge Ryman and hopefully he'll pull the kid's license for a while."

"Shoot, Jimmy, you think that'll stop him from driving? He's one of those entitled kids and thinks he can get away with anything."

Weber couldn't disagree with that. Richard Owens was a well-to-do real estate developer who had come to town three years earlier and expanded his fortune by buying up tracts of land and building elaborate summer homes on them. People called them their cabins, but many of them were close to 2,000 square feet and did not resemble any cabin Weber had ever been in when he was growing up in Big Lake. Judith Owens was fifteen years younger than her husband, just one of the trophies that a rich man like Richard could afford. Gary, their only child, was as spoiled as one might expect, and every time Weber had talked to the teenager, he had been surly at best. He had obviously never been taught to respect authority or anyone else.

Leaving the body shop, Weber made his habitual pass through town, part of his morning routine just to let the citizens know the sheriff was on the job and ready to serve them in any way needed. When he got back to the office, it was time to take Todd Norton to his arraignment before Judge Ryman.

"Really? Handcuffs? What do you think I'm gonna do, try to escape?"

"It's standard procedure," Weber said. "Don't make a big deal out of it."

"Oh, I'm gonna make a big deal out of it, don't you worry about that," Todd said. "You might feel big and tough walking in that courtroom, Sheriff, but when my lawyer gets done with you, you'll be singing a different tune when you walk out."

"Hey, Todd. Do you remember that whole thing about your rights, including the right to remain silent?"

"Yeah?"

"How about you do that? How about you just keep quiet and tell your story to the judge."

"Enjoy being in charge while you can," Norton said. "It's all going to be over with real soon now."

"Hey, Todd."

"Yeah?"

"Shut up."

Chapter 28

If the prisoner thought the attorney he had hired was going to do him any good, he was sadly mistaken. When Weber saw who Norton had retained to represent him, he couldn't help shaking his head. It seemed like the most obnoxious man in town had managed to hire the most obnoxious lawyer around. They made an excellent pair.

Like his client, Grover Recker was a small man with an abrasive attitude. He had barely made it through law school, finishing at the very bottom of his class at the University of Arizona. It had taken him three attempts before he finally passed the Bar examination to get his license to practice law, and he made his living taking on any case he thought he could make a quick settlement on and get out, usually with a hefty percentage of whatever payment came his clients' way. He and Weber had been in the same classes all through grade school and high school, and the sheriff didn't like him as an adult any better than he had as a kid. As soon as the Town's Attorney, Bob Bennett, read the charges against his client, Grover went on the attack.

"Your Honor, everything Mr. Bennett just told you is a lie!"

"I beg your pardon," Bennett said. "Those are the charges against Mr. Norton."

"And they are false charges. False charges filed by this man," he said, pointing an accusing finger at the sheriff. "False charges that we will prove have absolutely no basis in fact. Charges that

Sheriff Weber pulled out of thin air because of his personal animosity toward my client. Charges that have destroyed my client's reputation. Charges that have caused him to be unlawfully imprisoned. Charges for which I'm going to file a lawsuit against Sheriff Weber and the Town of Big Lake!"

By now Grover was shouting for emphasis and the judge rapped his gavel. "Enough with the theatrics, Mr. Recker. This isn't television. You don't have to put on a show."

"Your Honor, I am only trying to make the point that this entire proceeding is a gross miscarriage of justice. My client was a victim of assault in his own business by this ninja that has been terrorizing Big Lake. A bloodthirsty maniac that has already attacked another member of this community not once, but twice. But instead of searching for the real criminal, Sheriff Weber decided to take the easy way out and fabricate an elaborate story that makes poor Mr. Norton look like the bad guy. I ask that you dismiss the charges against my client immediately so we can proceed with our civil suit to seek reparations for harm done to this poor man."

If the judge was impressed by the attorney's comments, he didn't show it.

"The motion for dismissal is denied, Mr. Recker."

"But, Your Honor..."

"I said the motion was denied," the judge said crossly. "I'm not going to sit here and listen to a bunch of nonsense about how Sheriff Weber framed your client. If you want to tell fairytales, I believe the library has a story hour for kids this summer. Take it over there. Mr. Bennett, are you ready to proceed?"

"Yes, I am, Your Honor."

"Then let's get this show on the road."

Bennett explained the charges against Todd Norton and then called Weber as his first witness. The sheriff, and then all of the deputies who had been at the scene, gave their accounts of what had happened, including the discovery of the pistol hidden under the counter, the nature of Norton's wounds, where they had found the bullet and spent cartridge after the shooting, and the fact that fingerprints taken from the pistol matched those of Todd Norton taken from his earlier arrest. Dolan also testified that the defendant's right hand, the one not injured in the shooting, had tested positive for gunshot residue. The prosecution also submitted a statement by the doctor who had treated Norton's wounds stating that, based upon his experience and the nature of the injuries, he believed they were self-inflicted. Through it all, Recker kept objecting and the judge continued to overrule him.

Recker cross examined each witness at length, going over their testimony word by word, asking about their experience and training as police officers, and repeatedly asking them if they didn't believe it was possible that Todd Norton's story was true and that a ninja had actually attacked him. When it was Weber's turn to be grilled, Recker asked him why he had immediately discounted the defendant's explanation of what had happened to him and decided instead that it had been Norton himself who had fired the shot that injured him.

"For several reasons," Weber replied. "First of all, Mr. Norton described the ninja as being a large man, about the size of Deputy Wright there. Every report we've had about the ninja indicates that it was a small person, probably a teenager. Secondly, ninjas don't use guns, as far as I know."

"As far as you know, Sheriff. Do you consider yourself to be an expert on ninjas?"

"No, but I've learned a lot about them in the last couple of weeks," Weber said.

"But you're no expert?"

"I already said that."

"I'll ask you again, Sheriff Weber. Are you an expert on ninjas?"

"Objection, Your Honor," Bob Bennett said. "This question has already been asked and answered more than once."

"Sustained," Judge Ryman said.

"If you're not an expert on ninjas, Sheriff Weber, are you an expert on gunshot wounds?"

"I've seen plenty of them in my time," Weber replied.

"Really? I've seen plenty of pine trees in my time, Sheriff, but that doesn't make me an expert arborist."

"Objection."

"Sustained. We're not here to listen to a bunch of sarcasm, Mr. Recker. Get to your point."

"I will, Your Honor. Sheriff, are you an expert on gunshot wounds?"

"Objection, Your Honor."

"I will allow this line of questioning to continue for a moment, but don't waste this court's time or your own, Mr. Recker," the judge warned.

"Answer the question, Sheriff Weber. Are you an expert on gunshot wounds?"

"I don't know what qualifies someone as an expert," the sheriff said.

"It's a simple yes or no answer. Which is it? Are you or are you not an expert on gunshot wounds?"

"I guess the answer would have to be no."

"I see. So, you're not an expert on ninjas and you're not an expert on gunshot wounds, yet within a few moments of responding, you were able to determine that my client's wounds were self-inflicted and that there was no ninja in his store. Is that correct, Sheriff Weber?"

"Yes, that's correct."

"And how did you make that determination?"

"Objection, Your Honor," Bennett said. "Sheriff Weber has already testified as to how and why he reached the conclusions he did about how Mr. Norton was injured."

"Sustained."

Even given Recker's shady reputation and lack of character, Weber was still taken aback by his next line of questioning.

"Sheriff Weber, why do you hate my client?"

"Objection!"

"No, I'll answer," Weber said. "I don't hate anybody."

"I see. Would you say that you and my client are friends?"

"No, I wouldn't say that."

"Is it fair to say you have a strong dislike for him as a person."

"I'm not fond of him," Weber admitted. "But that doesn't have anything to do with the facts of this case, which are what I based my determination of what happened on."

"Sheriff, isn't it true that you are having or in the past had a sexual relationship with Jessica Norton, my client's ex-wife?"

"Objection," Bennett said. "That question is totally out of line."

"Your Honor, I'm trying to demonstrate that there is a reason for Sheriff Weber's animosity toward my client."

"I'm going to allow the question," Judge Ryman said, but gave the attorney a stern look. "You're skating on very thin ice, Counselor. You need to watch your step."

"Sheriff Weber, please answer my question."

"No, I have not had any kind of physical relationship with Jessica Norton. Not presently and not at any time in the past."

"Then can you explain to me why you urged her to hire a lawyer while she and my client were going through their divorce? Would you say that was part of your job description, Sheriff?"

"I believe that part of my job description is to see that the peace is maintained in Big Lake and that all of our citizens are treated fairly. When it came up in conversation that Mr. Norton was refusing to share any of their community property with his wife, I advised her to get an attorney. Just like I advise battered women to seek shelter at SafeHaven, to get a restraining order against their abuser, and to find an attorney to represent them."

"Wait a minute. There's no evidence at all that Mr. Norton ever abused his wife before, during, or after their divorce. I want that comment stricken from the record."

"I'm sorry, Mr. Recker," the judge said. "You opened this line of questioning. You've got only yourself to blame for that."

"I'm done with this witness," the attorney said, scowling at Weber as he left the witness stand.

When it was time for the defense to state their case, Norton took the stand and told the story of how a ninja had walked into his store and shot him without saying a word and then ran away. When he was finished, Bob Bennett cross-examined him.

179

"Mr. Norton, can you explain where the handgun came from that was found under the counter of your shop the day you were injured?"

"I never saw it before. I think the cops planted it there."

"We have already heard testimony that the bullet that injured you and was stuck in the wall of your store came from this handgun," Bennett said, holding up the pistol. "And we've already heard testimony that your fingerprints are on that handgun. Can you explain that?"

"That's bullshit…"

The judge rapped his gavel and said sternly, "Watch your language in my courtroom, Mr. Norton."

"I'm sorry, Your Honor. What I was saying is I don't believe that my fingerprints are on that gun."

"So what you're telling me is that these officers perjured themselves?"

"If that's what they're saying, I guess they did."

"Okay, Mr. Norton, can you explain this?"

Bennett handed him a piece of paper, which Norton looked at and shook his head, but from the look on his face, Weber could tell that he was not pleased by what he saw. Bennett took the paper from him and handed it to the judge.

"Your Honor, this is a receipt from Bill's Bang Room in Springerville made out to Mr. Norton for the purchase of an FIE Titan .25 semiautomatic pistol, and if you will note, the serial number on the receipt is the same as the number on the pistol entered into evidence here. The same pistol whose ballistics match the bullet found in the wall of Mr. Norton's store on the morning of the shooting. And I ask you to also note, Your Honor, that receipt is dated four years ago."

The judge read the receipt, took the pistol from Bennett, and compared the serial number on the pistol to the receipt.

"I find this very interesting, Mr. Norton. I very clearly told you that you are not to have any firearms while you're on probation for your previous shooting incident. Is that not correct?"

"I can explain, Your Honor."

"Okay, explain."

180

"Ahh... I forgot I even had that gun. It's been under the counter of the shop forever."

"Didn't you just testify that you had never seen this gun before?"

"Like I said, I forgot."

The judge shook his head and said, "Mr. Recker, is there anything else you want to say to waste our time this morning before I enter my judgment and pass sentence?"

"Your Honor, my client is a well-known and respected businessman in this community. He deserves better than this kangaroo court."

The judge rapped his gavel and said, "That's enough, Mr. Recker. One more comment from you like that and I will hold you in contempt. I have warned you before about your behavior in this courtroom, and I have no problem at all arranging for Sheriff Weber to have you as a guest at his jail for the next fourteen days. Do you understand me?"

"I understand, Your Honor."

"Fine. Do you have anything else to say?"

"No, sir," Recker said somewhat sheepishly. "Defense rests."

"Wait a minute," Norton shouted. "That's it? That's the best you can do for me, you shyster?"

"That's enough out of you," the judge said, pointing his finger at the defendant. "Mr. Norton, please stand while I announce my judgment."

Norton shuffled to his feet defiantly.

"Todd Norton, I find you guilty of filing a false police report, of perjury, and of violating your earlier probation. Do you have anything to say before I pass sentence?"

"I keep telling you people, it didn't happen the way Sheriff Weber said it did. A fricking ninja came in my store and shot me!"

"You're only digging your grave deeper," the judge said. "I'm fining you $5,000 plus $750 Court cost. I'm extending your probation for two more years, including my earlier stipulation that you not possess any firearms, and I'm sentencing you to 45 days in jail. And I'm warning you right now, Mr. Norton, I'm going to have Sheriff Weber keep a close eye on you. If you so much as change lanes without signaling, if you spit on the sidewalk, if you do anything at all, I'm going to have him haul you back in here and I'm going to send you to prison. Do you understand me?"

"45 days? How am I supposed to run my business if I'm locked up?"

The judge looked at Bennett and Weber and said, "He's got a point. Any suggestions, gentlemen?"

The Town's Attorney and the sheriff had a quick whispered conversation, and then Bennett said, "Your Honor, Sheriff Weber and I would be in agreement to you allowing Mr. Norton some sort of work release, if it pleases the Court."

"What are the hours at your store, Mr. Norton?"

"I open at eight in the morning and I close at six at night, Monday through Saturday," Norton said.

"Do you have any employees who could run the store in your absence?"

"No. Business sucks so bad I can't afford to pay myself, let alone any hired help. And if I did, they'd probably steal me blind anyway."

"You certainly have a miserable life, don't you Mr. Norton?"

"Yeah, and this don't help."

"You have only yourself to blame for your present situation," the judge said. "I'm going to agree to allow you to leave the jail and run your store Monday through Saturday during the hours you specified. But that means you go to work and then you go back to jail. No place else. Do you understand me?"

"Am I supposed to wear the same clothes every day?"

The judge sighed and said, "You have to push everything every inch of the way, don't you?"

"I'm just saying, I can't wear an orange jumpsuit in my shop, and I don't have a change of clothes."

"Sheriff Weber, when you leave here please have a deputy take Mr. Norton to his house and let him gather up any clothing and personal items he may need and take him to drop them off at his store. Anything else? Fine. We're done here."

The judge rapped his gavel and left the bench, going back to his private office.

"Do you really need the handcuffs? He's not going anywhere," Recker said as Dan Wright pulled cuffs from the pouch on his belt.

"That's the way we do things," Weber said. "He gets handcuffed anytime he's out of his cell."

"How can he run his business if he's handcuffed?"

"We'll take them off when we take him to the store every day," Weber said. "But when it's time to go back to jail, the cuffs go back on."

"Let's go pack you some stuff," Dan said, leading Norton out the door.

"I'll send you my bill," Recker shouted to his client's retreating back.

Weber looked at Bob Bennett and said, "If I was that little turd, I wouldn't hold my breath waiting for a check to show up."

Bennett nodded in agreement and they left the courtroom.

Chapter 29

News spreads fast in a small town, and a dozen people in stores and on the street asked Weber if he and Robyn were okay and expressed relief that they had not been injured in the accident the night before. And each and every one of them reminded him that it could have been worse. Almost that many people who were on a first name basis with the Sheriff went out of their way to bust his chops about the accident. When he returned to the office, some clown had hung a sign that said "Don't Hurt Me!!!" in bold red letters around the neck of the mounted elk head that had hung in his office since Pete Caitlin was the sheriff.

"I don't know, Jimmy, maybe you should have got one of those little chrome bulldogs for a hood ornament instead of a whole damn elk," Buz said.

"Hey boss, is it true that you and Archer are having a contest to see who can wreck the most units in a week?" Dolan wanted to know.

"If I had known you were going hunting, I would have loaned you my .270. It does just as good a job as an Explorer does, and it's easier to clean afterward," Chad Summers said.

"You guys laugh all you want," Weber told him, going along with the fun good-naturedly. "Just remember, I'm the one that makes out the schedules around here. The way I hear it, there's a lot of things happening on the graveyard shift. I may need all of you out there working it for the next month or two."

"Do you hear that, Dolan? We get to go hunting, too," Buz said.

Weber laughed with them, knowing that if it were anybody else in the hot seat, he would be the one making jokes.

Things were no better when he went across the street to the newspaper office, where Paul Lewis said, "I hear you joined the Elks lodge last night."

"You're a funny little fat man," Weber told his friend. "I come over to ask if you want to go to lunch and you give me this kind of crap?"

"Sure, let's go," Paul said "Do you want to go to the Frontier Café or the ButterCup? Or we could just go to your place and throw a couple of elk steaks on the grill."

Weber gave him the finger and Paul asked, "Was that too soon?"

There was more to come at the restaurant, where Harvey Clayton asked Weber what kind of camouflage clothing he wore when he was elk hunting with an SUV, and Lester Eubanks held his fingers over his head in a poor imitation of a set of elk antlers and bellowed a sound that Weber had to admit was very close to that of a bull elk in rut.

"So, enough with the elk," Paul said. "What happened with Todd Norton in court?"

"The judge gave him a big fine, extended his probation two more years, and sentenced him to 45 days in jail."

"Wait a minute. He's going to be in your jail for 45 days?"

"He gets off for work release every day, and then he comes right back," Weber said.

"Man, what did you do to piss off the judge that he'd subject you to that kind of punishment?"

"What can I say, Paul? It seems to be my week in the barrel."

Weber's phone rang and he looked at the display. Pat Schroeder was calling.

"What's up, Pat?"

"Well, I've got bad news and maybe good news."

"Let's hear it."

"It looks like the grill will be here on time, but the bumper and hood are on back order. My supplier says maybe as much as three or four weeks."

Weber groaned and Pat continued. "However, the good news is, if you're agreeable, I found the parts we needed at a junk yard in Gallup, New Mexico. Someone had an Explorer that got rear-ended and totaled, but the front end is in perfect condition. I know the guy who owns the place and he said since it was for law enforcement, if we'll pay for the gas here and back he'll have one of his guys take them off and he can have them here tomorrow."

"That's great, Pat! I appreciate it. And tell your friend thanks for me, too,"

"Will do, Jimmy. I'll keep you posted on what's happening."

Weber ended the call and told Paul the good news.

"That's good of Pat to go the extra mile. Anything new on the ninja?"

"We had an incident last night. He was peeping through Imogene Buckley's window. Dan Wright chased him through the woods, but he got away."

Weber didn't feel the need to tell the newspaperman the rest of the story. Paul was his friend, but as far as he was concerned, what his deputy and his lady friend did behind closed doors was nobody's business.

"Imogene again?"

"What can I say, Paul? She's a pretty girl. If they had teachers like that when we were in school, I imagine if we were still pimply faced kids we might be peeking in her window."

"Yeah, why didn't they have teachers like that back then?"

"Are you kidding me? I had a hard enough time getting out of that place as it was after twelve years," Weber said. "If they had women like that teaching, I'd still be there."

"I've got to tell you, Jimmy, I'm hearing a lot of things that bother me about this ninja thing."

"What do you mean?"

"I've had more than one person tell me they bought a gun, or they are keeping the ones they have loaded. I know you keep saying that it's probably kids doing all of this, but there are a lot of

187

people out there with itchy trigger fingers. This could turn out real bad."

"You're not telling me anything I don't already know," Weber said. "And to be honest with you, Paul, that scares the hell out of me."

Chapter 30

The Town Council chambers were packed when Weber arrived for the weekly meeting that night, and several people stopped him to ask for any updates on the ninja and what his department was doing to catch him. Weber gave them his standard answer, "We're working on it," but knew it wasn't enough to satisfy their fears.

Kirby Templeton called the meeting to order and there were the standard preliminaries, including the Council secretary's reading of the minutes from the previous week's meeting and a report from the Treasurer on the Town's financial status, which was at an all time high. With those tasks out of the way, Chamber of Commerce Director Juliette Murdoch gave a brief report on the upcoming annual Pioneers Days celebration. When she was finished, she asked if there are any questions.

"Yeah, I've got a question," Harley Willits said. "What kind of entertainment are you planning this year?"

"We'll have the usual events for children like the sack race and pin the tail on the donkey and other games," Juliet said. "There will also be plenty for the adults to do. We've got the arm wrestling competition, pie eating contest, barbecue cookoff, horseshoes, three different bands, the crowning of this year's Miss Big Lake, and of course, the fireworks to celebrate the Fourth of July."

"Can I make a suggestion?"

"We're always open to new ideas," Julie replied. "What did you have in mind?"

"How about a ninja fashion show? I hear black is all the rage these days."

It seemed like everyone in the crowd laughed, and Arnold Foster had to get his two cents worth when he stood up and said, "I'm for any kind of a costume that makes Harley wear a mask over his ugly mug!"

"You ain't no Prince Charming yourself," Harley retorted.

"Screw you. If I had a dog that looked like you, I would shave its ass and make it walk backwards."

"Okay guys, that's enough," Kirby said, wrapping his gavel once the laughter had died down.

"Yeah, when are we going to do something about these ninjas? I heard one shot Todd Norton the other day," Cliff deCarlo said.

There were other comments from the crowd expressing their fears and frustrations over the phantom ninjas. Kirby rapped his gavel again and said, "All right people, calm down. Sheriff Weber will have a report on all of that in just a moment. Meanwhile, Ms. Murdoch, do you have anything else to share with us about Pioneer Days?"

"No, except I hope everybody comes out and has a good time."

"Thank you, Ms. Murdoch," Kirby said. "Moving right along, Sheriff Weber, what can you tell us about this ninja business?"

Weber walked up to the speaker's platform and said, "First of all, let me clear the air about something. Todd Norton was not, and let me emphasize that, he was *not* shot by a ninja."

"That's what I heard," Gloria Miller said. "I heard he came in his shop and shot him four or five times and walked out the door."

"I don't care what you heard, that's not what happened," Weber replied. "Mr. Norton accidentally shot himself and was subsequently arrested and was convicted this morning of filing a false police report, among other things."

"I wouldn't blame anybody for shooting that SOB," Troy Coppage said. "He more than doubled the price on a starter for my pickup because I told him I had to have it in a hurry."

"That's enough," Kirby said. "Sheriff, please continue."

"Anyway, the rumors you heard about the ninja shooting Todd Norton are not true."

"What about the attacks on Doug Mullins? Are you telling us those didn't happen either?"

"No, sir, I'm not," Weber replied. "Those attacks did happen and we're still trying to find out who is responsible for them."

"Bastard comes around my place I'm going to shoot first and ask questions later," someone said from the back of the room.

"That's enough of that," Kirby said, wrapping his gavel. "Don't make me order the sheriff to clear this room so we can continue."

There was some grumbling from the crowd, but Weber continued. "We believe that the attacks on Mr. Mullins and the other ninja sightings around town are completely separate."

"Why do you think that, Sheriff?"

"That's a good question, Ms. McGill," Weber told one of the newer Town Council members. "Several reasons. First of all, the pattern is different. Most of the ninja sightings have been, from want of a better word, teenage pranks. Running through backyards, peeking in windows, that sort of thing. They are irritating, but we don't believe the person or persons doing them is a threat to anybody. As for the attacks on Mr. Mullins, the pattern is just so different. In every other instance, the ninja has fled immediately upon being spotted and not shown any kind of aggressiveness whatsoever."

"Then why Doug Mullins? Why was he singled out, if that's what's happening?"

"I wish I had an answer for you, Ms. McGill. We have looked at Mr. Mullins' background, his interactions with other members of the community, and his business dealings. We can't find anything that would indicate why someone wants to do him harm."

"Yet somebody is trying to hurt him. Or at least scare him to death."

"It would seem that way. I won't lie to you, we have no idea why. It's still an active case and we continue to investigate it."

"What about the other ninja sightings, Sheriff? Are your people making any headway on that? Because as you can see, this community is very concerned about them right now," Kirby said.

"I understand everybody's concerns. I really do. But let me emphasize again, we really believe that the sightings are some kind of teenage prank. I know people are frightened, I know they're on edge, but please, please. Don't do something stupid in response to a stupid prank. I hear people talking about shooting first and asking questions later. Spouting off like that may make you feel better, but the reality is, if you shoot somebody because they're trespassing or even looking in your windows, you're going to go to jail."

"I've got a right to defend myself and my family," Ross Sinclair said. "This is still America."

"Yes, you do have a right to defend yourself and your family," Weber replied. "However, that means you can defend against an aggressor who means to do you bodily harm. The things we're talking about, peeking in windows and that kind of nonsense, those are not lethal threats to you and you cannot use lethal force in response."

"I can shoot them in the ass if I want to!"

"You can do that, Ross. But if you do, you're going be sitting in a jail cell and you're going to answer to the judge for it. Not to mention the fact that you're probably going to get sued and lose everything you have."

"That's bullshit, Sheriff. A man's got rights!"

Kirby rapped his gavel again and said, "Okay, enough Mr. Sinclair. This is not the time or place for a debate like this. Anybody else who wants to go down this route, you might as well leave now and save the sheriff from having to remove you."

"So free speech is gone, too? It wasn't like this when Chet Wingate was the mayor."

There were murmurs and comments back and forth, and Kirby rapped his gavel yet again. "Enough, people. Mr. Sinclair, this is your last warning, sit down and be quiet or leave."

The man sat down, but from the look on his face he was not happy about it.

"Is there anything else you can tell us about this ninja thing, Sheriff?"

"I wish I had more to tell you, but we don't at this time," Weber told him. "All I can say is I've got every deputy on the lookout all the time and we are fielding lots of calls from people saying they saw the ninja. Unfortunately, by the time we get to the scene, whoever they saw is long gone."

"Thank you, Sheriff Weber. I know you and your people are doing the best you can with what you have to work with," Kirby said. "On another note, I believe you have some news to share with us about an incident that occurred last night."

"Yes, I do. Last night, actually early this morning, I hit an elk in my Department vehicle. Deputy Fuchette was with me, and while neither of us were injured, the vehicle suffered quite a bit of damage to the front end, and I had to euthanize the animal because it's injuries were so severe."

"That's unfortunate," Kirby said, "but we all know it happens around here. I'm just glad neither one of you were hurt. Is your vehicle salvageable?"

"Yes, it is. Randy Laird towed it to Pat Schroeder's body shop and Pat has already provided me with an estimate for repairs. At first he said he would have the parts in two or three days, then he called a little while ago and said some were on back order. But he located some used parts at a junkyard that will donate them, which saves us a bunch of money. He said getting it back on the road will be a priority."

"May I see the estimate?"

Weber handed it to the interim mayor and reminded him that the actual cost would be less the bumper and hood that were being donated. Kirby passed it among the other councilmembers.

"This looks appropriate to me," Councilman Mel Walker said. "I hit one last winter and it's about what it cost to get my car put back together."

"I have a question," Councilwoman Smith-Abbot said. "Who is going to pay for these repairs?"

"It will come out of the Sheriff's Department's discretionary budget," Weber replied.

"So the taxpayers are paying for it."

"I guess you could say that," Weber agreed.

"Then what you're telling us is that we've got a big bill to pay, due to your negligence, Sheriff. Is that right?"

Kirby spoke up before Weber could answer and said, "Gretchen, according to the police report, there was no negligence involved. Sheriff Weber was going under the speed limit on that road when the incident occurred."

"A report filed by his own deputies. That's not good enough for me. Why wasn't an outside agency called in to investigate the accident, Sheriff Weber? What are you trying to hide?"

"This was a routine accident with no injuries," the sheriff said. "We don't typically call in an outside agency to investigate something like that."

"This smells like a cover-up to me!"

"That's enough, Gretchen," Kirby said. "We're not going to sit here and listen to you start the same old finger pointing game. Does any other councilmember have any questions for the sheriff about this unfortunate incident?"

"I do," Janet McGill said. "Sheriff Weber, first of all, I'm glad that you and your wife were not injured. I'm just curious, being a relative newcomer to the area. What happens when you have to put an animal down like that? I mean, is it just pulled off the side of the road and left to rot, or is there some kind of a disposal you take it to?"

"That's a good question," Weber said. "For game animals like elk and deer and bear, if we can, we salvage the meat. In last night's case, I called Jean Du Plessis. He runs the Mountain Food Bank and he and his son came to pick up the animal and took it home to process. The meat will go to needy families here in Big Lake."

"I'm glad to hear that." Janet said. "At least something good came out of what happened."

"Any other questions for the sheriff from the Council or from anybody in the crowd?"

"Yeah, I've got a question," Arnold Foster said, waving his hand in the air.

194

Kirby sighed and asked, "What is it now, Arnold?"

"Sheriff, instead of running over elk, why don't you find the ninja and run over him?"

There was both laughter and groans from the crowd and Kirby waited for it to die down and then asked, "Does anybody have a serious question for the sheriff?" Before anybody could raise their hand or speak up, he continued, saying. "Okay, that's enough for this week's meeting. I make a motion that we adjourn."

The motion was quickly seconded by Mel Walker and the rest of the Council agreed. Kirby rapped his gavel one final time to signify the end of the meeting and people began to get up from their seats, some milling around to discuss the meeting or gossip, others heading for the door.

"Well, it could have been worse," Councilman Frank Gauger said, joining Weber on the floor.

"We've seen worse in here, no question about that," Weber agreed. "It's been a long day, Frank, and I didn't get a lot of sleep last night. I'm headed for home."

When Weber walked out of the Town Council chambers, he had no idea that he was in for yet another sleepless night.

Chapter 31

A week earlier Coop had invited them to have dinner with him and his girlfriend, attorney Roberta Jensen, but they were both so tired that Robyn called and begged off. They ate a light dinner and were in bed just after 9 o'clock, both of them too tired to keep their eyes open.

"You know what you said last night about leaving me sleep while you have sex and covering me up afterward?"

"Yeah."

"Be sure my feet are covered, too," Robyn said.

"If it's all the same to you, how about…"

When he didn't finish the sentence, Robyn asked. "How about what, Jimmy."

The only response she got was her husband snoring.

Robyn kissed his cheek and said, "I'll be damned. I guess the honeymoon really is over." She snuggled up to his side and was soon fast asleep herself.

Weber was dreaming that he was sitting at his desk surrounded by stacks of reports and requisition slips and other paperwork that all needed his attention, each stack as tall as he was. He loathed paperwork and tried to avoid it at every opportunity. Mary Caitlin was a hard taskmaster who never let up in her demands that he

197

keep it up to date. In his dream, Mary was wheeling in stack after stack of paperwork on a refrigerator dolly and his office was so full that he couldn't see the door any longer. Meanwhile, he was sitting at the desk with a stub of a broken pencil in his hand that was badly in need of sharpening. For some reason there was an irritating trilling noise in the background that kept getting louder and louder. When Robyn called his name he came awake, realizing it was his phone and that it was Dispatch calling.

"Answer the phone, Jimmy."

"Huh? Okay. He fumbled for the phone and pressed the button.

"Yeah, what is it?"

"I hate to wake you up two nights in a row," Judy Troutman said. "But Dan caught the ninja."

"What?" Weber was instantly awake. He looked at the clock on Robyn's nightstand, which said it was 1:45 AM. "He did? Where?"

"He was back peeking in Imogene Buckley's window again. But this time Dan was waiting for him and chased him down."

"Where are they at?"

"Back at Imogene's."

"Tell Dan I'm on my way."

"10-4, Sheriff."

Robyn was awake by then and asked, "What's going on?"

"Dan caught the ninja. Apparently he was back at Imogene's place again."

"Two nights in a row? Damn, he's as horny as you are!"

"Are you talking about Dan or the ninja?"

"Both, I guess."

Robyn got up and pulled a pair of panties from her dresser drawer.

"What are you doing?"

"My mother said to always wear clean underwear in case I was in an accident."

"My mom told me that, too," Weber replied. "I told her if I was ever in an accident, I'd probably crap my pants anyway."

"You must've been a fun child to raise."

"I like to think so. You know, you don't have to go."

"After all this, do you think I would miss out on seeing who this creep is?"

They took Robyn's patrol car, since the headlights were so feeble on the LTD that it wasn't worth turning them on. When they got to the place where Weber had hit the elk less than 24 hours earlier, Robyn slowed down instinctively, both of them knowing that there was really no reason to do so and neither of them mentioning it.

Jordan and Tommy's patrol cars were both parked in Imogene's driveway, along with Dan's motorcycle and her Mazda. The lights were on in the house and in the yard, and Jordan opened the door when he saw them coming.

"What's going on?"

"Dan caught him, Jimmy. Caught him red-handed, looking in the window."

In the living room Dan, dressed in black pants and a long sleeve black T-shirt with some kind of camouflage paint covering his hands and face, towered over a young boy dressed in black clothing with short brown hair and a miserable expression on his face. The kid looked like he would welcome finding a hole he could fall into and pull the earth in on top of him.

"What happened, Dan?"

"I figured if this little rat would come twice, he might come here a third time. Especially after the eyeful he got last night. So I had Imogene leave the window open a little bit like before and the light on, and I hid out in the backyard on the roof of that utility shed out there waiting for him with night vision goggles. Damn mosquitoes about ate me alive, but it was worth it. Sure enough, he came sneaking out of the woods and up to her bedroom window. I guess he heard me jumping off of the shed, because when I did, he took off running. He never made it as far as the woods. I tackled him right there in the backyard."

While Weber wasn't pleased that one of his deputies had taken on a clandestine surveillance without telling him about it ahead of time, he was pleased with the results.

"What's his name?"

"Coulter Odell," Imogene said. "He's one of my students. I thought he was a good kid, until now."

The boy hung his head, not looking at any of them.

Weber stepped in front of him and said, "Coulter. Look at me."

The boy shook his head and Weber reached down and put his hand under his chin and lifted gently. There were tears in the boy's eyes, and in spite of all the mischief he had caused, Weber couldn't help feeling a little bit sorry for him.

"It looks like you got yourself in some trouble, son. Do you have anything to say for yourself?"

He shook his head.

"Why have you been doing this stuff?"

The boy mumbled something and Weber said, "Speak up. None of this is going to go away just because you got caught. Now, I'm asking you again. Why have you been doing this?"

"I don't know."

"Yeah, you do know. We can talk here or we can take you down to the police station and call your parents and they can hear all of it. Which is it going to be?"

"I'm sorry, Ms. Buckley. I'm really sorry."

Imogene looked at him with a mixture of sympathy and anger on her face.

"Look, this isn't the end of the world," Weber told the boy, "even if it feels like it. But you need to start talking to me because it's only going to go downhill from here if you don't. Now, why have you been running around doing this crap?"

"It just started out as fun. Then it got out of hand."

"How did it get out of hand, Coulter?"

The boy shrugged his shoulders. "I don't know. We were just goofing off and then one night I saw the window open in Ms. Buckley's bedroom. I know I shouldn't have, but I couldn't help it."

"You said 'we were just goofing off.' Who else is involved in this?"

The boy hung his head again and Weber repeated this question. "Coulter, who else?"

"I'm not going to tell you that."

"Yes, you are. It may take a while, but you're going to tell me everything about it. The only question is, how miserable do you have to get before you reach that point?"

"You can take me to jail or whatever you want, but I'm not ratting out anybody."

"We're going to find out one way or the other," Weber told him. "How about you make life easier on all of us and tell me."

The boy was crying now, but he shook his head stubbornly. "I can't."

"You can't, or you won't?"

"Just take me to jail."

"Okay, that's your choice. Stand up."

"Do you have to call my dad and tell him what happened?"

"You're a juvenile. What do you think?"

"Please don't do that."

"I don't have any choice, son. Now stand up."

Coulter got to his feet and Weber said, "Jordan, give me your handcuffs.

The boy flinched when the cold steel bracelets locked around his wrists but didn't say anything.

"Take him in. We'll see you at the office."

Tommy led the boy out the door to his patrol car, his head still hung low.

Chapter 32

"Coulter, what the hell were you thinking? You could have got yourself shot pulling crazy shit like this!"

"I'm sorry, Dad."

"You're sorry? Do you know how many people in this town are freaked out because of these stunts you've been pulling? Do you know how easy it would've been for someone to shoot you and claim you were trying to break into their house?"

"I wasn't trying to break in anyplace. I swear I wasn't! I was just…"

"You were just what, Coulter? Peeking in people's windows like a little pervert?"

Weber couldn't help but feel sorry for Wayne Odell. Coulter's mother had run off to "find herself" when the boy was in third grade, and except for an occasional phone call or a card at Christmas or on his birthday, they never heard from her again. Wayne, who worked long hours installing and servicing garage doors for a company out of Albuquerque, New Mexico, was responsible for a large area that included the twin towns of Springville/Eager, near the state line west to Pinetop/Lakeside and Show Low, and as far as Holbrook, Arizona. Wayne had never pictured himself in the role of a father, let alone a single father, but he tried his best to provide for his son and give him a good home life.

"I'm sorry, Dad."

"Yeah, I heard you the first time. But what I want to hear from you is the answers to the   questions Sheriff Weber has been asking you. Now, who else is involved in this stupid crap with you?"

"I'm sorry, Dad. I'll answer any question except that. I just can't."

Weber could see the anger in Wayne's face and didn't want things to get out of hand.

"Okay, let's just take that question off the table for right now, Coulter. How did all of this start?"

"I don't know. I've always liked ninja movies. When I heard about the Ninja World down in Tucson we went to check it out."

Weber was tempted to try to trick the boy up by asking who he had gone to the convention with, but before he could ask, Wayne said, "Wait a minute. You went to Tucson? When did this happen?"

"I don't know, Dad. Three or four weeks ago, I guess. It was when you had to go to that work thing in Albuquerque."

"When I went to the weekend training seminar?"

"Yeah."

"You were supposed to be staying with your buddy Richey. Is he who you were doing this stuff with?"

"No. After you left town, I called Richey and told him there been a change of plans and you weren't going to go, so I was staying home."

"And then you snuck off to Tucson?"

"Yes, sir."

"How did you get to Tucson and back?"

"We were hitchhiking and some lady gave us a ride."

"Some lady? What's this lady's name?"

"I don't know. She was just some old lady."

"Who were you with, Coulter?"

"You can beat me or they can lock me up or whatever they want, but I'm not going to tell you. I can't."

Weber was truly afraid that Wayne might strike the boy, and even though Coulter probably had it coming, he spoke up and changed the subject.

"Okay, so you went off to Tucson with whoever and you came back as ninjas. And since then you've been running around town doing this stupid stuff, right?"

"Yeah."

"Coulter, you know looking in people's windows is wrong, don't you?"

"Yeah."

"How would you feel if someone was looking in the window at your mother when she was getting dressed?"

He could immediately tell that was the wrong question to ask. The boy's jaw clenched and he said, "Anybody who wants to look at that bitch can, as far as I'm concerned. I hate her!"

"That's enough of that kind of language," his father said.

"Well, it's true, Dad. You know that as much as I do."

"No matter what she's done, she still your mother, son. You need to show some respect."

"For what, Dad? Leaving us like she did? Never being here?"

Weber couldn't help but admire the fact that Wayne didn't trash talk his ex-wife to his son, but he wanted to get the interview back on track.

"Coulter, what's the deal with Doug Mullins?"

"Who?"

"Doug Mullins. The man you or whoever is involved in this stuff with you tried to kill."

"That's crazy! We never tried to kill anybody. We were just goofing around."

"Going after someone with a sword isn't goofing around, Coulter. Neither is slinging one of those throwing stars at him. Not to mention cutting his brake lines."

"Wait a minute. Are you saying he was involved in the stuff that happened to Mullins?"

"Somebody dressed like a ninja did it," Weber said. "And so far, this is the only ninja we've caught."

"Coulter, you tell the man what he wants to know right now. I mean it. No more of this bullshit. Why in the world would you try to hurt somebody like Doug Mullins?"

"I never did! I don't even know who he is."

"Then it's your partner in crime," Weber said.

"No! I swear to God, we were just goofing off. We never tried to hurt anybody."

"Somebody said they saw two ninjas fighting with swords a while back. Tell me about that."

"They weren't swords, they were just sticks."

"Do you have any swords, Coulter? Or throwing stars?"

He shook his head. "I tried to buy some throwing stars at Ninja World but they wouldn't sell them to me because I wasn't eighteen."

Weber had thought all along that the ninjas seen peeking in windows and running around town were not related to the attacks on Doug Mullins, but he didn't want to reveal that information just yet. One way or the other, he intended to find out who else was involved with Coulter. But as it turned out, even though the boy continued to refuse to give them that information, they would soon learn the answer from a different source. But it wouldn't come easily.

It was after 4 AM and they had taken a break in questioning Coulter when Judy Troutman at the dispatch desk said, "Sheriff, somebody else just caught a ninja. His wife said he's fighting with him out in the back yard!"

Chapter 33

Red and blue lights from the light bars on top of three Big Lake police cars swept across the trees and houses on Arapahoe Way. Weber and Robyn jumped out of her unit and ran toward the backyard of a brick ranch style house where they could hear the sounds of a battle going on. When they came around the corner of the house, they both skidded to a stop when they saw the sight before them.

Jordan and Tommy were tangled up in a heap on the ground, along with what appeared to be a large naked man and a smaller person wearing a black ninja costume with a hood over his head and a mask covering his face.

"Let go of me, God dammit. I'm going to strangle this little dipshit!"

"I said that's enough," Jordan said, trying to pull the large man away from the much smaller ninja. "We'll handle it from here."

"No way! I know what's gonna happen. The judge is gonna give him a slap on the wrist and that's it. I'm putting a stop to this right now."

"Back off," Jordan ordered, but the enraged man was half again the young deputy's size, throwing him away like he was no more than a child and grabbing the squirming ninja before he could get away. Jordan went high, jumping and looping an arm around the man's neck, while Tommy went low, grabbing his knees and throwing him off his feet.

Weber knew he should try to help, but it was all he could do to keep from laughing out loud as he watched the tableau unfold before him. At one point, Tommy was pinned to the ground, his face firmly planted in the cheek of the man's fish belly white ass as they thrashed around.

"You really need to go help those guys," Robyn said, laughing so hard she could hardly talk.

"I'm not going to do it. You do it."

"I'm off duty. And even if I was, you couldn't order me to do that."

Tommy, pinned under a huge mound of flabby flesh, had the ninja by an ankle with one hand and was slapping at the naked man with the other, seemingly having no effect.

While Robyn and Weber proved useless in breaking up the melee, the man's wife apparently had enough because she came out of the house wearing pink stretch pants that hadn't quite stretched enough and an old worn out brassiere that was doing its best to hold things inside but wasn't quite making it. She picked up a garden hose and turned it on, spraying the four combatants, who yelped and broke apart. Struggling to get to his feet, Tommy lost his grip on the ninja's ankle but managed to get hold of it again and hung on so he couldn't get away.

Sensing it was safe to approach, Weber and Robyn went into action, her grabbing the ninja and handcuffing him while Weber got in front of the naked man and pushed him backwards when he tried to go after the prisoner again.

"That's enough," the sheriff ordered. It was only then that he realized the man wasn't completely naked. A pair of boxer shorts hung off of one of his ankles. "Pull your drawers up."

"Don't worry about me, worry about that little asshole! I should've shot him, sneaking around in my backyard like that."

"Well, let's be glad you didn't. Now go in the house and get some clothes on. I'll talk to you later. Tommy, go with him and make sure he doesn't do anything stupid."

After the homeowner and his wife went in the house, with Tommy accompanying them, Weber stepped in front of the ninja and said, "Okay, boy, take off the hood and mask."

208

When there was no response, he said, "No problem, I'll do it for you."

The hood and face mask were a one piece affair, and when he grabbed the top of it and pulled it off the boy's head, he was greeted by long dark hair and the realization that the boy ninja wasn't a boy after all!

~~~***~~~

Amy Druzniac sat sullen faced and handcuffed in the back of Robyn's patrol car while Weber talked to the homeowners.

"We heard all about this ninja crap that was happening, and I told Samantha here that if I caught the little son of a bitch, I was gonna pop his head like a pimple. And sure enough, I got out of bed to take a leak and I heard something outside. I looked out and that little puke was sneaking through my backyard. Who knows what he was up to? Probably peeking in the windows at us 'cause we usually sleep naked when it's hot out like this."

Of all the mental pictures Weber didn't want to have, the image of Louie and Samantha Tubbs being naked was real close to the top of the list. Louie, whom everybody called Tubby because he tipped the scales at 300 pounds in his senior year of high school and hadn't lost an ounce since then, worked as a butcher at the supermarket, while his equally large wife was a stay-at-home mom to several yappy little Shih Tzus, none of which had stopped barking since he had entered the house. He didn't know if it was the late hour, the lack of sleep, or the noisy dogs that were giving him a headache, but either way, he just wanted to get out of there.

"Okay, so you heard a noise in your back yard and you looked out and saw the ninja? Is that correct?"

"Yeah, that's what happened," Tubby said. "I didn't have time to get dressed, so I pulled on some underwear and went out the back door after him. At least I thought it was a him. Why in the world would a girl be dressed up and doing shit like this, Sheriff?"

"We don't know that yet, but we intend to find out," Weber replied. "What happened when you got out in the backyard?"

"He ran right into the clothesline and it knocked him on his ass. At least I thought it was a him at the time. I jumped right on top of him and yelled for Sam to call the police. He or she or whatever it was was trying to get away and I was holding on tight. The next thing I knew, those two deputies were on top of me, too."

"Why didn't you obey their orders and stop fighting? You could've gotten yourself Tazed or something."

"I don't know, Sheriff. I was so pissed off at the idea that that little puke was spying on us. I don't think I even realized they were cops."

"What happens now? Is my husband under arrest? All he was trying to do was catch the ninja."

"It's okay, Mrs. Tubbs," Weber told her. "Neither one of my deputies were hurt, and as warm as it is, they probably appreciated the shower you gave them. But Tubby, do me a favor, will you? The next time something like this happens, stay inside and call 911 and let us handle it. Okay?"

Tubby had pulled on a pair of sweatpants that were cut off at the knees, and he was dripping wet both from the garden hose and the exertion of chasing down and tangling with the ninja.

"Yeah, okay, Sheriff. I should'a done that in the first place. But I was so mad that I just reacted. I'm glad I didn't have a gun or it might have been a whole lot worse!"

Weber didn't disagree with that. While he was a strong supporter of the Second Amendment and believed every law-abiding, mentally competent citizen had the right to own as many firearms as they wanted, and to use them in self-defense if it came down to it, he also believed that there were far too many people running around with guns who had never taken the time to get any kind of proper training in how to handle and use them.

"Okay, that's enough for now," he said, handing Tubby and his wife both witness statement forms. "I'd appreciate both of you filling these out and either dropping them by the office or else giving us a call and I'll send someone out to pick them up if you can't get away. We'll get out of your hair for now."

He stood up and one of the little dogs grabbed the hem of his pant leg, pulling determinedly on it as it growled ferociously. Or at least as ferocious as an eleven pound ball of noise could growl. The dog hung on all the way to the door before it finally let go. Weber was glad it did because he couldn't decide if he was going to have to kick it off or drag it all the way out to Robyn's patrol car.

~~~***~~~

"Well, it was a busy night, but it looks like we caught our ninjas," Weber said two hours later when Mary Caitlin arrived to start her day.

"You did?"

"Well, actually Dan caught one of them and Tubby Tubbs caught the other."

"You're kidding me? There were two of them?"

"Yeah, and you're never gonna believe who one is," Weber said. "Come with me."

Amy Druzniac looked up when Weber opened the door to the interview room.

"Amy? Is that you?"

"Yes, Mrs. Caitlin, it's me."

"What are you doing involved in all this?"

The girl shrugged her shoulders and didn't answer.

"Are you all right, Amy? Do you need anything?"

She did not reply, just looked down at the table and shook her head.

Weber closed the door again and they walked back down the hall to the office.

"Have you called her parents yet, Jimmy?"

"Yeah. Her mother was working the night shift at the hospital in Show Low and her dad was so wasted he never knew she left the house. I'm still not sure he understood what I was telling him when I called. Her mom's on the way here now."

"I can't believe my own next door neighbor was mixed up in all of this. My Lord, I've known Amy since the day she was born!"

211

"I think I have, too." Weber said. "I never took her for a wild child. Her partner in all this is Coulter Odell, if you can believe that."

"You're kidding me? I always thought both of them were just nerds."

"I guess every nerd has a secret side, Mary."

"I feel so sorry for Sheila," Mary said. "Clark is a lush who can't hold a job, so the poor woman is working double shifts and doing everything else she can just to make ends meet. And now this."

"Yeah, I kind of feel that way about Wayne Odell. His wife runs off and he's raising the kid alone, and then this happens."

"Do you see the pattern here? We've got two kids that are pretty much social misfits and come from families where one parent is either gone or might as well not be in the picture for all the good they do, and the other parent is busting their butt to pay the bills and provide a home," Robyn said. "I guess it's no wonder the two of them found each other. They say great minds think alike. Maybe miserable hearts do, too."

Weber couldn't disagree with her, but he also couldn't picture a more unlikely couple than Coulter and Amy. He was 15 and she was almost 17, she was a head taller than him, and while she never bothered with makeup, and wore her hair straight without any kind of curling or highlights, she was more than plain, if not quite pretty. Coulter's face was a roadmap of acne, his teeth badly needed attention, and it seemed like he didn't put much effort into his personal hygiene. Neither of them really fit in with the other kids their ages, so maybe that's what drew them together.

A few minutes later a harried looking Sheila Druzniac arrived.

"Where's Amy? Is she okay?"

"She's fine, Sheila," Mary assured her, giving her neighbor a comforting hug.

"What happened? Someone called and said she was under arrest because she was involved in this ninja business?"

"I'm afraid that's right," Weber told her. "She was caught sneaking through somebody's backyard a few hours ago. He ran outside and caught her and there was a bit of a struggle before deputies arrived."

"A struggle? Like a fight?"

"Well, it really wasn't much of a fight," Weber said. "It was Tubby Tubbs who caught her."

"Tubby? The butcher?"

"Yes, ma'am. And it may have been a somewhat traumatic experience for her. Tubby was only wearing boxer shorts when he chased her down and tackled her."

Sheila put her head down and massaged her temples for a moment. "Please tell me you're kidding me."

"I wish I was," Weber told her.

"Can I see her?"

"Sure. I'll take you back to where she is."

He led the way down the hall to the interview room and opened the door. Amy looked up, and when she saw her mother, she burst into tears and ran into her arms.

"I'm so sorry, Mom. Please don't tell Daddy. He'll kill me."

"Are you okay?"

"I guess. I just want to go home."

She looked at her daughter and asked, "Why is your hair wet? And where did you get those clothes?"

"That's a long story," Weber said. "We don't have all the answers yet. I'm hoping you can convince Amy to talk to us."

"Oh, she'll talk all right," Sheila assured him. "She'll tell you everything she knows. I'll see to that!"

Chapter 34

"So apparently these two nerdy kids got fascinated with ninja movies and martial arts crap," Weber said at a hastily called staff meeting later that morning. "When they heard about that Ninja World thing down in Tucson, they snuck away and hitchhiked a ride down there. They came back thinking they were full-fledged ninjas. They've been doing their thing ever since. From what we've been able to find out so far, they started out together last night and went back to Imogene Buckley's place to see what they could see. The girl was waiting in the woods while the boy went to check to make sure the coast was clear and see what was going on."

"I don't usually think of teenage girls as being Peeping Toms," Chad Summers said. "The boy? I can understand that, I guess. But why would the girl be there with him?"

"I don't know," Weber replied. "They're nerds. Maybe they needed to figure out where Part A goes into Part B. Anyway, they weren't expecting Dan to be up on the roof of Imogene's shed, and when he came down off of it, they both made a run for it. He caught the boy and never knew the girl was there. She got away and said she was hiding in the woods for a long time and got lost while she was trying to get home. That's when she took a shortcut through Tubby's back yard and got caught."

"Do you think that's true, or was she peeking in their window, too?"

"Have you seen Tubby and Samantha? Why would anybody want to see that?"

"I know I saw a lot more than I wanted to see of him," Jordan said. "I always dreamed about being a cop, but I never pictured myself wrestling with fat naked guys."

Everyone laughed out loud at that, and had a bigger laugh when Weber asked, "Did you two learn anything from the experience?"

"Yeah, I learned something," Tommy said. "When I was on the ground with my face pushed into that guy's ass, I learned that there is no question about it. I'm definitely not gay."

~~~***~~~

"Congratulations. I heard you solved the great Big Lake ninja case," Parks said when Weber walked into the small trailer at the back of the Sheriff's Department's parking lot that served as the FBI's field office.

"Yeah, just like I thought, it was a couple of dumb kids."

"Hopefully, that will ease people's minds around here and they won't be shooting stray cats and dogs every time they hear a noise in the night."

"Yeah, I was able to catch Paul Lewis as he was starting his press run for this week's paper. He pissed and moaned a little bit, but he rebuilt the front page with a big banner across the top saying the ninjas were caught."

"So that's it? All wrapped up in a tidy ball?"

"Not quite," Weber said. "The kids go to see Judge Ryman today and he'll do with them what he feels like he needs to do. But we still don't know who has been trying to kill Doug Mullins."

"There's no question about it? The kids weren't involved?"

Weber shook his head. "They were doing some stupid stuff, but neither one of them are really bad kids. More like kids with dysfunctional families who don't fit in with anybody else and kinda found each other."

"Sounds like one of those TV love stories to me," Parks said. "Assuming they make movies about ninja love."

216

"I don't know about that," Weber told him. "I think the boy has a major crush on the girl, but I'm not sure she feels the same way."

"See? There you go? Unrequited young ninja love. I'm telling you, Jimmy, if there's not a movie out about that already, we need to write the screenplay."

"You know, I kind of feel sorry for both of them. In both cases they've got one parent working themselves to death to pay the bills and keep a roof over their head, and another parent is either completely out of the picture or isn't worth a damn even though they're there. I'll say this for the boy, he's loyal. He admitted his involvement right away, but no matter how many times I asked him or how much his dad threatened him, he wouldn't give up his girlfriend. He was willing to take the fall for both of them."

"I can see it right now. We're going to be up on stage getting an Emmy for this, Jimmy. In fact, screw television, we're going to take this to the big screen. Can't you see them rolling out the red carpet for us at the Oscars, Jimmy? We'll be rubbing shoulders with celebrities and hobnobbing with the beautiful people."

"You go without me," Weber said. "I don't think I'd fit in with that crowd very well."

"I know, but that's why you got me, Bubba! I'll be the front man. People are going to see my good looks and how sophisticated I am and you'll just fade into the background. But don't you worry. In our Oscar acceptance speech, I'll be sure to let everybody know that you did your part, too."

"You're a real friend, aren't you, Parks?"

"The best you'll ever have, that's for damn sure!"

"I'd love to sit here and listen to you blow smoke up your own ass, but I've got real work to do," Weber said.

"That's it? You just came here to gloat because you're the town's hero today?"

"You know what they say," Weber told him, "today's hero is tomorrow's zero."

"Here's an idea," Parks suggested. "You could buy me lunch."

"What? Here in Big Lake? You're not gonna find any of those fancy restaurants like you do in Hollywood around here. The best we've got is Chez Roadkill."

"Look at you, talking French and all that! I'll tell you what, Jimmy. You just might fit in with the Hollywood crowd after all."

They walked down the sidewalk to the Cross Eyed Cricket, a submarine sandwich shop that had opened a few weeks earlier that they had not had a chance to try out yet. An attractive woman in her 40s smiled at them from behind the counter and said, "Welcome. Have a seat anywhere, guys."

They sat down at a table in the corner, where Weber could keep his back to the wall and watch who was coming in the door and what was going on out in the street. Big Lake was not a particularly dangerous town and it wasn't like he expected to be assaulted by anyone, but it always helped to be cognizant of situational awareness, just in case.

The woman brought them menus and asked, "What would you like to drink, gentlemen?"

"I'd like an ice cold Budweiser in a longneck bottle," Parks said. "But I don't suppose that's on the menu."

"Sorry, but we've got some killer iced tea."

"That sounds good to me," Parks told her, and Weber agreed.

"I'm afraid we haven't met yet, ma'am. I'm Sheriff Weber and this is FBI Special Agent Larry Parks."

"Nice to make your acquaintance," she said, shaking both of their hands. "I'm Diane Wenzel and that guy in the back is my husband Tim."

The man heard his name called and looked up and waved from the prep table behind the counter.

"So, you folks are newcomers to Big Lake," Weber said.

"Isn't everybody?"

"These days it almost seems that way," he agreed. He could not remember the sleepy days before Big Lake was discovered by the outside world. Many of the old timers around town resented the newcomers and longed for the good old days, seeming to forget the fact that during the "good old days" it had been incredibly hard for many people to make a living and the town's young people usually left for greener pastures as soon as they got out of high school. While it was true that many still struggled in the changing economy, some working two or three minimum-wage jobs just to get by, the new seasonal residents and the businesses they attracted had definitely brought changes, both positive and negative, to the community. Land prices had gone sky high, rental units were hard to come by, and many young people working in the service industry found themselves sharing an apartment with two, three, or even four friends. And there had definitely been an increase in both traffic and crime over the last few years.

"Where do you folks come from?"

"We lived in Denver for the past ten years," Diane said. "Before that we were in Abilene, Texas. We always wanted to live in the mountains but Denver just got to be too big and too busy for us. We thought about moving up toward Vail, but you have to be rich to be able to open a business there, if you can even find a space available. So we started looking and ended up here."

"What do you think of our little community so far?"

"We love it! Just busy enough to be a challenge, but not so much that it's overwhelming."

"Well, welcome to town. If you need anything at all, you just give my office a call," Weber told her.

"I'll do that. Let me get your teas for you."

She went away and was back soon with two tall glasses of tea with lemon wedges stuck on the rims. "Any idea what you want?"

"I think I'll go with the pastrami on Swiss," Weber said, while Parks went for a turkey club sandwich. The food was excellent and Diane had been right, the iced tea was killer to be sure. They were partway through their lunch when Tim Wetzel came to the table and introduced himself and thanked them for stopping in. Weber liked both of them immediately and had a feeling they were going to be a good addition to the community.

While they were chatting, Parks noticed activity outside and said, "I wonder what's going on there?"

Weber looked up to see two women standing on the sidewalk next to a blue Accura MDX looking distressed.

"I guess I ought to go see."

He walked out to the sidewalk and couldn't help but notice that both young women were not only attractive but dressed in expensive clothes. They also both seemed to be nearly frantic.

"Hello, ladies. I'm Sheriff Weber. You look like you've got some kind of problem. Is there anything I can do to help?"

"I can't unlock my car," one of the women, a brunette whose hair was perfectly coiffed, told him. "I forgot and left my key fob in my slacks and it went through the laundry. I'm always doing something silly like that, and I know when I call my husband and tell him I'm going to need a locksmith, he's not going to be happy."

Weber tried the doors on the SUV and they were indeed locked.

"May I see your key fob, please?"

"Sure, but it's not going to do you any good. I pressed the button a dozen times and it won't work."

Just for the heck of it, Weber pressed the unlock button on the key fob, and just like the woman had predicted, it didn't work.

"Oh, James is going to be so mad at me," the woman said.

Her friend tried to console her, saying, "It's no big deal. We'll figure it out one way or another."

While they were talking, Weber stuck the key in the door's lock and turned it and then opened the door.

"Here you go, ladies. All fixed."

"My God, what did you do? I tried that thing over and over again."

"I just used the key to unlock it," Weber told her, handing the key and fob back to her.

"Oh, I love you! You are amazing," the woman said, throwing her arms around Weber and hugging him tightly, kissing his cheek. "Thank you, thank you, thank you! I just knew my husband was going to throw a fit when he found out what I did. You're my hero!"

Weber chuckled and said, "No problem, it's all in a day's work. You ladies have a nice day."

He went back into the restaurant and Diane clapped her hands. "Nice work, Sheriff."

"Yes, ma'am. That's some real police work we just saw there," Parks said. "That's our sheriff, busting ninjas at night and rescuing damsels in distress during the day."

"Wait a minute. You caught the ninjas?"

"Yes, ma'am. We got both of them last night."

"Who was it? Not that I know anybody in town yet."

"Just a couple of kids acting stupid," Weber told her.

"Well, that's good. Some of the things I heard people saying about all that really scared me."

"Nothing to worry about," Weber assured her, "they were just kids."

"I wasn't as worried about the ninja as I was about how people were talking about shooting them if they saw them prowling around their houses some night."

"Believe me, I was even more worried about something like that happening than you were," Weber said.

"Where we lived in Denver, people never talked about shooting someone and things like that. It's kind of a different mindset here, isn't it?"

"Sometimes," Weber agreed. "There's still a bit of the Old West alive and well in this part of the country."

"Well, at least the ninja thing is over with and nobody got hurt," Diane said. "We can all be thankful for that."

But, of course, things didn't turn out that way. In Big Lake there always seemed to be more surprises and more aggravation awaiting Sheriff Weber and his deputies.

Chapter 35

In spite of the fact that their actions had put the town's nerves on edge and could have turned out tragically, just as Weber expected, Judge Ryman showed mercy when Coulter Odell and Amy Druzniac were brought before him to answer charges of disorderly conduct and trespassing. While Imogene Buckley had declined to press charges against either of the teenagers, Tubby and Samantha Tubbs were not as forgiving.

The pair's parents had agreed to a single trial for both of them, and after both had entered guilty pleas the judge sentenced each of them to 200 hours of community service, with their duties to be determined by the sheriff, along with placing both of them on probation for a year. Before releasing them, he gave them a stern talking to, telling them how easy it would have been for some frightened homeowner to shoot one of them when they were discovered on their property at night. He warned them that if either one got into any kind of trouble again, he would come down on them so hard that they would regret the day they were born. Properly chastised, Coulter and Amy were released to their parents.

"Some people might say I was too lenient on those kids," the judge told Weber afterward. "But from what I know about them, neither one has ever been in any kind of trouble before this. I think that in spite of what they were doing they are both pretty good kids. And I have to admit, the boy impressed me by not telling you or his father who his accomplice was. I mean, from your standpoint it made your job harder, but it shows a lot of loyalty on his part, don't you think?"

"Gee, I never thought of you as being a romantic, Judge."

"Are you kidding me? My two favorite movies are *West Side Story* and *Love Story*."

"Really? I'd have never guessed that."

"What can I say, Sheriff? I'm an old softy. I just hope those two don't prove me wrong."

"I don't think they will," Weber said. "I know that Wayne Odell and Sheila Druzniac are both good people who made some poor choices in marriage partners. But both of them want the best for their kids, and both of them are going to work hard to make sure they stay out of trouble. And to be honest with you, I think a wake-up call like this will keep those kids on the straight and narrow."

"Sheriff, do you ever wish you had the power to rearrange things in life?"

"I'm not sure what you mean, sir."

"I mean, you've got Wayne Odell, a hard-working man who is just trying to raise his son the best way he can all by himself. And then you've got Sheila Druzniac stuck with a drunk for a husband doing the same thing. Do you ever wish you could take could a couple of people like that and pluck them out of the situation they're in and put them together?"

"What are you saying, sir? Are you thinking about playing matchmaker?"

"Oh heavens, no. I've got more than enough going on to keep me busy as it is. And I don't know if that's the proper term for it or not," the judge said. "It just seems like sometimes life deals a bad hand to some folks, and somebody ought to be able to shuffle the deck and give them a do-over."

"Yeah, that would be nice," Weber told him. "There's a lot of things in life I wish I could change for people to make their lives better."

"Are you a religious man, Sheriff?"

"I don't know that I would say I'm religious, sir. I mean, I don't go to church, but I remember the way I was raised and I try to live right and treat people the right way. I believe there is some kind of higher power. You can't walk through these mountains or stand by the lake and not feel that something bigger than all of us created all this. But I don't believe that I have to sit in a building every Sunday morning to connect with that power. One time, Robyn told me that I'm not particularly religious, but I am spiritual. I guess that's as good an answer as any."

"I guess so," the judge said. "I never miss a Sunday service. I believe there's a heaven and there's a hell. But I've got to tell you, Sheriff, if I ever make it to heaven, and I truly hope I do, I want to sit down with God and have a long talk. Because sitting on this bench all these years, I've seen a lot of things that just don't make any sense to me at all. People say He has a plan for everything, and I believe that's true. But I'd sure like to have him explain some of the things I've seen."

"Me too," Weber said. "Me too."

~~~***~~~

True to his word, within just a couple of days Pat Schroeder called Weber to tell him that his Explorer was ready to go.

"It looks great! Can't even tell it was in an accident," Weber said when he got to the body shop. "How did you get it done so quick?"

"We had most of it put together by the end of the day yesterday. Then me and Chuck stayed up most of the night painting the hood and making sure everything was finished," Pat said, pointing his thumb over his shoulder toward his helper. "I took it by Mayfield's Tire Shop first thing this morning and had him check the alignment in case the impact screwed anything up in the suspension. I didn't think it did, but I wanted to be sure."

"Well, you sure went the extra mile for me, Pat," Weber said. "And I really appreciate it."

"Anytime, Jimmy."

Randy Laird had joined them and Weber said, "That old LTD I've been running around in is really a piece of crap. It'll be nice to be back in this thing."

"If you want me to, I can tune up that LTD," Randy offered. "It'll never be new again, but at least I might be able to make it run halfway decent for you."

"That's a good idea," Weber told him. "The headlights suck, too. Could you check those out while you're at it?"

"No problem. If you want, I can ride back to your office with you and pick it up and bring it back."

"Yeah, let's do that, if you've got time."

"I've got more time than money, Jimmy."

Back at the Sheriff's Office, Weber transferred everything from the LTD back to the Explorer, then handed Randy the keys. "How about once you're done with this one, see if you get that Chevy running, too? I know the battery is dead for one thing."

"I'm on it," Randy told him.

"Hey, guy, I really appreciate your help," Weber said again. "But neither one of these are a priority. They've been sitting forever. Work them in around all of your other stuff."

"Will do, Jimmy."

"I'm serious," Weber told him, "Don't be pulling any all-nighters to get these things running, okay? They don't get used that much."

"Yeah, I'm getting too old to do that night stuff too many times in a row," Randy told him, getting into the LTD.

Watching him drive away, Weber was glad that even with all the newcomers, Big Lake still had some people who went out of their way to make things easier for others. He didn't know what it would cost to get the two outdated cars running decently again, but he figured that with what Pat had saved the Town on the Explorer's repairs, they would still come out ahead.

Chapter 36

Things seemed to have fallen back into a routine, and Weber was enjoying not being jolted awake by the telephone in the middle of the night. Unfortunately, that only lasted for a while. Five days after Coulter Odell and Amy Druzniac were sentenced by Judge Ryman, Weber and Robyn finally had their delayed dinner with Coop and Roberta. She had fixed a delicious pot roast, along with assorted vegetables, dinner rolls, and homemade mango ice cream. Weber was surprised that a blind person could cook that well, but then again he didn't know all that many blind people, and everything Roberta did impressed him, from the way she ran her law office to her culinary skills.

After dinner they visited for another hour or two before calling it an evening. Robyn's Mustang was low on gas, so on the way home they pulled into the Fast Stop and he filled the tank. He was just putting the hose away at the pump when Robyn said, "Look over there, Jimmy," pointing across the convenience store's parking lot to where a young man had gotten out of a white over green pickup truck and was swaying unsteadily on his feet. "Tell me that's not Levi Bischoff."

"I'll be damned," Weber said. "He's at it again."

They walked across the parking lot and Weber asked, "How you doing, Levi?"

He looked at them bleary-eyed, trying to figure out who they were, then laughed and said, "I know you! How you doin', Sheriff? How you doin', Deputy? I don't recognize you with your clothes off. I don't mean clothes. I mean your uniforms. What's that they call it when cops don't wear their uniforms? Chevys. That's what it is, you're wearing Chevys!"

"I think the word you're looking for is civvies," Weber said, reaching out a hand to steady the young man before he fell.

"That's right, civvies. You're wearing civvies!" He looked around cautiously, then lowered his voice and burped something foul before he asked, "Are you guys working undercover? Did I just blow your cover? I'm sorry."

"No, Levi, we're just off duty," Weber said. "It kind of looks to me like you've been drinking, my friend."

"Who? Me?"

"It seems that way to me."

"I was shelebratin," Levi said, slurring his words.

"Oh yeah? What were you celebrating, Levi."

He grinned and asked, "Does there have to be a reason to shelebrate?"

"I guess not," Weber told him.

"No! No." He said, waving a finger at them. "I know what I was shelebratin. You too just got married, didn't you?"

"A while back," Weber said.

"Well, that's what I was shelebratin!" Levi smiled, proud of himself for coming up with the answer.

"Well, we do appreciate that," Weber told him. "But I'm kinda worried about you being wasted and driving a car."

"What car? This ain't a car, Sheriff. No, sir," Levi said turning to slap the fender of the truck and almost falling down in the process. Fortunately, Weber caught him before he completely lost his balance and helped steady him. "No, sir, this here is a Chevy pickup truck. This was my daddy's truck back when he was about my age. Did you know that?"

"No, Levi, I didn't know that."

"Hey, how come... how come I didn't get invited to your wedding? Don't you guys like me?"

"We like you just fine, Levi," Robyn said. "It was just a small wedding, just family."

"Oh, okay," he said, seeming to accept her explanation. "Hey, you know what?"

"What's that, Levi?"

"I never got to kiss the bride."

"No, I'm afraid you didn't."

He turned to Weber and asked, "Sir, may I kiss your bride?"

"I'm not sure that's a good idea, Levi. I mean, the wedding's been over for a while now."

"Well that's a damn shame, Sheriff. A damn shame. I don't mean no disrespect. I hope you don't mind me asking. What the hell, it don't hurt too ask, does it? She's my buddy, did you know that, Sheriff?"

"She is, is she?"

"Yes, sir. Do you know that one time when I was drunk and being an idiot at the Brewpub, this little lady here put me right down on the floor and handcuffed me and dragged my drunk ass out of there? That's the truth, Sheriff, I swear." Levi raised his right hand up, palm forward. "If I'm lyin', I'm dyin'."

"Yeah, I heard about that," Weber said.

Under normal circumstances Robyn wouldn't have appreciated the "little lady" comment, but for some reason she had developed a certain fondness for Levi. Yes, he drank too much, and yes, sometimes he got rowdy. But in spite of all that, he had a steady job and a good heart. After Robyn had taken him down that night at the Brewpub, he always spoke highly of her in spite of the fact that his buddies razzed him for a long time about being arrested by the little lady with the pink handcuffs.

"Hey, if I can't kiss the bride, can I at least shake her hand?"

"Yeah, I think that's okay," Robyn told him.

He ceremoniously took her hand and shook it, then turned to Weber and fist bumped the sheriff.

"So, what are we going to do with you, Levi? You know you shouldn't be drinking and driving."

"Who, me? I'm not driving, I'm standing here talkin' to you. Did you see me drive?"

Weber looked to Robyn, who shook her head and said, "To be honest, I didn't see him drive in, Jimmy."

"Well, he damn sure didn't fly here," Weber said.

"No, but if I didn't see him driving and you didn't see him driving…"

"Yeah, okay," Weber said. "We've got a couple of choices here, Levi. We don't have grounds to arrest you right now, but as soon as you get in that truck and start it up, we do. I don't think any of us wants to see that happen, do we?"

Levi burped again, a nasty smell of stale beer and something he had eaten at some time in the last couple of hours. "I don't know about you, but I don't want that to happen."

"Are you still living at your trailer?"

"Yes, sir. Hey, how come you never come by to hang out with me?"

"I don't know, Levi. I guess because I'm busy a lot."

"Well, you should. I could fire up the grill and throw some brats on it and we could have a few beers."

"Yeah, we'll have to do that sometime," Weber said, knowing it would never happen, and knowing that Levi wouldn't remember the invitation when he woke up the next day. "In the meantime, how about if I drive you home and park your truck in your driveway, and you promise me you won't go out anymore tonight."

"Sorry, can't do that," Levi said shaking his head.

"Why not?"

"Because I need to get some more beer. Can't sit home with no beer, can I?

"I'm not sure you need any more beer, Levi."

"Can't never have too much beer, Sheriff."

Weber sighed, trying to be patient and ignoring the smirk Robyn was giving him.

"Okay, go inside and get your beer then come out and I'll take you home. Fair enough?"

"You're a good man, Sheriff Weber. You're a damn good man. And anybody says otherwise is gonna hafta answer to me!"

"Yeah, that's good to know. I appreciate that, Levi. But we've had a long day and we're tired, so go inside and get your beer and I'll take you home, okay?"

It was only a couple of miles to Levi's house, but it was long enough for him to tell Weber what a great buddy he was, how lucky he was to find a fox like Robyn, to apologize for calling Robyn a fox and to assure the sheriff he had meant no disrespect, and to tell Weber they needed to go fishing together sometime because he knew of a couple of good honey holes in the lake where they would pull in some big ones. Once Weber got him to his mobile home and safely inside, he took the pickup's keys and left a note on the table telling Levi he could come to the sheriff's office in the morning and retrieve them. He thought about telling him about the note, but he was pretty sure Levi wouldn't remember by the next day.

He looked at Levi, who had crashed face down on his tattered old sofa and was off to dreamland. Weber shook his head, wondering why a hard working, basically decent young man like him couldn't stay off the booze and out of trouble. But then Weber remembered that he, too, had once had a problem with alcohol and the words, "there but for the grace of God go I." He locked the door behind him and went out to where Robyn was waiting for him in her Mustang.

"Thank you, Jimmy," she said when he got in beside her. "I knew we could have run him in, but for some reason I like the damn fool. Hopefully he won't be out getting in any more trouble tonight."

"He passed out on the couch the minute I got him in the door. Let's make a quick pass through town and drop his keys off with the dispatcher before we head home."

At the office, he gave the dispatcher the keys and told her to make sure that Mary got them first thing in the morning, then told her they were calling it a night and heading for home. "Get some rest, Sheriff," Judy Troutman said as he went out the door. At the time, neither Weber nor the dispatcher knew that they would be talking again within the next couple of hours.

231

Chapter 37

They were cuddled together, sound asleep, when the dispatcher called.

"If that's your girlfriend calling, tell her you're married and to leave you alone," Robyn mumbled. "And if it's my boyfriend, tell him to call back in the morning."

Weber answered the phone and he could tell by the tone of Judy's voice that something bad had happened. But he had no idea just how bad it would be until she told him.

"Sheriff, you need to get to the Mullins' place. He just shot a ninja."

Still half asleep, Weber wasn't sure he understood what Judy was telling him. "What are you talking about? What happened?"

"I just got a 911 call. Tracy Mullins said a ninja broke into their house and her husband shot him. I've got units and an ambulance responding."

"I'm on my way," Weber told her, pulling on his clothes before he even put the telephone down.

"What's going on?"

Robyn was sitting up in bed, a sheet pulled to her waist but bare breasted.

"Doug Mullins just shot a ninja."

"Damn! I was hoping this stuff was over," Robyn said, springing out of bed and getting dressed as she spoke. "Do you think it was one of those two kids again?"

"No, I said all along that the two things were not connected," Weber said.

They were out the door and racing toward town with the light bar on top of Weber's Explorer and the blue lights in the grill flashing while the siren screamed out a warning to anything that might be in their path. Weber didn't even think about the elk he had hit recently or that there were plenty more of them in the forest around Big Lake.

By the time they got to the Mullins house the circular driveway in front was filled with emergency vehicles. They went in without knocking to find Rusty Heinz doing CPR on Doug Mullins on the living room floor while Pat Price was holding a pair of defibrillator paddles. Sweat dripped off of Rusty's bald head and his face was red from exertion.

"Let me try again," Pat said and Rusty raised his hands. Pat put the paddles on Doug's bare chest, called "clear" and shocked him. The unconscious man's body spasmed and then was still again. Pat pulled the paddles off and looked at Weber, shaking his head while Rusty resumed CPR.

"What happened here?"

"It was terrible, Sheriff," Tracy said, holding her husband's hand in both of hers. "I was sound asleep and I woke up when I heard Doug yelling at somebody. This crazy person was standing in the hallway with a sword. I don't know where Doug got the gun. I didn't even know he had a gun! The next thing I knew, he shot him and yelled for me to call 911."

"It was a ninja?"

"I… I guess so. He was wearing all black and he had a sword, just like Doug described the first time it happened."

"Where is he?"

"In the hallway."

Tracy looked down at her husband and begged, "Doug, don't you leave me! Come on, baby, come back to me!"

Weber went to the hallway, where he saw Dan Wright and Chad Summers standing over a body dressed all in black that was laying on its left side. A long sword was on the floor next to the body. A large and messy hole in its back signified the exit wound from a heavy caliber firearm. "What have we got, guys?"

"I checked for a pulse and there wasn't one. Then I backed off. We didn't want to mess with anything until Buz and Dolan got here to process the scene," Chad said.

The two experienced deputies were well schooled in crime scene investigations and Weber knew Chad, himself a veteran of many years with the Sheriff's Department, had done the right thing. Based on what he knew already, there was no question in his mind that it was a justifiable shooting in self-defense, but they always wanted to make sure all the i's were dotted and the t's crossed.

"Did you get a statement from Tracy yet?"

"No, sorry, Jimmy. When we got here Doug was out there on the living room floor and she was frantic. I performed CPR, hoping to get him breathing, while Dan made sure the house was secure. Once the paramedics got here, I went to help Dan."

"What a mess," Weber said.

"How's Doug doing?"

"I don't think it's good. I'm not sure they're going to be able to bring him back."

Just then they heard a loud wail from the living room and Tracy screaming, "Don't die on me, Doug. Please, baby, don't die!"

Weber went back to the living room, where Rusty was still performing CPR, but he could tell the paramedic was just going through the motions at that point. Pat wheeled a stretcher in and Weber and Chad helped move Doug onto it.

"Please, please don't die, Doug. Please don't."

They started out the door, Tracy holding onto her husband's hand, not willing to let go, not willing to give up yet. But Weber could tell by the grim look on the paramedics' faces that it was too late. They loaded Doug into the back of the ambulance and Tracy got in with Rusty, who was still performing CPR while Pat sped away toward the Medical Center, lights and siren clearing the path.

Dolan and Buz had arrived and he pointed them toward the hallway. After taking photographs from every angle they could in the narrow confines of the hallway, they rolled the body onto its back. They took more photographs and then Dolan said, "Let's see who this clown is."

He removed the hood and mask combination from the body and studied the face, then looked up and asked, "Do any of you know this guy?"

None of them could identify the dead man. He looked to be in his mid to late 20s, with sandy brown hair and a sparse mustache and beard. Weber noted a large caliber bullet hole in the center of his chest that was covered with blood. Even though they couldn't see it because of the dark clothing he wore, the smell and the damp puddle on the floor told them that the dead man's bladder had released when he died.

"Does he have any identification on him?"

Dolan patted the body down and shook his head. "Apparently ninjas don't have pockets. I can't find anything."

Weber pulled his phone from his pocket and took a picture of the man's face, knowing it might be necessary to share with the news media to identify him. Then he called Robyn's name and told her, "I need you to go to Judge Ryman's place. Tell him you're sorry to wake him up, but we need a search warrant signed."

"I found the weapon," Buz said from the bedroom, holding up a Taurus .357 magnum revolver with a pencil through the trigger guard. "It was laying on the floor next to the bed."

Weber went out in the hallway again and looked at the walls and ceiling. "I think the bullet ended up there," he said pointing at a hole in the wall opposite the bedroom doorway.

"Yeah, I saw that, and I've got pictures," Dolan told him.

It seemed like every deputy in the Department was there by then, called in from home to deal with such a major crime. Once they knew the house was secure and that there were no other intruders hiding anywhere, Weber moved everybody outside to await the search warrant. Though it was an active crime scene, he knew that in a major case like this they needed to do everything by the book.

It only took Robyn half an hour to drive to the judge's house, wake him up, get a search warrant signed, and get back. More than once Weber had been grateful that they had a judge who trusted the Sheriff's Department and did not force them to jump through endless bureaucratic hoops to get their job done.

While Tommy and Archer directed traffic and kept the curious crowd back behind the line of yellow police tape surrounding the crime scene, Coop and Dan searched the outside of the property, looking for any clues.

Back inside, Buz asked, "So, who is this guy? And why the hell was he trying to kill Doug, of all people?"

"I don't know," Weber said. "But we're damn sure going to find out."

"According to what I could get out of Tracy, she was asleep and woke up when she heard Doug yelling at somebody. She could see a dark shape in the bedroom doorway, and the next thing she knew there was a shot. They turned on the light and found this guy here in the hall."

"Well, whoever he is, he won't be bothering Doug Mullins anymore," Buz said.

Weber's phone rang and he answered it. He listened for a moment and said, "Thanks for letting me know." He ended the call and said, "Unfortunately, nobody will be bothering Doug anymore. The EMTs did all they could, but he was DOA when they got him to the Medical Center."

"Oh man, that sucks," Dolan said.

"Yes, it does."

"I'm a little bit confused," Dan said. "Was Mr. Mullins injured by the ninja, or did his heart give out?"

"Looks like it was his heart," Weber told him. "The poor guy was in bad shape already, and every time the ninja came after him, it caused more stress. And then that thing with his brakes going out and the accident, none of that helped. I think this was the straw that broke the camel's back. But either way, he knew he was living on borrowed time."

"Hell of a way for a good guy like him to go out. Sometimes life just doesn't seem fair, does it?"

"No, Dolan, it doesn't. I can't count the times I've asked myself why a nice person like Doug dies and yet some maggot who is always out abusing people and doing bad shit lives."

"Hey, Jimmy, can you come here a minute?"

Weber walked out to the living room, where Robyn was standing in the doorway.

"Jessica Norton is here. She says she's related to the Mullins."

Weber followed her outside to the crime scene tape that was holding the crowd of neighbors and gawkers back.

"Is it true, Sheriff? Did someone break in and kill Doug?"

Weber lifted the tape and waved her forward, walking away to be out of earshot of others.

"Someone broke in and there was a shooting."

"Oh my God! He killed Doug?"

"It wasn't Doug that was shot. Doug shot the intruder. Then he apparently had a heart attack. The paramedics did all they could, but he was gone by the time they got him to the hospital."

"No! Oh God, no!"

"I'm sorry," Weber said.

"What about Tracy? Is she okay?"

"She wasn't injured. She's at the hospital with Doug."

"I have to go there! I have to go be with her."

"I understand that," Weber told her. "But first, can I ask you to look at something?"

"Please tell me it's not a dead body. I'm sorry, but I'm kind of squeamish."

"Actually, all I need you to do is look at a photograph of the person's face, to see if you know who it was who broke in."

"Will there be any blood?"

"No, I promise. It's just a face of somebody who looks like they're sleeping."

"Okay," Jessica said hesitantly.

Weber took out his phone and pulled up the picture of the dead man inside the house.

"Have you ever seen this man before?"

The woman studied the picture, seeming to relax a bit when she realized there was no gore showing. She shook her head. "No, I don't remember ever seeing anybody who looks like that."

"When was the last time you talked to Doug or Tracy?"

"Just this evening. I came by to drop off some peanut butter cookies I made. They were always Doug's...." Her voice broke and she had to swallow hard and wiped tears away before she could continue. "They were always Doug's favorite. Tracy didn't like him eating too many sweets, with his health problems and all, but he kept saying what was the difference, he was going to die anyway. So they compromised and he would eat one, maybe two cookies every day or so." She started crying again and Weber gave her a moment to compose herself before she continued. "I just can't believe he's gone. I don't know what Tracy's going to do without him. They loved each other so much."

"I know you guys were close, even after you and Todd got divorced," Weber said.

At the mention of her ex-husband's name, Jessica frowned. "I heard that fool shot himself. Would I be a terrible person if I said I wish it was him that died instead of Doug? I know that sounds horrible, but…"

"It's not horrible to think that way," Weber assured her. "Just a few minutes ago I was telling my deputies that I wonder how life can be so unfair. That we can lose good people, but yet bad people seem to stick around forever."

"That's so true, Sheriff."

"Jessica, I know you want to get to the hospital, and you need to be there for Tracy. But before you go, do you know of anybody who would want to hurt Doug?"

"Oh God, no! He was one of the nicest guys I've ever known. When Todd and I were going through our divorce and he was acting so shitty to me, Doug and Tracy were right there for me. They gave me a place to stay, they kept telling me that everything was going to be okay and reassuring me I wasn't the bad guy. And at that time, I really needed to hear that because Todd spent so much time telling me I was stupid and fat and an idiot and worthless. But those two kept pumping me up, telling me I was a good person and I deserved to be happy."

"Did they say anything to you about this whole ninja business?"

"Yeah. It had them both freaked out. Doug was already under so much stress, knowing how little time he had left, and he was obsessed with making things better for Tracy after he was gone. She kept trying to get him to slow down, but he just wouldn't do it. Then this whole ninja stuff started and it was like he was looking in six directions at once, afraid of what was going to happen next. They kept asking themselves who they could have made so mad that they would try to hurt him like that."

"Did they have any ideas who it might be?"

"No. That's the thing, there's nobody in the world who could want to cause Doug any kind of harm. He was nice to everybody, he ran his business on the up and up, and he was always doing something for somebody. Not for any money, just because that's the kind of guy he was."

Weber had heard those stories about Doug Mullins himself and knew they were true. From putting up a dog run at SafeHaven to building a ramp for an elderly woman in a wheelchair, and more things than Weber could count, Doug Mullins had always exhibited the very picture of being a good citizen and a good neighbor.

"Okay, Jessica, that's all I need. Will you be okay to drive to the hospital, or do I need to have someone take you?"

"No, I'll be okay."

"All right," Weber said. "I'll be along in just a few minutes to talk to Tracy. I may need to ask you some questions later."

"If there's anything I can do to help you find out who's responsible for all of this, just let me know, Sheriff."

Chapter 38

Weber spent a few more minutes at the crime scene, but knowing his deputies had everything under control and were more than capable of investigating on their own, he drove to the Medical Center. On the way he saw the ambulance coming back in the opposite direction and he flashed his lights to flag them down.

"I'm sorry, Sheriff," Pat Price said from across the cab when Weber leaned on the open window on the passenger's side of the ambulance. "We did everything we could. I think he was already gone when we got there."

"Sometimes it works out that way," Weber said. "How you doing, Rusty?"

They had turned on the interior light in the cab and Weber could tell that the paramedic was having a hard time of it. In a small town where everybody knew everybody, first responders often found themselves trying to save the lives of people they knew well and were sometimes friends or family members of. They learned to put a hard shell around themselves so they could perform their jobs and still stay sane. But sometimes that shell cracked. Weber had experienced it himself on more than one occasion. He had seen in his deputies, and now he was seeing it in the paramedic.

"You okay, guy?"

"Not really," Rusty said closing his eyes and looking upward. "I tried, Jimmy. I tried so hard."

Tears were rolling down his face and Weber put a comforting hand on his arm.

"I know you did, buddy. But I think it's like Pat said, he was probably gone when you guys got there."

"There are times when I hate this job," Rusty said. "Times like this, I wonder what good I'm doing? Am I really accomplishing anything out here?"

"Rusty, look at me."

The man kept his eyes closed and shook his head.

"Rusty, look at me," Weber said firmly.

He turned his head and opened his eyes and Weber could see the pain in them.

"I know how you're feeling. I've asked myself the same questions a million times. Believe me, I have. But you have to look at the successes. What was it, a week or two ago that you guys pulled that little girl out of the lake? We thought she was gone, but you got to her in time and brought her back. Last week when Eloise McConnell fell and broke her hip, you guys got her to the hospital before she laid there and maybe died all by herself. I've seen the good you do, what both of you guys do. Those successes are what you have to focus on, Rusty. Yeah, you're going to lose one now and then. It sucks, but that's the way it is. You and I both know that. And it sucks even worse when it's a nice guy like Doug Mullins. But a lot of people are alive today because of what you do. This community needs you on the job. *I* need you on the job."

Rusty nodded his head, unable to speak, but he put his hand on Weber's and squeezed. They stayed that way for a long moment, communicating without speaking. Then Rusty pulled his hand back and said, "I guess we'd better go pick up the dead guy if your deputies are done."

"You may have a bit of a wait, but hopefully it won't be too long," Weber told him. He stepped back from the ambulance and Pat nodded at him, then put it in gear and drove away. Watching the boxy vehicle go down the road until its lights disappeared in the darkness, Weber looked up toward the stars and wondered himself why life was so unfair.

~~~***~~~

Dr. Patel, looking tired and somewhat defeated, nodded at him when he came down the hallway.

"How are you doing, Doctor?"

"It's been a rough shift. Six broken bones, a bad case of sunburn, an attack of appendicitis, somebody cut two of his fingers off with a power saw, and then Mr. Mullins. Tell me again, Sheriff, why did I come here to get away from the big city?"

"Because we need you," Weber told her.

She smiled tiredly at him.

"How is Mrs. Mullins doing?"

"She's taking it very hard. Her sister-in-law is with her, and I gave her a sedative to try to help her calm down a little bit. She keeps saying it's all a bad dream. She keeps saying that she just wants to wake up and have it all be different."

"I know that feeling," Weber told her. "Right now, I feel the same way."

"I understand someone was shot at the Mullins house."

"Yeah, but there's nothing you can do for him. It looks like he was killed instantly."

"I don't understand any of this, Sheriff. This whole ninja thing… it's like something out of a bad movie."

"It is," Weber agreed. "We're just trying to sort it all out. Can I see Mrs. Mullins now?"

"Certainly."

She let him down the hallway to an examining room where Tracy was standing slumped over the bed, holding her husband's body. Jessica Norton stood beside her, her hand on her sister-in-law's back, murmuring comforting words. Words that Weber knew were well intended but probably not even heard.

"Tracy, I'm so sorry to bother you right now," Weber said. "But I have to ask you some questions."

"Wake up, Doug. Please wake up," she sobbed.

"Come on, honey. Sit down here, okay?"

Jessica gently tried to pull Tracy away from the dead man and guide her to a chair at his bedside, but the grieving woman shook her off.

"No! No, I can't let go of him. I can't!" She shook her husband's body and wailed, "Wake up, Doug. Please, please, just wake up!"

Jessica tried again, and with Weber's help they were able to get Tracy into a chair. Weber knelt down in front of her and took her hands in his. "Tracy, I am so sorry. I know this is the worst night of your life, and I hate to have to make it harder for you, but I have to ask you some questions. It's very important."

She stared at him as if she was unable to comprehend his words.

"Tracy, can you tell me what happened tonight."

"Huh?"

"I need to know what happened at your house tonight. Can you tell me?"

"I was asleep," she said dully. "Doug went to bed first, about 10:30 I guess. I watched the rest of the news and then I went to bed. I must've fallen right asleep, because I don't remember anything else until I heard Doug yelling at somebody. I sat up and Doug was standing next to the bed. And there was somebody..." She broke down and began crying again. Weber looked at Jessica and could tell by the pained look in her eyes that she was suffering, too.

Finally, Tracy managed to speak again, saying, "Somebody was standing in the bedroom doorway."

"Could you see who it was, Tracy?"

She shook her head. "There was a night light on in the hallway, but all I could see was a big black shadow."

"Did he say anything? Anything at all?"

"I don't think so. If he did, I'd remember. All I remember is Doug yelling at him, asking him why. And then he shot him. I didn't even know he had a gun! Where did he get a gun? I don't think Doug ever shot a gun before in his life!"

"We'll figure that part out," Weber told her. "What happened after Doug shot this person?"

"I don't know. It all happened so fast. One minute I was sound asleep and the next minute I was awake and there was yelling and then Doug shot him."

"Please, try to remember," Weber said. "It's important."

She closed her eyes, reliving the horrible scene in her head. "I think I turned on the light on the nightstand. I'm not really sure. Why can't I remember that?"

"It's okay. Just tell me what you can remember, Tracy."

"The light came on and there was this man laying there in the hallway."

"Did he say anything that you can remember?"

"I don't think so. Wait, I think he maybe moaned or groaned or something. It wasn't words, just sound. I remember Doug saying to call 911, then he went out to the living room. I didn't want him to go, but he said he had to make sure nobody else was there. I kept calling his name and he didn't answer. Then I…" She gulped and Weber wondered if she was going to throw up, but she was able to continue. "I heard this noise, this loud noise like something getting knocked over. I was afraid of the person on the floor. I didn't know if he was alive or dead, and I kept calling Doug and he wouldn't answer. So I got past the person and ran down the hall. That's when I saw Doug. He was on the floor and he wasn't moving. I kept shaking him and trying to get him to wake up, but…" She began crying again and couldn't continue.

Jessica, sitting beside her, put her arm around Tracy and pulled her close, the two women crying together.

"Mrs. Mullins. Tracy. Tracy, I'm sorry, but we need to take Doug into the other room now."

"No! No, please don't take him!"

"It's okay," Jessica said. "It's okay, honey. Let them do what they have to do."

"No," Tracy shrieked, jumping up and throwing her arms around her husband's body again. "Please don't take him. Not yet! Please, just a little more time."

Dr. Patel looked at Weber and subtly shook her head. They both knew there was never a time when a grieving spouse or parent was ready to let go. But they both knew it had to be done.

"Tracy, we are all going to go out in the hallway for a few minutes and let you have some time with Doug," the doctor said. "Okay? We'll be right outside the door."

They left her there to say her goodbyes, knowing that a few minutes or a few hours or a few days would never be enough.

Chapter 39

Weber called Chad and asked if they had been able to find any information about the dead man.

"Not yet, Jimmy. We looked for two or three blocks around and haven't been able to find a car that doesn't belong. If his fingerprints aren't on file somewhere, I think we're going to have to release his picture to the media to see if anybody recognizes him."

"Okay, keep doing your thing," Weber said.

Not knowing what else to do, he took a long shot and drove to Wayne Odell's house. It was still dark out, but there was a hint of a glow to the east. He had to knock several times on the door of the small wood framed house before a light came on and he heard someone moving inside.

"Who is it?"

"It's Sheriff Weber, Wayne."

The porch light came on and the door opened. Wayne, looking half-asleep, was wearing a pair of Levi's and was barefooted and bare chested.

"What's going on, Sheriff?"

"I'm sorry to wake you at this hour, but I really need to talk to your son."

"Coulter? Don't tell me he's slipped out and done something else. I swear, if he did I'm going to nail his window shut and put some kind of lock on the door he can't get open."

"No, it's nothing like that," Weber said, though for a minute he wondered if that was true. The way things are going down, he wasn't sure about anything anymore. "I just need to ask him a couple of questions."

"Okay." Wayne stepped back and waved Weber in, then led him across the small living room to a closed door and knocked on it. "Coulter. Coulter, wake up."

He opened the door and the bedroom was small, like the rest of the house. A single bed and a nightstand that didn't match, a beaten up old chest of drawers, and a shelf made of cinderblocks and wooden planks that held a cheap stereo, some model airplanes and one of the Starship *Enterprise,* and a few books. Coulter was sleeping on his stomach, wearing just white undershorts, and had pushed the sheet off his body. One leg dangled off the side of the bed.

"Coulter, wake up," his father said, shaking the boy's foot.

Coulter mumbled something but didn't respond beyond that.

"Coulter, wake up," his father said again, louder, and shook his foot vigorously.

"What? What?"

"Wake up, son. The sheriff is here and he needs to talk to you."

The boy rolled over and sat up in bed, bleary eyed and confused.

"What's going on?"

"Are you awake, Coulter?"

"Sheriff?" The boy blinked, trying to comprehend what was happening.

"Coulter, are you awake? I need to talk to you," Weber said.

He blinked his eyes again, then rubbed them with the heels of his hands. "What's happening?"

"Are you awake?"

"Yeah, I guess so."

"What's my name?"

"Your name?"

"Yes, Coulter. Do you know my name?"

"Sheriff Weber."

"Where are you?"

"Huh? I'm at home."

Deciding the boy was awake enough to answer his questions, Weber took out his phone and showed Coulter the picture of the intruder at the Mullins house.

"Coulter, do you know who this is?"

The boy looked at the image on the screen and shook his head.

"I need you to look real careful, and I need you to think real hard," Weber told him, "because this is very important. Are you sure you don't know who this man is?"

Coulter took the phone and studied it, then shook his head again. "No, I've never seen him before."

"Are you absolutely sure?"

"Yeah, I'm sure. What's going on?" A look of panic crossed his face and he asked, "Is Amy, okay?"

"She's fine," Weber told him. "Besides you and Amy, was anybody else involved with this ninja stuff you two were doing? Anybody else?"

"No, it was just us."

"Are you sure, Coulter? You're not covering up for any other friends?"

The boy frowned and said, "I don't have any friends except Amy. Everybody else in this town treats me like shit."

If the boy's father had a problem with his language, he didn't say anything. Instead he asked, "Sheriff, what's going on? I know Coulter hasn't been out of the house. I've been keeping a close eye on him after that crap he pulled."

Instead of answering the father, Weber addressed the boy again. "Coulter, do you know a man named Doug Mullins?"

"Who?"

"Mullins. Doug Mullins."

"I think I've heard the name. Wait. Is that the guy the ninja tried to kill?"

"Yes. That's who I'm talking about."

"No, I don't know him. I mean, I know who he is because everybody in town was talking about the ninja coming after him. But I've never seen him."

"Are you absolutely sure?"

"Yeah, I'm sure. I swear to God, Sheriff, me and Amy were just goofing around. We never tried to hurt nobody and we never knew that guy that the ninja tried to kill."

"Sheriff, I want to know what's going on," Wayne said.

"Unfortunately, somebody dressed as a ninja broke into the Mullins house in the middle of the night," Weber said.

"Oh, my God. Is Doug okay?"

"No, unfortunately not. He shot the intruder and then he had a heart attack. Both of them died. This fellow here in the picture, he's the one that broke in."

"That's crazy. That's just absolutely crazy." Wayne looked at his son and the expression on his face told Weber that he was not going to tolerate any nonsense or deception. "Coulter, you listen to me and you listen good. If you know anything at all about this, you tell the sheriff right now. I mean it, don't be trying to cover for your girlfriend or anybody else."

"I don't, Dad. I promise, I don't. Amy would never hurt anybody, and neither would I."

"I swear, Coulter, if you're lying to me…"

"Dad, I'm not. I'm not!"

"Okay. I believe you," Weber said. "Wayne, I'm sorry to bother you about something like this so early in the morning, but we just need to get to the bottom of it."

"I understand. Jesus, I didn't know Doug well, but sometimes he would be putting up fences at a new place where I was installing the garage doors and we would talk once in a while. He always seemed like such a nice guy."

"He was a nice guy. We're just trying to figure out who wanted him dead. And why."

They had left Coulter in his bedroom and were back in the living room. Looking around, Weber could see that nobody had put much effort into decorating the house. The furnishings were modest, and probably secondhand, but it was fairly clean even if it didn't show a woman's touch. He could tell that while Wayne Odell might work long hours and wasn't always at home with his son, the man was doing the best he could.

"Let me get out of your hair," the sheriff said. "Again, I'm sorry to bother you."

"Do you think Coulter and that girl had anything to do with this. Because I've got to be honest with you, Sheriff, I don't see that happening. I mean, I know they were doing that goofy ninja shit. But this... this is a whole different ballgame."

"To be honest with you, I don't think either one of them had anything to do with what happened last night," Weber told him. "I really don't. Yeah, your boy was doing something stupid running around playing ninja, but I don't think he has a mean bone in his body. More than anything, I was hoping he might have seen this guy around."

"If there's anything we can do, Sheriff, anything to help you get to the bottom of this, or to help Doug's wife, you just let me know. I mean it, anything."

"I appreciate that," Weber said, shaking his hand. "Just do one thing for me, if you will, Wayne?"

"Name it."

"Don't be too hard on your boy, okay? I think he's a pretty good kid in spite of what happened."

"I try to be a good father, Sheriff. I do. But I've got to tell you, sometimes it's not easy to know what to do. This sounds terrible, but I never wanted kids. That was my wife's thing. She just knew that having a baby would make her feel complete. So okay, we had a baby. Turns out that wasn't what she wanted. She didn't want me and she didn't want Coulter," Wayne said, looking at his son's closed bedroom door.

Weber knew some of what the man was going through. When his own parents had died in an automobile accident years before, he had taken an early discharge from the Army and came home to finish raising his sixteen year old sister. He knew more than anybody how much effort it took. And he knew that sometimes, no matter what you did or how hard you tried, things did not always work out the way you had hoped.

"You're doing a good job," Weber told him. "I've been in a lot of houses where both parents are there, and they're not doing nearly as well with their kids as you are with your son. Don't beat yourself up over all of this, Wayne. That boy is going to turn out all right. He's got a fine role model."

Chapter 40

It was daylight and the lights were on at the Druzniac house. Sheila opened the door wearing hospital scrubs when he rang the bell.

"Sheriff? What's wrong?"

"I'm sorry to bother you this early," Weber said. "Are you going to work or just getting home?"

"I just walked in the door. What's happening?"

Weber told her what had happened at the Mullins house and explained that he needed to show Amy a picture of the intruder to see if she recognized him."

"I know my daughter is not a little kid, but is this something that's going to traumatize her?"

"There's no blood or anything showing, it's just a face picture," Weber told her, and showed her on his phone.

"That's the guy that's been threatening Doug Mullins?"

"Apparently so."

"Sheila? Who the hell you talkin' to so loud this early in the morning? Can't a man get some sleep in his own damn house?"

She looked toward the sound and Weber saw a fearful expression on her face. "It's nothing, Clark," she said. "I'm sorry to wake you. Go back to sleep."

A moment later a man shuffled down the hall to the living room wearing just flannel pajama bottoms.

"How the hell am I supposed to sleep with all this noise goin' on?" He looked at Weber, then came closer. "Who the hell are you and what are you doin' in my house?"

Weber hadn't bothered to put on a uniform when they got the call about the shooting and was dressed in jeans and a dark blue T-shirt with the word Sheriff emblazoned across the front and back in bold yellow.

"How are you doing, Mr. Druzniac? I'm Sheriff Weber. Sorry to bother you so early in the morning."

By now the man was standing just a few feet away and the smell of alcohol seemed to ooze from every pore of his body. He looked like he hadn't shaved in at least a couple of days, and he smelled like it had been even longer since he had bathed.

"I don't care who you are. I want to know what you're doin' in my house with my wife!"

"It's okay, honey. The sheriff just had to ask me a couple of questions about something."

"I know what's happenin' here. You two think I'm stupid? How long's this been goin' on?"

"Clark, nothing is going on," Sheila said evenly. "Just go back to bed, okay? Like I said, the sheriff just needed to ask me a couple of questions."

"I'm not stupid. You're slippin' the pork to my wife, ain't you?"

"It's nothing like that," Weber told him. "Like she said, I need to ask her some questions about an investigation. That's all. Now, why don't you go back to bed like she told you to do?"

"You go to hell, you son of a bitch! You can't come in my house and tell me what to do while you're screwin' my wife behind my back. Yeah, Sheila, that's right. I know what's goin' on. You keep sayin' you're workin' extra shifts, but that's all bullshit. I want to know how long you've been cheatin' on me."

"Clark, nothing is going on. How many times do I have to tell you…"

She never got to finish, because her husband backhanded her across the face, sending her reeling backward, where she tripped over a footstool and fell to the floor.

"There, bitch. Take that. And there's a lot more where that came from, you no good slut. I'm goin' to…"

Whatever Clark Druzniac wanted to tell his wife about what he was going to do, he never got the chance. Weber grabbed the man and spun him around, forcing his face into the wall and pulling his right arm up behind him.

"That's enough! That stuff ends right now," Weber said.

"Let go of me!"

Weber pushed the man's face against the wall and pulled upward on his arm, getting a howl of pain in response. "Stop resisting."

"You can't…"

Weber pulled on his arm again and the man screamed, "You're breakin' my damn arm!"

"You're lucky I don't break it off and beat you with it," Weber said. He pulled his handcuffs from his belt and locked one end around the man's right wrist, then pulled his left arm behind him and locked it as well.

Sitting on the floor wiping blood from her nose and split lips, Sheila watched her husband being handcuffed with wide eyes. The look on her face was one the sheriff knew well. He had seen it on women living in run down house trailers where he had to be careful of stepping on toddlers in diapers playing with dogs on dirty floors, and he had seen it on the faces of women who drove expensive imported sportscars and spent their summers in lavish summer homes with stainless steel appliances in the kitchen along with all of the latest high tech gadgets. Abuse knew no economic boundaries.

And every time he saw it, Weber had to remind himself that he was there as a neutral third party. It was his job to end the abuse and seek justice for the victims through the legal system. But that didn't mean that there were not times he wished he could deal out a little one on one justice, too. He knew it was wrong, but he had stepped over that line a time or two. And right now he wanted nothing more than to take the handcuffs off of Clark Druzniac and see how well the drunken loser could handle hitting a man instead of a woman.

Weber was tired and angry and frustrated, and he came very close to doing exactly that, but then Amy stepped into the living room wearing loose fitting pajamas with some kind of pink flowers on them, rubbing sleep from her eyes and asked, "Mom, what's going on?"

~~~***~~~

"I can't tell you how many times Pete has been tempted to do the same thing," Mary Caitlin said, referring to her husband, Big Lake's retired sheriff and Weber's predecessor. "I never understood why Sheila would put up with that kind of abuse from him. Clark has always been a good for nothing, and when he gets on a roll you can hear him ranting and raving clear over at our place. Poor Sheila, she tries so hard, and all he does is drink, raise hell, and cause trouble for her."

"Well, he won't be bothering her for a while at least."

"Are Sheila and Amy okay?"

"Yeah. They were both a little shaken up by it, but they'll be okay. She tried to get me to let him go, kept saying he was just upset because we woke him up. But I explained to her that she doesn't have any choice in the matter. Under state law, I can't ignore domestic abuse. Especially not when it happens right in front of me."

"That's so damn typical," Mary said, shaking her head. "We see that time and time again with abused women. And over and over we arrest them and they get out and the same thing happens again."

Weber knew that was true and had had several conversations with Christine Ridgway at SafeHaven about it. Christine had tried to explain it by saying, "Sometimes the devil you know is better than the devil you don't know." It was a sad phenomenon that allowed the cycle of abuse to continue.

"How is Tracy Mullins doing?"

"She's having a hard time of it," Weber said. "That's to be expected."

"This whole thing is so crazy. I just can't imagine why anybody would do something like that."

"It makes no sense to me, either," Weber said. "I have not found one person, Mary, not one person, who ever had a bad word to say about Doug. Everybody liked him, everybody had some story about how he helped them or somebody else out with some problem without ever being asked to. If you can accurately describe a person as a saint, it was Doug Mullins."

"Did Coulter Odell or Amy recognize the guy that Doug shot?"

"No, neither one of them did. Once I got Clark out in the back of my Explorer and secured him, I went back in to talk to Amy. Her and Sheila were pretty shaken up, obviously, but she said she never saw the guy before. I don't have any reason to doubt either one of them."

"Maybe we'll get something off of fingerprints," Mary said hopefully.

The office door opened and Buz came in, looking worn out, as Weber knew all of his deputies were. As he himself was.

"What's going on, Buz?"

"I had Mary call some of our Citizen Volunteers to come out and help with crowd control at the Mullins house and sent a couple of guys home to get some rest."

"Good call," Weber said. "I should've thought of that."

"I went to the hospital and did a gunshot residue test on Doug's hands, and on Tracy's. Both tested positive, Doug more so than her. I'm sure some transferred onto her hands because she was holding his while the paramedics were working on him. I know I should have bagged him right then, Jimmy, but she was already doing it when I got there."

"That's okay, I don't have any reason to doubt her story. Do you?"

"No, I think the shooting happened just like she said."

There was a look on his deputy's face. It was a look Weber had seen before and had come to trust. Something was bothering Buz, no question about that.

"What is it?"

"Huh?"

"You've got something on your mind, Buz. What is it?"

"I'm not sure, Jimmy. I keep going over this whole thing in my head, trying to figure out how something this crazy could happen in a town like Big Lake. And not only happen here, but happen to Doug Mullins, of all people. Why?"

"I don't know why, yet, Buz. But it's our job to find out."

"Once they got the dead guy to the hospital, I took his fingerprints. I'm going to run them through the system and see if I can identify him."

"Let me know what you find out," Weber said. "I'm going to head back to the house and see if the guys there came up with anything."

Chapter 41

Coop's eyes were a spider web of red veins that looked like a roadmap of Texas. He took the coffee Weber handed him and sank down on the couch in the Mullins living room while the rest of his exhausted deputies took a break to drink their coffee and eat the breakfast burritos the sheriff had brought.

"You guys look like I feel," Weber said.

"Then they ought to bury all of us," Dolan Reed replied.

"How's Tracy?"

"When I saw her at the hospital she was falling apart, Robyn," Weber told her. "Her sister-in-law's there with her. Man, I feel for that lady. Her and Doug were so close. I know that with his health condition they knew it could happen any minute, but is anybody ever really prepared for that?"

Coop and Dolan exchanged looks and Weber could tell there was something on their minds.

"What is it, guys?"

"Well, Jimmy, things just don't add up here," Coop said.

"What do you mean?"

"Come with me, I want to show you something."

Weber followed him out to the attached garage off the kitchen, where Tracy's Honda was parked. It was a small garage, with just enough room for the car and a cluttered workbench along one wall that held an assortment of tools. There was an open window above the workbench.

"Tracy said the house was locked up. She said ever since the ninja attacks started, Doug was a fanatic about keeping the doors locked. She said he got up two or three times a night just to be sure."

"I remember somebody saying something about that a while back," Weber said. "I remembered thinking then that there was a time when nobody around here ever locked their doors. Especially people who had been here a long time like Doug and Tracy. I think I said to Robyn later that it was one more example of how much Big Lake has changed."

"Yeah, well, the perp had to get in some way, and if all the doors were locked, I wondered if the garage might be how he did it. And I came out here and this window was open."

"Okay. And?"

"Think about it, Jimmy. If Doug was so worried about security, and he damn sure had a right to be, why would he keep making sure all the doors in the house were locked but leave this window open?"

"You're thinking that's how the perp got in?"

"Unless he just appeared like magic, how else did he do it?"

"That makes sense," Weber said.

"I'm not sure it does. Look here, Jimmy," Coop said, stepping back a few feet. "See all the tools on top of the workbench?"

It looked like even though Doug Mullins was well respected in town for his honesty, his integrity when doing business, and his kindness to others, he may not have been as conscientious about his own workbench. There was a hammer, several screwdrivers, a few nuts and bolts and some other things littering the top of the bench. Weber's father had always taught him to put a tool away when he was done with it, a habit that he had carried on to adulthood, but the sheriff knew not everybody did things like he did.

"Now, come here and look at this," Coop said, and they walked back up to the workbench. His deputy pointed at the windowsill. "See that dust? It looks like this window has been closed a long time. See all the stuff on top of the bench right here under the window? Tell me, Jimmy, how does somebody open a window in a house that is supposedly completely secured, how do they crawl through that window without leaving any kind of indication they did in that dust, and how do they get from the window across the bench and down onto the floor without knocking something over? Something like this little tray of washers, or one of those tools?"

"What are you saying, Coop?"

"I'm not saying, I'm asking, Jimmy. And once the perp was inside the garage, what about the kitchen door? The front and back door were both locked. Why wasn't the kitchen door?"

"I don't know. Maybe Doug figured that if the garage was locked and the window was down, that was enough."

"Was it, Jimmy?"

"Obviously not."

Before coming to Big Lake, Coop had spent 20 years as an Army MP, many of them as a special investigator. The experience and skills he brought to the Sheriff's Department had been a major asset to the organization.

"Tell me what you're thinking, Coop."

"I don't know what I'm thinking, Jimmy. But whoever that dead guy is, I don't believe that he gained access to the house through that window or through this garage."

"Did you find a key on him? Any kind of lock pick or anything?"

"He didn't have a thing on him, Jimmy. I reminded Buz to look through all of his clothes once they had him stripped at the hospital, and he didn't find anything. Not so much as a paperclip."

"But yet he got in this place somehow."

"Yeah, Jimmy, he did."

~~~***~~~

Jessica had taken Tracy to her small apartment when they left the hospital, and when Weber knocked on the door, she put her

finger to her lips and stepped out into the hallway, closing the door
behind her.

"I couldn't get her to leave the hospital. Even after they took
Doug away, she just wouldn't leave. That doctor finally gave her
a shot, and by the time I got her here, she was having trouble
keeping her eyes open. She's finally sleeping."

"Good. That's the best thing she can do right now," Weber
said. "How are you holding up?"

Jessica folded her arms under her breasts and shuddered like
she was cold, even though the day was already warming up. "I
don't know, to be honest with you. I kind of feel numb. Like I'm
sleepwalking or something."

"That's a common reaction in situations like this. I need to ask
you some questions if you're up to it, Jessica."

"Sure. Can we talk out here? My apartment isn't very big and
I don't want to wake Tracy up."

"Here is fine," Weber said. "I know we've been over all of
this before and everybody's been asking himself the same question
ever since all this craziness started. But do you know anybody,
anybody at all, who might want to harm Doug?"

"No! We talked about this over and over, Doug and Tracy and
me. We kept asking ourselves who would have it in for him for
some reason, and the only people we could remotely think about
was either Marvin Harris or that guy he fired. I think his name was
J.T."

"Doug thought Marvin might be behind this? Or J.T. Mercer?"

"No, Tracy was the one who kept suspecting one of those two.
Doug is… Doug was the kind of guy who couldn't believe
anything bad about anybody. Tracy would say it had to be one of
those two, they were the only ones who had any reason to be mad
at Doug, and he kept pooh-poohing that and telling her that neither
one of them would do something like that to him."

Weber didn't believe Marvin Harris would do anything to
harm Doug Mullins. Everything he had seen or heard about the
relationship between the two men had been good, even though they
had been competitors. But he made a mental note to talk to Marvin
again, just to cover all the bases. As for J.T., as worthless a human

being as he was, Weber didn't think he was smart enough to pull off something like this either. But he would talk to him again, too.

"Were you ever out in the garage at Doug and Tracy's house?"

"The garage? Yeah, I guess."

"What does that mean, Jessica?"

"Sometimes if Tracy and I went someplace together we would use her car. If it was in the garage, we'd go out that way through the kitchen."

"Do you recall a workbench on the wall there, the outside wall?"

"Yeah. That's where Doug would work on small stuff and get ready for his jobs out in the field."

"How much do you know about that workbench, Jessica?"

She shrugged her shoulders and looked confused. "I don't know, it was just a workbench. What's there to know about it?"

"Would you say Doug was one of those neatniks where everything had a place and he put his tools away when he was done using them?"

Jessica laughed and shook her head. "Are you kidding me? Tracy and I were always teasing him because his workbench was always a mess. He was always dropping something or knocking something over and picking it up off the floor. Tracy would tell him that if his workbench wasn't such a mess, he wouldn't have to do that all the time, and Doug would tell her to leave him alone, it was part of his exercise program. His workbench and his desk were both like that. She'd laugh and say she didn't know how he ever got anything done and threaten to clean it all up, and he'd tell her he had a system and not to mess with his system."

"One more question about the garage. There's a window above that workbench. Do you recall ever seeing that window open?"

Jessica laughed and said, "Not in years."

"Why is that funny?"

"Oh, it's silly. One time, years ago, Doug was doing something out there in the garage and had the window open. While he was standing there at the workbench a bee or a wasp or something like that flew in and stung him right on the end of his nose. I remember because Tracy and I were in the living room doing something and he let out a yell like a bear was after him. He came running in the house pointing at his nose and trying to talk and we were both laughing so hard, we just couldn't help ourselves. Poor guy. After that, I don't think that window ever got opened again. Why are you asking me all these questions about the garage, Sheriff?"

"We're just trying to figure out how that guy got inside the house. The way I hear it, Doug had become really concerned about making sure all the doors were locked."

"Oh, he did. After this ninja stuff started, that place was like Fort Knox."

"What about the kitchen door, Jessica? The one that goes from the kitchen to the garage? Did he make sure that one was locked, too?"

"I guess, but I really don't know. I know it was never locked during the day, it was usually open."

"I know I showed you this picture before, at the hospital," Weber said, "but let me show you again. Jessica, have you ever seen this man before?"

He handed her the phone and she carefully studied the image of the dead man, then shook her head.

"I'm sorry, I never have. I'm pretty good with faces and almost never forget one. But this guy," she shook her head again, "I've never seen him before."

"Tracy kept saying she didn't even know Doug had a gun. Did you know about it?"

"No. I never saw a gun and I never heard either one of them ever talking about a gun."

"Okay. Look, I know you're tired and I don't want to keep you any longer than I have to. Thank you for your time, Jessica." Weber handed her one of his business cards and said, "When Tracy wakes up, can you give me a call?"

"Sure. I could wake her up now if you want me to, but the poor thing has been through so much…"

"No, let her sleep. Just call me when she wakes up, okay?"

Weber started to turn away when a thought came to mind and he turned back to Jessica. "I meant to ask you something else. I know that your ex-husband had a falling out with Doug and Tracy. What do you know about that?"

"Tracy and Todd never got along very well," Jessica said. "I was really against it when he borrowed all that money from his parents to start the store. I knew that he would never pay them back. Todd is the most selfish, self-centered person I've ever known. And I'm not just saying that because he's my ex. It's true. And Tracy never hesitated to tell him what she thought about him and the way he had taken advantage of their parents. But Todd never gave a damn what anybody thought about him. After both of their parents were dead, he thought he was going to move right in and take over everything. Well, Tracy put a stop to that right now! And she should have. She went to court and she made sure that not only did she get half of their estate, but that the money that Todd owed came out of his half. Man, that set him off big time!"

"Do you think there's any chance that Todd could be behind all of this, Jessica?"

She thought about it for a moment. "No, I don't think so," she said. "You've dealt with Todd before, Sheriff. You know how he is. He gets mad and he explodes. He doesn't exactly think things through. He's a miserable son of a bitch. But to be honest with you, I don't think he's smart enough to pull off something like this."

Chapter 42

"It's a damn shame," Marvin Harris said as he dumped a roll of chain-link fencing from his shoulder into the back of a Dodge pickup truck. "Man, it just breaks my heart to think about Doug being gone. I mean, we knew it was coming, what with his bad heart and all. But for something like this to happen? That's a damn shame. How's Tracy doing?"

"She's having a real hard time of it," Weber told him.

"Poor thing. If there's anything I can do to help, just let me know."

"When was the last time you talked to Doug, Marvin?"

"I don't know, Jimmy. Yeah, wait, I do know. After he had his accident, I took one of my pickups over to their place for him to use."

"How did he seem to you then?"

"He looked bad. I'm not gonna lie to you, he looked like he could check out at any minute right then and there. I kept telling him to take it easy, but he was raring to get back to work. That's the way Doug was. All he cared about was making enough money that Tracy could get by when he was gone."

"Did he ever talk to you about that?"

"Yeah, as a matter fact he did. Here, let me show you something."

Marvin led the way through the back of his shop past racks holding fencing materials, hardware, and tools to a corner where a

267

desk and two filing cabinets stood. He opened one of the cabinets, thumbed through folders for a moment and selected one, handing it to Weber.

"What's this?"

"Take a look and see for yourself."

Weber open the folder and looked through the three neatly typed pages inside.

"You bought Doug's company?"

"Not yet, but that's a sales contract effective the date of his death."

"I don't know much about the fencing business, Marvin, but Doug seem like a small operation. Was it really worth $30,000?"

"Nope. What did he own? A few tools and a wrecked truck? The best thing Doug had going for him was an outstanding reputation. Basically, what I was buying was blue sky."

"Why would you do that? Doug was your only competitor, and with him dead, why shell out that kind of money?"

Marvin looked him in the eye and said, "Because I had a tremendous amount of respect for the man, Sheriff. When we were both starting out, before things got so busy around here, there were times when I was in a bind and Doug would help me out, and there were times when he needed some help and I'd step up to the plate for him. I've been fortunate and I've made a bit of money. It's not going to break me. I don't know if Tracy could sell the company name for anything or not, but I just felt it was the right thing to do."

"And how did Doug feel about it?"

"Doug was a practical man, Jimmy. He knew he didn't have anything to leave behind as far as the business was concerned. Yeah, maybe Tracy could hire someone to do the work and try to run it herself. She already took care of the books and all that. But he didn't want her to have to mess with any of it. We both knew his outfit wasn't worth what I agreed to pay him for it, and he told me he didn't want charity. But I told him that it wasn't about money, it was about friendship. And even though Tracy doesn't like me very much, Doug Mullins was my friend."

"Why is it that Tracy doesn't like you, Marvin?"

"It's stupid, Jimmy. Do you remember Angela?"

"Your ex-wife?"

"Yeah. Her and Tracy were best friends for a long time. When Angela and I split up, Tracy right away decided I was the bad guy. I don't know what all Angela told her, and I don't really care. But for whatever reason, Tracy has held that against me ever since."

Weber showed Marvin the picture of the dead man and asked if he had ever seen him before. Like everyone else, he shook his head. "Not anybody I've ever seen, Jimmy."

"Okay, I know you've got work to do. I appreciate your time, Marvin."

"No problem."

Weber started for the door and Marvin said, "Hey, Jimmy. I know this is probably not the time to be asking a question like this, and I don't even know how these kind of things work, but will I ever get my gun back?"

"Your gun?"

"Yeah, that .357 I loaned Doug. I'm assuming that's the gun he shot that guy with."

"Wait a minute," Weber said. "You gave Doug the gun?"

"Yeah. A Taurus .357. I mean, I didn't give it to him, I loaned it to him."

"When did that happen, Marvin?"

"After that fool threw that star thing into his door. He was really shook up by that and I told him he should get a gun in case the asshole came back. Doug said he never shot a gun in his life and wouldn't even know what kind to buy. I've had that .357 here in my desk drawer forever. I told Doug to take it and hang on to it case he needed it. He wasn't too sure that that was a good idea at first, said he couldn't picture himself ever shooting anybody. But I told him that whoever was after him might try to hurt Tracy, too. He thought about that for a minute and said yeah, he'd take the gun. I had no idea he'd really have to use it."

~~~***~~~

269

Weber's head was pounding from running on adrenaline and caffeine, but he knew it was going to be a long time before he got any rest. When he got back to the office, Mary had already called the Medical Examiner's Office in Tucson and arranged to have both Doug Mullins and the man he had killed transported down there for autopsies. While there was no question that Doug's death had been a heart attack, it was still normal procedure when someone died at their home as part of a violent crime.

"I didn't get any hits from the fingerprints," Buz told him. "So we still don't know who the guy Doug shot is."

"Dennis Pearlman," said Parks, who had just come to the door.

"What?"

"Your dead guy. His name is Dennis Pearlman."

"How did you find that out?"

"Buz gave me a copy of his picture and I ran it through our facial recognition program. Don't forget Jimmy, I'm the FBI. I have powers you can't begin to imagine."

"Yeah, I know, Parks, you're a legend in your own mind."

"So who the hell is Dennis Pearlman? And what's he doing breaking into a house in Big Lake in the middle of the night in a Halloween costume?"

"He's a nobody, Buz," Parks said. "Worked in an office for an insurance company down in Tempe, pushing paperwork."

"A ninja insurance agent? That's a new one on me," Weber said.

"No, from what I was able to find out, he's not an agent. Or wasn't an agent, I guess I should say."

"Did you talk to anybody where he worked?"

"I got a receptionist, but she wouldn't tell me anything. She said I needed to talk to a Mr. Chapman, who is her boss, but he was in a meeting. She said he'd be available after 10:30."

Weber looked at his watch. "Then he should be available now. What's the number, Parks?"

He may have been out of his meeting, but it still took a few minutes for Weber to work his way through several receptionists and operators before Ronald Chapman came on the line. Weber identified himself and told him about Dennis Pearlman's death.

"You're kidding me, right? Someone shot Dennis?"

Weber could hear the disbelief of the man's voice and said, "I'm afraid so."

"That's unbelievable. No way!"

"I'm sorry, but it's true," Weber told him.

"The first time Dennis ever missed a day of work and you're telling me someone shot him? I'm sorry, Sheriff, I'm trying to get that through my head, but it's so implausible."

"Why is that?"

"Did you ever meet Dennis?"

"No, sir. I never did."

"It's so hard to believe because Dennis is not the kind of person anybody would ever shoot."

"Tell me, Mr. Chapman, what kind of person *was* Dennis?"

There was silence on the line for a moment and Weber could tell the man was choosing his words. "How do I say this without seeming unkind? Dennis was just a… he was one of those people that are just in the background, if that makes any sense. Kind of like the potted plants here in the office and the piped in music they have playing. They are here, but you don't really notice them. Does that make any sense?"

"Yeah, it does," Weber said, knowing there were many people who went through life just like that, faceless cogs in some giant machine who went to work, did their jobs quietly, and went home at the end of the day, leaving no impression on anyone.

"How did Dennis get along with his coworkers, Mr. Chapman?"

"I don't know that he did. I don't mean like they were having problems, it was just like… the man was like wallpaper, Sheriff. He was here, he did his job, but I don't think he had any friends anywhere in the office. I never remember him having lunch with anybody, to be honest with you, I never recall ever seeing him having a conversation with anybody, any more than a word or two about a file he was working on. It's not that anybody disliked him, it's more like he just didn't make an impression on anybody."

"What was his job there, sir?"

"He was an account verification specialist."

"What does that mean?"

"It sounds more important than it is. He reviewed new accounts and made sure all of the paperwork was done properly. No names misspelled, no incorrect addresses, or anything left out. If there were any questions about a policy, it was his job to follow up with the agent and the client to get them answered. Then he filed everything away and went on to the next one. If there was a claim, he would help our adjusters review it and answer any questions they might have about the account. That's it."

"Is there anybody else there that might have worked with Mr. Pearlman? Anybody who might give me any insight into his personality at all?"

The man thought for a moment and then said, "if there was anybody, it would be Holli Harshbarger. She shared a cubicle with Dennis."

"Would it be possible to talk to her?"

"Yes, I don't see any reason why not. If you want to hold on, I'll have the operator connect you to her desk."

"I appreciate that," Weber said, "and I'm sorry for your loss."

"Like I said, I don't want to sound insensitive, but it's no loss to me or the company. Dennis was just... wallpaper."

Holli Harshbarger seemed just as surprised as her boss had been when Weber told her about what had happened to her coworker.

"That's just insane. Freaking insane."

"Ms. Harshbarger, what can you tell me about Dennis Pearlman?"

"Not a lot," she replied. "I shared a cubicle with him for the last three years, but I didn't really know the guy at all."

"Did you ever talk about anything besides work? Your lives away from the office, anything like that?"

"Not really. I think it was just about a year ago that my cat died. I found him dead when I got up that morning, and I took it kind of hard. I called the office and said I'd be in late, and when I did get here, Dennis just looked at me and said, 'You're late.' I told him yeah, and told him about Mr. Bojangles. That was my cat's name. You'd expect something from somebody you tell them that kind of news, wouldn't you? I mean at least an 'I'm sorry' or something. But there was nothing, he just picked up the next file and started going through it like it was any other day."

"Did you notice any changes in Mr. Pearlman lately?"

"Changes? What kind of changes, Sheriff?"

"I don't know. Did he seem moody, or maybe happy or depressed or anything like that?"

"Not really. I mean if he ever had a mood it was just... I don't know. He didn't seem happy about anything, but he didn't seem particularly sad, either."

"All right, I appreciate your time. One final question, Ms. Harshbarger. Do you know of any friends that Mr. Pearlman had there at the office or anywhere else I might talk to?"

"I'm sorry, I don't. Sometimes when we would have office get-togethers here at work, like a cake for somebody's birthday or something like that, Dennis would come and have a piece. But more likely than not he would take it back to the cubicle and not stay and talk to anybody. He was a weird duck."

"Okay, I appreciate your time," Weber said.

He started to hang up, but just before he did he heard the woman say, "Oh, wait a minute. This may be nothing at all, and it probably isn't. But the last couple of weeks Dennis was acting kind of... I don't know, sneaky for want of a better word."

"What do you mean?"

"The only time he ever got phone calls were work-related. But lately it seemed like he was getting personal calls."

"Do you know who they were from?"

"No, but if his phone rang and I was there, he would say he couldn't talk right then and hang up. Or if I came into our cubicle and he was on the phone he would get off quick. And a couple of times I would walk in and he would hit the mouse and change the screen on his computer. Like he was looking at something that wasn't work-related. To be honest, I kind of wondered if he was looking at porn on the internet and calling one of those 900 talk lines or whatever they call them. But I didn't give it much thought because Dennis was the kind of guy that you just don't see as having a girlfriend or a sex life. Or really any kind of life, if you know what I mean."

Chapter 43

It was late afternoon before they finished processing the crime scene and Weber sent his exhausted deputies home to sleep. Tommy and Archer, whom Buz had sent home earlier to get some rest, were back on the street, and two of the Citizen Volunteers were stationed at the house just in case any morbid curiosity seeker came too close. Weber himself had slept for an hour or two on the couch in his office and was awakened when Mary knocked on his door.

"Jimmy, Tracy Mullins is on the phone. She said you came by her sister-in-law's place and wanted to talk to her earlier."

"Thanks," Weber said, getting up and going to his desk. He pushed the button for the flashing light on his phone and asked, "How are you doing, Tracy?"

"I don't know, Sheriff. I just don't know anything right now. I'm awake, but I still feel like all of this is just a bad dream and I can't wake up from it."

"I understand," he told her. "I need to come by and talk to you if it's okay. Are you still at Jessica's?"

"Yeah. I don't know if I can ever go home again. I just feel like… I don't know if I can ever go back there again."

Weber understood that completely. After his own sister had committed her crimes, crimes that left good people dead, he had been unable to step through the door of the family home they had both been raised in and where Debbie had lived with her husband Mike, who became her first victim.

"I'll be there in just a few minutes," he told her.

He took off his shirt and went into the small bathroom in his private office. He brushed his teeth, then splashed water on his face and used a washcloth to give himself a quickie cleanup. Putting his shirt back on and looking in the mirror, he guessed he look presentable enough to be seen in public. But he sure did not feel it. He went out into the outer office, where he was surprised to see Coop working at his desk.

"I thought I sent all you guys home to get some rest."

"I got a couple of hours, Jimmy. But then I woke up and couldn't sleep. Here, you need to look at something I found."

Weber walked up behind his deputy and looked over his shoulder at the screen of a laptop computer that he didn't recognize.

"Where did you get this?"

"We took two laptops from the office in one of the Mullins' bedrooms. I found something in the email files on this one. Here, look at this."

Weber read what was on the screen. "Son of a bitch."

"And there are a lot more just like this one. Here," Coop said, clicking a screen icon and calling up another file, "see what I mean?"

Weber read the file and shook his head.

"I couldn't believe it either when I saw it," Coop told him.

~~~***~~~

Tracy Mullins may have slept for a while, but Weber couldn't tell it by looking at her. There were deep circles under her eyes, her hair was a snarled mess, and she was obviously wearing some of Jessica's clothing, which were too big for her.

"I know I said I was going to be right over when we talked on the phone," Weber said. "But something came up. I apologize."

"That's okay," Tracy said. "I don't even know what time it is, to be honest with you."

"It's a little after five," Weber told her.

"Do you guys want some coffee?"

"No, thanks, Jessica. Right now I think we've both got more coffee in our veins then blood," Weber said. Seeing Tracy shudder at the word, he apologized for being insensitive.

"Tracy, I know we've asked you this before, but can you run through the whole thing for us again. We need to make sure we have all the facts straight about what happened last night."

"I don't know what else there is to tell you," she said. "It was just a typical night. Doug wasn't feeling well. Ever since all that stuff started with the ninja, and then the accident, it seemed like he was going downhill more every day. We were watching the news and he fell asleep in his recliner. I woke him up and told him to take his meds and go to bed. Doug always took a shower before he went to sleep at night, but he was so tired he didn't bother. I finished watching the news and I went to bed, too. He was so out of it, I don't even know if he knew I was there." She paused for a moment and wiped tears away from her eyes. "That really bothers me, not knowing if he knew I was there beside him."

"It's okay, hon," Jessica said, sitting on the arm of the couch and squeezing Tracy's shoulder. "Doug knew you were there. He always knew you were there for him."

"So, you went to bed and then what?"

"I told you guys all this before."

"I know, Tracy. I hate to keep asking these questions, but sometimes people remember some little thing that they didn't before."

She closed her eyes for a moment, replaying the terrible scene in her head again, then opened them and said, "I woke up and Doug was yelling at someone. There was somebody all dressed in black in the bedroom doorway and Doug was yelling at him."

"Do you remember what he said, Tracy?"

"I don't know. Maybe he was asking who he was or asking him why he was there. I just don't know!"

She began crying. Weber looked at Coop while Jessica comforted her. When she was able to get herself composed again, Tracy said, "The next thing I knew there was a shot. It sounded like a cannon going off in our bedroom. Then someone turned on the light, I don't remember if it was me or Doug. And there was this guy there in the hallway, dead. At least I thought he was dead. I don't know if he was dead for sure or not then. Doug told me to call 911 and said he was going to check the rest of the house, and I kept begging him to stay with me. But he went down the hall and then I heard him falling and..." she started crying again. "I tried to save him! I tried so hard. I took a CPR class when his heart problem started being so bad. I thought if something happened, I could help him. But I couldn't. I don't know if I did something wrong or if I wasn't doing it right, I just don't know. I tried so hard and I failed him."

She was weeping again and Jessica handed her a tissue from a box on the coffee table and held her close.

Weber gave her some time, then asked, "Tracy, when you went to bed, do you know if all the doors were locked?"

"I guess so. We never used to lock our doors before. But after all this started, Doug wanted them locked all the time."

"How about the kitchen door, the one that goes out into the garage? Do you know if it was locked?"

"It was closed, but I don't know if it was locked or not. Probably so. Why?"

Weber pulled out his phone and showed her a picture of the garage with the open window over her husband's workbench. "Do you know why this window would be open, Tracy?"

"No. It was never open. Was that how he got in?"

"That's the way it looks."

"I don't know if that window was locked or not, and I don't know if the kitchen door was locked or not. I just assumed they were because Doug was always locking everything up. Oh, God, could I have left the kitchen door unlocked? Is it my fault he got in that way?"

Weber didn't answer her, he just showed her the picture of the man her husband shot and asked, "Tracy, I know you've seen this picture before, but I have to ask you again, now that you've had some time to rest. Do you know this person?"

278

She looked at the picture and shook her head. "No. I have no idea who it is."

"His name was Dennis Pearlman. Does that sound familiar to you?"

"No. Should it?"

"That's what we're trying to figure out," Weber said.

"What's to figure out? Like I said, I don't ever remember seeing him anywhere."

"What we're trying to figure out," Weber said, "is why Dennis Pearlman's clothes and wallet were in the trunk of your Honda, Tracy."

"In my car? That doesn't make any sense. Why would his clothes be in the trunk of my car?"

"I don't know," Weber replied. "Maybe for the same reason that you've been exchanging emails with him for over three months now?"

"What? What are you talking about?"

Weber stood up and pulled his handcuffs from his belt. "Stand up."

"What? What's happening?"

"Tracy Mullins, you're under arrest for the murder of your husband and Dennis Pearlman."

Chapter 44

"Why, Jimmy? The man was already dying. Why was she trying to make it happen sooner than it already would?"

"I don't know what to tell you, Mary. Why does anybody do the things they do? Maybe she knew that as he went downhill, he was going to need more and more care. There was going to come a time when Doug had to go in the hospital, and with no insurance, where was the money going to come from? Maybe she got tired of waiting. Maybe she got greedy. Who knows?"

"I just can't believe any of this," Robyn said. "They seemed like such a good couple."

"I've been at this work long enough to know that you never really know what goes on in people's minds," Weber said.

"Tracy was actually the ninja who was trying to kill Doug, not this Pearlman guy?"

"We found a ninja costume in the crawlspace of their attic," Weber said. "I don't think she was trying to kill him. I think she was trying to scare him to death. When that didn't happen, she decided to bring Pearlman into the picture."

"But from everything we've heard about him, I don't see him being a killer."

"He didn't go there to kill Doug Mullins that night," Weber said. "He was a patsy that Tracy set up. Doug was hanging by a thread, but the guy was so damn stubborn he wouldn't let go. According to the emails between her and Pearlman, she was telling him that she had this fantasy about a ninja breaking into the house and ravishing her. The more they talked about it, the more he got into it. I think he believed Tracy was going to be the answer to every dream he ever had. He didn't know that Doug was going to be there. She told him Doug was already in the hospital and was out of the picture."

"But when he got there and saw the man, then what?"

"I don't know, Robyn. The plan was that Doug would have a heart attack and be gone, and I guess she figured Pearlman was so infatuated by her that he would roll with the punches. She laid it out step by step in her emails. Told him to come in from the back yard and be real quiet so as not to destroy the fantasy, go through the kitchen to the garage, and that she would have a ninja outfit and a sword in the trunk of her car for him to change into. All to make her fantasy come true. I think to him, that's what was happening, kinky role playing."

"And he got himself shot for his troubles," Mary said.

"For all I know, Tracy may have known about Marvin Harris giving Doug the gun. Maybe she figured it would happen just the way it did, that Doug would shoot him and have a heart attack. Maybe she thought they would get into a fight and Doug would die, then she would shoot Pearlman and claim self-defense. She thought she had a pretty solid plan put together, but there were a lot of holes in it. Once Coop found the emails between Tracy and Pearlman, he dug deeper and found where she had ordered the ninja costumes and swords and all of that online."

"Where did she come up with such a crazy idea anyway?"

"When she finally broke down and started talking, she said she kept seeing the ads on TV for that Ninja World event that was going around and that got her thinking."

"She should have thought a lot more," Robyn said.

"If people thought more about what they were going to do, we'd be out of a job," Weber said.

"It still doesn't explain why," Mary said. "He was dying anyhow. Why not just wait for it to happen?"

"You know how everybody knew about Doug working so hard to put money away to take care of Tracy when he was gone?

Well, as it turns out, Tracy was worried about her future, too. They incorporated their little company years ago, and over a year ago, Tracy took out what's called key man insurance on both her and Doug."

"What's key man insurance?"

"It's a policy that protects a company in case one of the principals dies suddenly, to ensure that the company can continue to operate."

"And Pearlman worked for an insurance company," Mary said, recognition suddenly coming into her face.

"Yep. Part of his job was double checking all the facts on new policies and looking into any kind of discrepancies or questions there might be. I don't know when Tracy hooked up with him, but Pearlman is the one that went through their policy and rubberstamped it as good to go. He was supposed to confirm any questions about health, and nothing on the policy talked about Doug's heart problems. Convenient, wasn't it?"

"How much was the policy for?"

"$850,000," Weber said.

"Wow, that's a lot of money."

"Yes, it is. That, combined with a regular life insurance policy they had on both of them and the money Doug had been socking away comes out to just over a million bucks. And Tracy didn't want to spend a bunch of that money on hospital bills as Doug's health declined."

"Do you think he knew about the key man policy?"

"I'm sure he didn't," Weber said. "If he did, I don't know that he would be working that hard toward the end. Then again, maybe so. We both know that Doug Mullins was more concerned about other people than he was himself. And he loved Tracy more than anything in the world. I guess we'll never know."

"You know, everybody talks about what a jerk Todd Norton is," Robyn said. "And no question about it, he's a first-class A-hole. But it seems like as bad as he is, his sister is even worse. At least he's right in your face about things. This… this is just so much worse."

"I guess it's like you said, Jimmy. None of us really know what's in someone else's heart, do we?"

Weber thought about Todd Norton with his explosive temper, and about Todd's sister, Tracy, who had always seemed to be the exact opposite of him. He thought about how she had been responsible for her husband's death, as well as indirectly being responsible for the death of Dennis Pearlman, a nobody who thought he had found a chance at happiness and a normal life with someone he met online. Someone who may have had some kinky fantasies, but who's to say Pearlman didn't have his own? Then he thought about Debbie, his own sister, and how good everyone thought she was, but yet how much pain she had caused so many people.

"No, Mary, we don't. We look at the outside and we think we know somebody, but we don't. And we never will, until it's too late."

**Here is a sneak peek at *Big Lake Quarterback*,
coming soon from Nick Russell**

"I'm telling you, Sheriff Weber, this is going to revolutionize the way your people do their jobs here in Big Lake."

"I just don't see these as being something we need," Sheriff Jim Weber said.

"Of course you need them! Your people need them! Do you want to be the sheriff standing in front of a crowd of reporters telling them that one of your deputies was shot and killed when you know there was a way to prevent that?"

Weber never like talking to reporters. He didn't like it any more than he liked talking to pushy salesmen. And this guy was definitely pushy.

"Listen, Mr. Knight, we're a small town and a small department. It's not something we need, and it's not something we can afford."

"You're wrong about that, Sheriff. You *do* need our products. And as for affording them, how do you put a value on the lives of your deputies?"

The guy was persistent, Weber had to give him that. But he wasn't going to allow him to push any emotional buttons and convince him to spend money that wasn't in the budget for something the sheriff didn't feel they needed.

"I know this is a small town, Sheriff Weber," the salesman continued. "And we both know that bad things happen in small towns, too. I've done my homework. You've had more than your share of violent incidents here in Big Lake. Including having one of your deputies shot. Am I right?"

"That was an isolated incident."

"Right. An isolated incident. But to that deputy, it was still life or death."

285

Weber knew the incident the man was referring to could have turned out a lot worse, no question about that. If the teenage sociopath who had shot Deputy Buz Carelton had aimed for his head instead of his chest, if Buz hadn't been wearing his ballistic vest, if any of a number of things had been different, it could have been a tragedy. It was tragic enough as it was that Weber had been forced to shoot the young man. And the sheriff was well aware that things like that could happen at any time, in any place. But even given all of that, what the salesman was proposing was overkill.

"Mr. Knight, I'm not going to spend a lot of money on these ballistic shields and suits of armor of yours. It's not in the budget, and if I had that much money to spend, there are a lot of other things we need more."

"They're not suits of armor, Sheriff. They are personal protection equipment."

Weber looked at the fancy four-color brochure the man had brought with him. And if money were no object, he might say yes. But in a small town, budgetary concerns always played a role. Besides which, Weber knew his deputies, and he could not see any of them wearing the protective suits and the bullet resistant helmets complete with built in cameras, or carrying the protective shields the salesman was insisting they needed. To him, they looked like something out of a science fiction movie. Trying to lighten his rejection up, Weber said, "The name of your company is Knights Armor. I'm just going off of that."

"The name just signifies the strength of our products, Sheriff Weber."

"I get that. I don't care what you call it, it's out of our budget and I'm not interested."

"Sheriff, with all due respect, is that how little the safety of your people means to you?"

Weber had tried to remain pleasant but he didn't like being pushed. And this guy was coming off like a used car salesman who wouldn't take no for an answer. So much for being pleasant.

"This conversation is over, Mr. Knight. Thank you for your time, but don't bother coming by again."

"That's it? You're going to blow me off just like that?"

"Yes, sir. Apparently I am. I told you I'm not interested, and I don't appreciate the pushy attitude."

"Amazing, Sheriff Weber. It's amazing that you care so little for your people."

"That's enough," Weber said, getting up from the chair behind his desk and pointing at the door. "I've got work to do. Have a nice day, Mr. Knight."

The salesman, a short, bloated man with blotchy skin, a bad combover, and a pencil thin mustache, seemed like he was about to say something else. But the look on Weber's face told him that the best course of action he could take would be to follow the sheriff's advice and leave.

"I'll leave my brochure. Maybe you could let your deputies take a look at it and see if they are willing to invest their own money in their personal safety." The friendly tone he had used when he first sat down in the sheriff's office had left his voice.

"I'll pass it around them," Weber said. "Please close the door on your way out."

When he was alone, Weber picked up a brochure and looked at it, then threw it back on his desk. Yes, there might be a time when the man's equipment would come in handy. And if the Sheriff's Department's budget was unlimited he wouldn't hesitate to spend that kind of money if it would protect one of his deputies from harm. But the reality was, they couldn't afford it, and there were a lot of other things they needed more.

There was a knock on his door and then Mary Caitlin, his administrative assistant, poked her head in. "Got a minute, Jimmy?"

"I don't know. Are you trying to sell something?"

"No, but I need you out here. There's a problem."

"Please tell me Archer didn't stop up the toilet again. What is it that guy eats, anyway?"

"No, Jimmy, it's not that. We've got somebody pretty upset out here."

Mary was the wife of Weber's predecessor, Sheriff Pete Caitlin, and she had worked at the Department forever. Some might say she was the one who actually ran the place, and there were times when it certainly felt like that to Weber. Mary had been there longer than any deputy that he knew of, certainly longer than he had, and if something came up in the office that she couldn't handle, it definitely needed his attention.

He followed her out into the main office, where a short, plump woman seemed to be on the verge of hysterics.

"Why are you people just standing there? I'm telling you, something's wrong! My son wouldn't just disappear like this. It's not like him."

"Ma'am, I understand you're upset, and I understand you're worried," Deputy Chad Summers was saying, "but we're only talking about a few hours. Sometimes teenagers are off having fun and they lose track of time."

"No! You're not listening to me," the woman said slapping her hand down on the counter in frustration. "My son would never stay out overnight like this."

"When was the last time you saw him?"

"I don't know. Last night sometime. I just know that when I got up this morning he wasn't there."

"Isn't it possible he might have gotten up before you and taken off with some friends or something like that?"

"Are you kidding me? I have to drag him out of bed by the ankles every morning to get him to go to school! Something's wrong. I think he's been kidnapped… or worse."

"Excuse me, ma'am," Weber said, "I'm Sheriff Weber. "Who's missing?"

"My son, Gary. I think something bad has happened to him."

"Okay, let's just calm down for a minute. What your son's name?"

"Gary. Gary Gunkel."

"The football player?"

"Yes. You have to find him."

"Mrs. Gunkel, we're not trying to make light of your concerns. But like Deputy Summers said, sometimes teenagers lose track of time. They get busy with their friends or whatever they're doing, and before they know it, hours have gone by."

"That's not the case," the woman sobbed. "Something really bad has happened to my son."

"Aside from the fact that you don't know where he's at right this minute, do you have any reason to believe that it's something more than just an irresponsible teenager goofing off somewhere?"

"My son is not irresponsible, Sheriff!"

"I'm sorry. Poor choice of words," Weber said. "Anyway, what makes you think something bad has happened to your son?"

The woman was carrying an oversize cloth purse with wooden handles and some kind of design printed on it that reminded Weber of the knitting bag his mother used to keep next to her chair when he was a teenager living at home. She dug in it and pulled out four pieces of paper and slapped them down on the counter. "Read these. I know something is wrong because my son has been getting death threats! And I think they're real."

Weber looked at the papers. Each was a standard size sheet of white paper like one might use in a computer, and on each, crudely lettered with what appeared to be a red marker, somebody had threatened to kill the recipient in ways that Weber thought had to come from the mind of someone who wrote horror movies. He read them again, then handed them to Chad, watching the veteran deputy's face. When Chad set them back down on the counter, Weber knew that they both realized the woman might be serious. They had a missing teenager on their hands, and there was a very real possibility that something terrible had happened to him.

Made in the
USA
Monee, IL